ANGEL IN RED

She blinked and found herself staring into a pair of summer blue eyes. They were in the face of an angel and framed by hair the color of sunshine. She must be dead and the angels come for her. Either that or she was dreaming.

"Are you hurt, miss?" a deep, warm voice asked.

Izzy quickly sat up when she realized that a bright red coat covered the broad shoulders of the man instead of a pair of wings.

He held out a hand. "Can you stand?"

Izzy stared at the hand, aghast. Had a redcoat saved her?

"The ruffians are gone," he assured her. "They ran as soon as I appeared. I hope they left empty-handed. I wanted to give chase but hesitated to leave you alone."

"What?" Izzy asked. She felt like an idiot, but it was hard to follow his words with her head pounding so.

Gentle hands touched her forearms and pulled her to her feet. Her head swam and she fought against the urge to let darkness overcome her. Ewan would have a fit if he knew she'd fainted into the arms of a redcoat.

Cindy Holby

Fallen

LEISURE BOOKS NEW YORK CITY

For Dad, who fought the fight and won!

A LEISURE BOOK®

February 2009

Published by

Dorchester Publishing Co., Inc.
200 Madison Avenue
New York, NY 10016

ISBN 10: 0-8439-6026-4
ISBN 13: 978-0-8439-6026-6
E-ISBN: 1-4285-0598-9

The name "Leisure Books" and the stylized "L" with design are trademarks of Dorchester Publishing Co., Inc.

Printed in the United States of America.

10 9 8 7 6 5 4 3 2 1

Visit us on the web at www.dorchesterpub.com.

ACKNOWLEDGMENTS

Thank you to my wonderful friends Alyssa Day and Barb Ferrer who kept me going on days when I didn't think I could write another word. Ever again. Ever.

And also thank you to Laura and Chris who always gave me rah rahs when I needed them.

Fallen

Chapter One

Aberdeen, Scotland, 1773

A fine mist fell. John Murray could not help shivering in his shirtsleeves as he stepped out into the damp gray gloom of early morning. A shudder moved down his spine as his eyes fell upon the post planted in the middle of the courtyard at Castlehill. The ground around it was trampled, torn, mucky from a mix of rain and free-flowing blood. Ewan Ferguson's blood. No comfort for him there; his blood would soon join it.

Was she watching? His blue eyes scanned the ranks of his peers, all standing at attention in the despicable weather, all surely cursing his name because they'd been forced to rise early this miserable morning and watch his punishment.

Where was she? Surely they would force her to watch too, since it was her fault he was here in the first place. Surely they had made her watch her brother's lashing as it was his fault that two men now lay dead.

There. He saw her. She stood next to the general with her chin held high and her shoulders squared as if she had just handed down the sentence herself. In some strange turned-about way, she had. Luckily for her the general was magnanimous in his show of mercy. She was a woman, after all, nothing more than an instrument in the treachery of her clansmen.

Her hair was plastered down against her head instead of the usual mass of springy curls that framed her face like sunlight. This morning it seemed darker than its usual reddish blonde. Her dress was stained dark with blood and the neckline gaped open, torn by him in his haste the afternoon they were together. Of course she would have had no way to mend it, so it hung open, teasing him, tormenting him, just as she did the first time he met her. She had gotten into his head that day, damn her. She had no choice about the state of her dress, because her hands were tied before her. Even though the distance between them was great, he could feel her deep brown eyes upon him. Her gaze gave him a measure of satisfaction. A small measure, but something to hang on to.

If only they would lash her also. Did she not deserve it? Was not she as guilty as her brothers and her father in the planning and the plotting and the betrayal?

John's stomach clenched in anger at the thought. No. It would not do to rip her pale, delicate skin. Knowing her as he did, he understood that she would rather take the lashing herself than watch it. She would suffer more this way. She deserved to suffer for what she'd done.

"Best get on with it, lad," Sergeant Gordon said. "Dread only makes it worse."

John ripped his eyes from his desperate examination of her face and looked at the grizzled sergeant who served as his escort.

"Aye, lad," Gordon said in his hoarse croak. "I've felt the lash. 'Tis best not to think on it too much. Fear makes the muscles bunch across your shoulders and the pain is much worse."

John flexed his shoulders as he took the first step into the courtyard. "How can I not think on it?" He'd seen lashings. Plenty of them. Twenty lashes was the usual sentence for dereliction of duty.

But General Kensington had added another five because of the circumstances surrounding John's transgression. His punishment was to be a lesson to all. Do not be swayed by a pretty face and the offer of favors. When John considered the loss of his reputation and the damage to his career, the lashes were nothing in comparison.

Still, he knew they were coming, and with them would come pain. John flexed his shoulders again. The mist had turned into a drumming rain and his shirt was soaked through. He felt goose bumps on his flesh. He hoped it was the cold that caused them, and not fear.

"I know what you're thinking, lad," Sergeant Gordon continued as they walked the innumerable steps to the post. "You're wondering, how will it feel? Will I be able to stand it? Will I cry out like a babe?" Gordon was right all on accounts. John felt a newfound respect for the man as they continued the gut-wrenching walk across the yard.

Too soon they stood before the post and Gordon attached the hook to the bonds around John's wrists. Gordon nodded to a corporal, who jerked on a rope attached to a pulley, and John's arms were stretched above his head, pulling him against the post. His boots sank into the muck and the corporal pulled again so that he was stretched up onto his toes.

"Let him down a bit, lad," Gordon instructed. "Ye might find yerself in the same predicament some day." The corporal relented and John was able to place his feet more firmly on each side of the post.

Gordon looked beyond John to the burly man holding the lash. "He won't be happy unless you cry out," he said. "The man loves his job too well." Gordon spat into the mud by John's feet. "Sadistic bastard," he added. He slipped a piece of wood in John's mouth. "Bite down on it, lad. 'Twill help."

John nodded as he placed his cheek against the post. Gordon stepped behind him and ripped away his shirt. "Think on something else, lad," he added into his ear as the cold rain on his bare back let him know that Gordon had left.

Think on something else. . . . John blinked the rain off his eyelashes and looked toward General Kensington. He heard the sentence being read by Kensington's aide, a nephew of the general with a squeaky voice and bad skin.

"Do you understand your sentence?" the aide asked, his voice breaking on the last word.

John looked at the general and nodded. The general raised his hand. His face looked sad and John knew that the man was thinking about his father. They were friends. It was the reason Kensington had requested that John be assigned to him. What would Kensington have to say to his father about all of this?

Think on something else. He knew the lash was coming. He could sense it coiling and gathering. He heard it whistle through the air.

John looked at her. Isobel. Izzy. It was her fault. He'd trusted her with his life, with his soul, with his heart, and she'd betrayed him.

He felt the sting of the lash. His back burned as he was slammed against the post.

"One," the aide said.

Get on with it. . . .

The next one came from the opposite direction. Marking his back with an X as if he were a target. His eyes stayed on Izzy. How easy a target he'd been for her. He'd fallen like a rock into the sea. Sunk right into her plotting. Captured by a winsome smile and deep brown eyes that seemed to hold the secrets of time.

"Two."

The next one landed straight across, the tail of the whip caressing his rib cage and tearing at the skin on his side as it hit against the bone.

John let out a hiss but kept his eyes on Izzy. Her eyes seemed huge in her face. At one time he'd thought he could get lost in those eyes.

"Three."

Damn her eyes. Three lashes and his back felt as if it were on fire.

The next one struck straight down his spine. The man was thorough if nothing else. He seemed determined to flay every inch off John's back in the strokes allowed. John pressed his wrists against each other as pain shot through every inch of his body. He pushed against the post, his body automatically seeking escape from the next blow.

"Four."

Think on something else.

How could he not be tense when he knew the pain was coming? He heard the whistle of the lash once again. Felt his flesh tear. Felt the blood pour down his back. He groaned and clenched his teeth tighter into the wood.

"Five."

Twenty to go. How could he stand it? He had to. Crying wouldn't stop it. Begging wouldn't stop it. Screaming his anger at the heavens would not stop it any more than it would stop the rain that washed against his back and plastered his hair into his eyes.

Izzy. He stared at her, blinking against the rain. It was her fault. All her fault. Every bit of it. Izzy.

Izzy.

A month earlier

"Pride goeth before destruction, John Murray, and a haughty spirit before a fall."

John Murray lifted a blond eyebrow as his blue eyes switched from his own reflection in the small mirror to that of his friend.

"Quoting scripture again, Rory?" he asked. "Did you ever think that perhaps you should have pursued a career in the church instead of the king's army?"

"You forget, my friend, I have the misfortune of being a second son," Rory replied, shouldering John away from the mirror so he could arrange his own brown locks to his satisfaction. "Which means my life, alas, was predestined from the start." Rory placed his hat at a jaunty angle atop his head. "And since I have no control over Destiny, I will be off to see what she has in store for me." Rory threw him a mock salute and, with his hand on his sheathed saber to keep it from catching on the door, left the narrow room that the two men shared.

"Destiny is what we make of it!" John shouted after him, and returned to his perusal of his image. "Or so we tell ourselves," he reminded his reflection, speaking quietly lest someone catch him talking to himself. That would not do at all.

There would be no cause for gossip where Captain Jonathan James Markham Murray was concerned. Being the son of a bastard was a heavy enough cross to bear without the added burden of a damaged reputation. That was why he was very careful in everything he did. His father had bought him a commission in His Majesty's army, and John had readily embraced the life of a soldier. It was the only path open to him. It was his only chance for success and respect in spite of his doubtful heritage. He had made the rank of captain in good time and had also had the good luck of being fortunate in his postings. His father had friends who'd made a point of looking out for his son. John's most recent transfer to the prison built on the ruins of Castlehill was the result of his father's friendship with the post commander, General Kensington.

Even though his father was a bastard, he was a well-connected one. John's grandfather, the now deceased Lord Dunmore, had acknowledged his son and gifted him with his own commission several years before. James Murray had managed to achieve the high rank of general and was now serving His Majesty in the colonies. His father even had a close relationship with his younger, legitimate half brother, the current Lord Dunmore, who was governor of the Virginia colony in America.

John dusted an imagined piece of lint from the shoulder of his red coat, once more adjusted his stock, and pronounced himself ready to meet his future wife. That was, if she'd have him.

John practiced his most charming smile.

She'd have him, he assured himself. How could she resist his obvious charms? The smile quickly faded as John once more contemplated his reflection. Charm would only go so far when there was an obvious lack of wealth. As his mother had told him often enough, his good looks would eventually fade and then where would he be?

"You'd best seal the deal as soon as possible," John reminded himself as he heard the heavy limp of Sergeant Gordon in the hallway. "Before you wind up with missing body parts and massive scars from His Majesty's service."

Sergeant Gordon stuck his grizzled head into the open doorway. "Off to town, are ye?" he asked in his croaky voice. "Off to please the ladies?"

"Only one in particular," John said as he turned from the mirror. "The young Miss Edina Rabin."

"Is she rich?" Sergeant Gordon asked with a twinkle in his eye. The man presumed much with his betters, but John allowed the freedom as Sergeant Gordon had given much for king and country. His father had often advised him to listen to the men below him in rank, as well as the ones above. You never knew which man would hold your life in his hands, especially when you were on the field of battle.

"Her father owns the print shop," John replied obligingly. "General Kensington arranged an introduction." John was fortunate that his commanding officer held great regard for his father and was also well connected among the peerage. The general could open many doors that were usually closed to one with John's unfortunate credentials.

"Aye," Gordon said. "She'll do."

"She will indeed," John agreed.

He followed Gordon's chuckling form out of the barracks and made his way to the stables. The sound of hooves thrumming against wood alerted him that Sultan, his stallion, was rebelling against whatever poor private had drawn the dubious duty of saddling him.

"Be careful lest that beastly ghost horse be the end of ye," Gordon admonished as he disappeared into the mess hall.

John merely shook his head. Sultan was high spirited and temperamental, but the stud had every right to be. Snowy white, of Arabian descent, he was bred for stamina and speed and he happened to be the bet on the table the one night John had experienced an unbelievable run of luck. A run of luck that continued the next morning when the young and foolish Lord Afton had challenged him to a duel after losing the prize of his father's stables.

Lord Afton no longer required the services of Sultan, or any other stud, and his younger brother became the heir that day. Such was life.

Some were born lucky, the heirs to great fortunes and titles and all that went with them. But for the majority, it was hard work and taking your luck where you could find it. Sultan was a prize and John intended to take great care with him. He could amass a fortune just in stud fees, with the right connections.

Having the right connections could take a man a long way in this world.

"I take it he's being difficult," John said to the young man who stood before Sultan's stall with a saddle in hand and a grim look on his face. The lad couldn't be more than sixteen. He was stout and had a few stray hairs sprinkled on his chin. The boy wasn't even shaving yet.

"Yes, sir," the private replied.

"You just have to let him know who's in charge," John said. "Are you one of the new recruits?" he asked.

"Yes, sir," the young man said. He wanted to salute but had some trouble adjusting the saddle so that he could snap his hand in the proper matter. He settled for balancing the saddle on his knee while acknowledging John's rank. "Private Pearson, sir."

"Captain Murray." John returned his salute. "And this is Sultan."

"Yes, sir," Pearson said, lifting a dubious eyebrow. "We've met."

John laughed. "Not much experience with horses, then?"

"No, sir," Pearson replied. "My father is a baker. We live in the middle of London."

"And you wanted to see the world?" John finished for him.

"There must be more to it than narrow streets and tall buildings," Pearson said. "Though I can't say that Aberdeen is much different."

"Then look in the other direction," John said. "The country around you is magnificent although not as pleasing to the eye as other parts of Scotland."

"Yes, sir," Pearson agreed. "Or so I've heard. I've not had a chance to see much of it yet."

"I'll make sure you're included on my next patrol," John said, and Pearson grinned widely. John took the saddle from his arms. "Watch and learn," he instructed as he entered Sultan's stall.

With an outstretched hand he gentled the stallion. The horse tossed his silky mane and pawed the straw with his hoof. "Yes, you know you're going out," John murmured. "You're anxious to see new sights and perhaps eye a mare or two," he added. He rubbed the finely arched neck and attached a lead to the halter. Sultan looked at him with dark brown eyes and tossed his head in agreement.

"See, he thinks he's getting what he wants," John explained to Pearson as he quickly exchanged the halter for a bridle. Sultan champed at the bit while John saddled him. "But all the while, he's giving me what I want."

"Do you think he really understands you?" Pearson asked.

"He understands that he's getting out of here," John said as he led Sultan from the stall. "And he is particular about who rides him."

"He could sense I didn't know about horses and such," Pearson said.

"Exactly," John said, repeating the wisdom his father had passed down to him. "Animals seem to know right off if someone is good or bad. So if you're in doubt about a man, pay attention to how his horse or dog reacts to him."

"Yes, sir," Pearson said, and snapped a proper salute as John mounted.

"Practice saddling a gentler mount," John said. "It shouldn't take you long to figure it out." He gave Sultan a little kick in the flanks and the horse sprang forward, ready to run.

The weather was mild, and the sun shone in a nearly cloudless sky. It was a lovely early summer day and John decided to give Sultan a bit of a run before taking him into the narrow, twisted streets of Aberdeen.

They rode past the ruin of Aberdeen Castle, heading west,

where the land lay flat. John could well understand Pearson's frustration at not seeing much of the world. The land around Aberdeen was impressive with its deep mountains rising in the distance as if they were determined to split the land in two. But beyond impressive, it was also dangerous. Rebels still hid in the depths of the mountains.

John gave Sultan his head and the stallion stretched out in a run across the field of deep grass. John knew it was risky to let the stud gallop over the uneven terrain, but John was feeling a bit reckless, a change from his usual calm demeanor. A strange restlessness had been his constant companion since he'd come to Aberdeen two weeks earlier.

John shook his head at the strange feeling. "It is most likely the legends and the landscape," he said to himself as he heard Sultan's labored breathing. He slowed the stallion to a brisk walk. The horse fought against the bit, but John was firm. Sultan tossed his head and John rubbed the snowy arch of his neck as he looked around to see how far they'd run.

His eyes beheld a country as wild as its history, one where the peace was hard maintained. The most recent rebellion had occurred in John's own lifetime, and even though he was barely walking at the time of Culloden, to the Highlanders it felt as if it were yesterday. Of course the constant presence of the king's army reminded them that they were still being punished. Even after some twenty years, Highlanders outlawed since the rebellion remained hidden in the mountains. John and his comrades had been commanded to find them and bring them in for sentencing. More times than not, the sentences were harsh. Usually death or banishment to the colonies as a bondsman, which was as good as death for a Highlander.

They were an interesting people, these Scots: proud, stubborn, and extremely resourceful. Even the ones who'd been faithful to the king during the rebellion bore watching. Thank goodness his own Murray ancestors had had the foresight to throw in with the correct side long ago. Better to be the son of a bastard who served the king than one who was an outlaw.

John turned Sultan toward Aberdeen. His future awaited inside a granite house on King Street. It was time to see what he would make of it.

Chapter Two

"Come, then, Izzy, give me a coin," Donnie Ferguson implored his sister. "Please," he added.

"No, Donnie, I won't," Izzy said. "I hae none to give."

"Ewan said you'd lie to me."

Isobel Ferguson looked at her younger brother and released a long, frustrated sigh. His blue eyes were earnest, guileless, and innocent, as always. Just like his faith in Ewan. He believed everything their older brother said; there was nothing she could do to change his mind. "And, as always, you choose to believe Ewan over me," she retorted as she followed Donnie into the alleyway so they would not be jostled by the passersby on King Street.

"Ewan looks out for me," he said.

"A fine job he must be doing if ye are here begging coins from me," she said. Izzy's brown eyes took in the dirt on the sleeves of Donnie's shirt, the tear in the knee of his breeches, and the worn leather of his boots. He needed a shave and his golden hair, as untidy as her own reddish gold, hung in his eyes. She resisted the urge to push it back behind his ear. He was much too old for her sisterly ministrations now. "Did he send you to fetch a coin for himself?" she asked instead.

Donnie started to protest and Izzy threw up a hand to stop him. "Why aren't you at work?" she asked. The dealings of her brothers were enough to drive her to the madhouse at Woolmanhill; the less she knew, the better off she'd be. But she'd always been protective of Donnie. Since he was ten years old she'd mothered him, after their own mother died in childbirth, along with the baby girl just delivered. If only she could be confident that Ewan felt the same protective instincts for Donnie as she.

Izzy narrowed her eyes at Donnie. He should be at work instead of tracking her down in alleyways as she made her deliveries for Master Rabin. Donnie worked for the blacksmith. He had a magic hand with the horses and could calm the most skittish mount. It was a waste of his gifts, Izzy often thought. He should be in a stable somewhere, training horses, instead of standing by their heads while they were shoed. But life was hard and jobs were scarce, especially for the offspring of a known rebel who was God knows where. If not for Culloden and the uprising . . .

Izzy shook her head at her own foolishness. She sounded just like Ewan. Constantly lamenting about what should have been.

"The forge is broken," Donnie explained. "And there's no work for me until it is fixed. I just want a coin to go to the tavern."

Izzy felt her resolve melting beneath Donnie's blue-eyed gaze and she dipped into her bodice to retrieve the leather pouch that hung safely between her breasts.

Donnie coughed and turned away as a flush rose up his neck. Izzy rolled her eyes. She knew Donnie, with his good looks and sweet smile, had tumbled many a wench, but the thought of his sister being female was enough to mortify him.

Well, there was no help for it. She had no other place to hide her coin without fear of it being stolen. It wasn't as if she could leave her wages in her room. Not with the likes of Angus Fitzwarren, Master Rabin's first apprentice, snooping around every chance he got and watching her every move with his piggy little eyes.

"Take it, then," Izzy said, holding the coin out and dropping it into her brother's hand.

Donnie's fist closed tight over it and he gave her a roguish smile. "I knew you had some," he said. "Even though you denied it."

"I never denied having money," Izzy said. "I just said I had none to give you." Her toes curled within her worn shoes, feeling every stone through the thin soles. She had not lied. She was saving her wages for a new pair of shoes and hoped to have them before winter set in.

She quickly checked Donnie's boots to make sure they would get him through the winter. Maybe she should get Donnie a new pair instead of herself. Perhaps Master Rabin, who was always more than generous, had a pair he no longer used; then both she and her brother could have good shoes. The ones Donnie wore would not last much longer.

How had their mother managed through the years with three growing children and a husband who was outlawed? A husband who gave her nothing except some stolen coin, an occasional bit of game, and a new babe in her belly every time he managed to sneak home for a visit.

"Where is Ewan?" Izzy asked as Donnie turned to go.

"He's off," Donnie replied.

"To meet Da?"

"Aye."

"Where?" Izzy grabbed Donnie's arm. "When?"

"He said not to tell you," Donnie said, shaking off her arm. "He said you might let it slip."

"The only thing I'll let slip is my foot on his backside," Izzy protested. "He's a fool on a fool's mission. He'll hae all of us in the tollbooth before he's done with it."

"Are you talking of Da or Ewan?"

"Both," Izzy said as she shook her head in disgust. "Thank the heavens he didn't take ye with him."

"I wanted to go," Donnie insisted, as if that would change Izzy's opinion.

Izzy grabbed her brother's arms. She felt the heavy muscle beneath, built from swinging the hammer, pumping the bellows, lifting the iron. When had he grown so? When had his shoulders broadened so? When did he come to stand head and shoulders over her? The top of her head barely met his chin. She looked up into his eyes, and realized once more how much like Da he looked.

"Donnie," she said. "Stay away from Da. And whatever plans he puts into Ewan's head." Donnie tried to pull away and she tightened her grip. "Ewan has no sense where Da is concerned. And Da has no sense at all."

"He's our father, Iz. How can you speak so of him?"

"Because I ken what he is like. I ken that he still talks of the rebellion as if Bonnie Prince Charlie himself will come back and save us all and shower us with riches beyond measure. I ken that he believes he is right and the English living among us are the enemy. I've heard him speak of it my entire life."

"The English *are* the enemy," Donnie said carefully as if repeating what he'd heard.

Izzy looked toward the street behind him. No redcoats in sight, but that did not mean none were listening. Anyone might turn Donnie in for speaking treason. "Nay. They *were* the enemy," she said. "Now they are the victors, and they will not let us forget it." She moved her hands down his arms and gripped his fingers, twining them between her own. "Donnie, if ye are to have any kind of future, ye must look ahead and not listen to Da and Ewan."

"Iz . . ." Donnie said with his sweet smile. He was a charmer, just like their da. Da had used the same smile to sweep their mother off her feet. At one time, Donald Ferguson was tall and strong, golden and beautiful with eyes as blue as the summer sky and a smile as broad as the lochs. Or so their mother often said. It had not taken much for him to convince Ellyn MacDonald to run off with him. No matter that she was the youngest daughter of an earl and destined for the church. Her husband became her religion and she followed him to the edge of hell.

Love was blind and foolish as far as Izzy was concerned. The world would be better off without it. "Donae try to charm me, Donnie Ferguson," Izzy said, quickly dropping Donnie's hands. "Go to the tavern and give the whores a treat. Just make sure you donae catch the clap because I'll leave your carcass to rot in the gutter."

Donnie dropped a kiss on the top of her head and took off with a smile and a wave. Izzy watched until he disappeared from view into the bustle of pedestrians, horses, wagons, and carriages on busy King Street.

Izzy shook her head. Now she was sure to be late getting back to the shop. She had finished her deliveries for the morning, but there were sure to be more waiting for her, along with whatever work Angus pawned off on her. Tommy, the second apprentice, would need help with his chores and this afternoon Miss Edina wanted her to serve tea to an officer in the king's army.

No rest for the weary. If she went by the back alleys, she could save some time, so she turned to make her way behind the shop fronts. Even though it was midday, the height of the granite buildings blocked the sun. Izzy could not repress a shiver as she made her way down between the shops to the alley behind. She picked up her skirts to keep them from dragging in the slops thrown down from the windows above.

Not too long after she turned the corner behind the

building, Izzy knew she'd made a mistake. A rat scurried ahead of her, and then darted behind a barrel as a boy stepped in front of her. He was tall and thin, with ill-fitting clothes that looked as if they'd been scavenged. An orphan, most likely, and she did not have to turn to know there were more gathering behind her, making their way from behind crates, beneath staircases, and out of cellars. At one time she'd feared Donnie would get caught up in gangs such as these. Only her stubbornness had kept him safe.

But now she was the one in danger, alone, weaponless, with all her coin in a bag about her neck. Judging by the way the boy was looking toward her breasts, she guessed he'd seen her take it out earlier. Without conscious thought, Izzy's hand moved protectively to the neck of her shirt and she saw the boy grin wolfishly.

He wasn't as much of a boy as she'd first thought. It was the roundness of his cheeks that had fooled her. But the look in his eye told her. He must be close in age to Donnie. Old enough to be after more than her money. The sudden appearance of a knife in his hand led her to believe that he'd have no qualms about hurting her to get everything he wanted.

Izzy heard quiet laughter behind her. How many were there? Were the others armed also? What were her chances of coming out of this alive? Izzy looked around for a weapon but saw nothing. She had nothing but her wits and her two fleet feet. She decided to trust in the latter. She turned and took off running as hard as she could.

There were two more that she could see. They were smaller than the one with the knife, but there was no doubt in Izzy's mind that they were quick and strong. They had to be to survive on the streets. She put her shoulder down and barreled past one, but felt the other grab at her arm as she ran by. She felt her sleeve rip but did not stop. If she made the corner, the passersby on the street would surely see that she needed help. Or else her attackers would leave off for fear of being caught.

Izzy prayed she would make it. She reached the corner and felt a brush of air down her back. Then her ankle snagged and she fell forward. She landed on her hands and knees and screeched as she felt her leg being pulled back. She slid in the garbage that littered the ground and twisted as the hand moved up her calf. She lashed out with her free leg and landed a solid kick against the chin of the boy who held her. He fell back, but behind him was the one with the knife.

Izzy let out another screech as she scrambled to her feet and took off. She felt the hands reaching again and felt her body pitch forward when her skirts got tangled around her legs. She felt a sharp pain as her head hit the cornerstone of the building. Lights burst in her eyes, but still she staggered on until the hands dragged her back. One clamped over her mouth and she gagged at the smell emanating from the body that held her tight.

"Get her bag," one said, and hands clawed at her bodice. Izzy jerked and kicked out as the hands pinched and probed and the fabric gave way. Her head spun and waves of pain washed through her skull. She felt dizzy and sick, yet still she fought. Then suddenly she fell to the ground as the arms that had imprisoned her disappeared. Izzy lay in the dirt, gasping for breath, as a pair of shiny black boots came into view.

She blinked and found herself staring into a pair of summer blue eyes. They were set in the face of an angel and framed by hair the color of sunshine. She must be dead and the angels had come for her. Either that or she was dreaming.

"Are you hurt, miss?" a deep, warm voice asked.

Izzy quickly sat up when she realized that a bright red coat covered the broad shoulders of the man instead of a pair of wings.

He held out a hand. "Can you stand?"

Izzy stared at the hand, aghast. Had a redcoat saved her?

"The ruffians are gone," he assured her. "They ran as soon as I appeared. I hope they left empty-handed. I wanted to give chase but hesitated to leave you alone."

"What?" Izzy asked. She felt like an idiot, but it was hard to follow his words with her head pounding so.

Gentle hands touched her forearms and pulled her to her feet. Her head swam and she fought against the urge to let darkness overcome her. Ewan would have a fit if he knew she'd fainted into the arms of a redcoat.

"Did they take anything?"

Izzy released his arm long enough to reach for the bag between her breasts. "No," she said in surprise. How had she managed to keep it? "I still have it." She looked down and realized to her horror that her bodice was torn. The fabric fell away to reveal the swell of pale skin above her shift. She knew her cheeks were burning and felt the flush move down her neck to her breasts. She pulled her arms away from her rescuer and folded them modestly over her exposed skin.

"You are bleeding," he said. He touched a finger to her temple and when he pulled it away, she saw that she was indeed bleeding. "Should I take you to a physician?"

Izzy drew in a deep breath and looked up into those summer blue eyes. Genuine concern showed in them, as he took in her appearance and the extent of her injuries. She willed her trembling limbs to relax and found that her brain did not seem as muddled as before. Was it possible that her savior was nothing more than a kindhearted soul who happened to be in the service of the king? He was not an enemy; he had no idea that she was the daughter of an outlaw and had brothers who talked of sedition every chance they got?

"I think I shall be fine once I am home," she said with a

tremulous smile. She even managed a quick curtsey. "I thank you for your assistance, sir."

His smile brightened the alleyway as he swept her a deep bow. "Captain John Murray at your service, Miss. . .?"

"Izzy, er, Isobel . . ." She hesitated to say Ferguson and decided at the last minute to go with her mother's name. "MacDonald." Ferguson was a common enough name, but there was no need to alert the king's men that the daughter of a known rebel was residing in Aberdeen. She managed to cover up her deception with a slight cough as if still breathless from her attack.

"It will be my honor to see you safely home," Captain Murray said, offering her his arm.

A redcoat, concerned about her safety? She wondered if she was having a wee bit of a delusion of some sort. But the arm before her seemed steady enough, and the pain that throbbed at her temples was real, along with the trickle of blood she felt on her cheek.

As if Captain Murray knew what she was thinking, he procured a fresh white linen handkerchief from within his coat and she used it to dab at the blood on her cheek as she took his arm.

Izzy took a moment to thank the heavens above that Ewan was gone. If he saw her so, she'd never hear the end of it.

Never.

Chapter Three

It was her eyes that John noticed. They were dark and deep, a warm brown that seemed like windows he could look into. There was an uncompromising directness in them that made him blink, as if she could see into his soul too.

Or maybe it was just the shadows of the alley that created that illusion. The dark richness of her eyes was a sharp contrast to her ivory skin, and the cloud of strawberry-blonde hair. The dusting of freckles across her upturned nose seemed to rebel against the seriousness of her eyes.

When she spoke, her words added to the puzzle. He expected, by the worn state of her dress, that she would have the guttural accent of the serving class. Instead she sounded educated and her speech was laced with the musical flow of the Highlanders. She did seem a bit confused when she answered him. The blow to her head would explain that.

She dabbed at the blood on her temple with his handkerchief, and then quickly pulled up the torn side of her bodice. John stopped in his tracks and took off his coat. He swung it over her shoulders and kept his eyes focused on her forehead, even though he was sorely tempted to look at the creamy swells of her breasts above the worn fabric of her undergarment.

He was no stranger to such sights. He had a sister, after all, and he hoped that if Carrie ever found herself in such dire straits, she would be rescued by a gentleman. But knowing Carrie, chances were that the gentleman would need rescuing from her inherent clumsiness. He kept his eyes averted for the moment lest his body betray him. Above all else, John valued control, and having his nether regions react to a random woman was not something he could allow.

Think on something else.

John's lips curved as he filled his mind with memories of his sister's disastrous escapades. He grew serious as he realized that the young woman, Isobel, had made no effort to cover herself with his coat. Instead she stood rigid, as if the red wool carried the plague itself.

"I have a horse waiting," John said encouragingly. Lord help him if she fainted and he had to carry her out of this dark alley. The locals would be on him in a moment, accusing him of rape and protesting against the viciousness of the king's army. Which led him to question why he'd come to her aid in the first place. He'd been riding to his meeting with Miss Rabin, practicing polite conversation in his mind, when he'd heard the scream and seen the tussle in the alleyway. His first instinct was to help. He'd quickly dismounted, tied Sultan to a post, and run toward the young woman who was fighting so valiantly against her attackers.

The same young woman who now stood proud and silent beside him.

She didn't say a word as he swept his arm toward the street to indicate the way. Instead she grasped the lapels of his coat around her bodice, straightened her spine, and moved toward the bright light of midday that spilled forth from King Street.

Sultan tossed his head impatiently as they walked out of the alley. John couldn't help feeling pride at the stud's display of spirit.

"This is your horse?" Isobel asked. Once more she had stopped dead in her tracks, looking from him to the beautiful white animal standing before them.

"Do not be afraid," John said, and placed a hand on Sultan's proudly arched neck. "He won't hurt you as long as I am around."

She shoved his coat into his arms. " 'Tis not the beast that I fear," she said, and turned back toward the alley. Before John could speak, she was gone at a run, her skirts gathered up in her hands.

John stared after her for a moment, then shrugged his shoulders and pulled his coat on. The view of her retreating backside was not unpleasant for all that her behavior was strange.

"Highlanders," he said to Sultan as he released the horse from the post and mounted once more. "They are an odd breed indeed."

Izzy flew through the alleyways, and did not stop until she reached the back of the granite house that contained the print shop, the Rabins' residence, and the room in the attic that she called home. With one hand she covered the stitch in her side while she held her bodice up with the other, all the while praying that Angus would not notice the state or smell of her dress. She had enough problems keeping him at bay without his glimpsing her cleavage. The pig.

Of course, handling the unwanted attention of Master Rabin's first apprentice would be easier than having to explain to Ewan what she was doing on the back of a snowy white steed, wearing a red coat, and being led down King Street by an English soldier. Heaven forbid. She might as well strip naked and dance at the Mercat Cross for all of Aberdeen to see. Either one would have the same effect on Ewan. There would be hell to pay for both her and Captain John Murray of the golden hair and proper speech.

Ewan wouldn't even care about the why or what had led up to her being with Captain Murray of His Majesty's army.

He certainly wouldn't stop to consider that if he was more concerned about taking care of her and Donnie, instead of chasing after Da and his dreams, she would not have been in the predicament in the first place.

Such was life. There was no need mourning what could have or should have been. It was the lot she'd drawn and she'd better make the best of it.

She'd better be quick about it too. Izzy pounded up the back stairs, past the first floor, which housed the print shop and kitchen, the second, which was the main floor of the house, the third, which held the bedrooms of Master Rabin and his daughter, Edina. It was four full flights to the attic, where she had a room beneath the eaves, along with Katty Ann, the maid, and the two apprentices, Angus and Tommy. Cook had her own room off the kitchen, which Izzy passed by without so much as a response to Cook's screech about the tea.

"Yes, I know about the tea," Izzy panted as she burst into her room. She heard the pounding of boot heels behind her and she slammed her door shut as she quickly undid the buttons of her bodice and loosed the tie of her skirt. There was no time for mending it. She'd have to wear her one dress and repair the damage this evening when her chores were done. She just hoped she could get the stink washed out of her skirt by morning time.

"Izzy!" Tommy pounded on her door. "Izzy, come quick. Miss Edina is fit to be tied. Her gentleman is here and she wants you to serve tea."

"I know it, Tommy, I know it." Izzy stepped into her dress and pulled it up over her shoulders. "Where is Katty Ann that she can't do it?"

"Crying beneath the staircase." Tommy's voice showed his frustration. He was sweet on Katty Ann, who was as skittish as a mare in season. "Edina told her not to touch the service, as she is more likely to pour it in the gentleman's lap than in the cup itself."

"I need her to do up my dress," Izzy said.

"She'll not come out."

Izzy knew she wouldn't. She didn't need Tommy to tell her. When Katty Ann hid beneath the staircase, it often took hours to dislodge her and usually it took Tommy to do it, talking to her as if she were a wee kitten stuck up a tree. Luckily for all of them, Master Rabin had the patience of a saint. He had to possess it to put up with the madness of his household.

Izzy took a moment to look in the small cracked mirror that hung on the wall over a washstand. The bleeding on her temple had stopped and she used a cloth to wipe the dried blood away. She'd likely have a bruise by evening. Izzy pinched her cheeks to add a bit of color and retied the dark ribbon that held her unruly hair in check.

"Iz!" Tommy said a bit louder than before.

"I'm coming," she replied. She flung open the door. Tommy was leaning against it and his painfully thin frame practically tumbled upon her. Izzy pushed him upright as Tommy shoved back the flop of brown hair that was always falling into his eyes. She presented her back to him. "Do me up," she said, holding her hair out of his way.

Tommy's nimble fingers, which were quick and sure from handling the small tiles of the print trays, made quick work of it. Izzy didn't think twice about having Tommy do the service for her. He felt more like a brother to her at times than Ewan and was always on the lookout for her. Especially when it came to Angus. They'd learned long ago that they were stronger united against him. Unfortunately Master Rabin's leniency concerning the quirks of his household also extended to lecherous oafs who were sly about pawning their work off on others while taking full credit for the rewards. Angus also had no compunction whatsoever about helping himself to the possessions of others. Izzy figured that one day he would get his due. She just hoped she was around when it came to pass.

"Done!" Tommy announced.

Izzy tossed a thank-you over her shoulder as she clattered back down the stairs. No wonder her shoes were so worn. It was a wonder there was any soles left to them with all the running about she did.

She stopped at the bottom of the stairs to open the closet door. Katty Ann sat on an overturned bucket with her face buried in her apron. "It's not my fault the platter broke!" she wailed. "It's had a crack in it forever!"

"Katty Ann," Izzy said firmly. "Can ye help me with something?"

Katty Ann rubbed her hands across her tear-streaked face and looked up at Izzy with red-rimmed brown eyes. "Of course," she said.

Izzy arched an eyebrow in surprise. She had hoped to distract Katty Ann from her tears lest Edina complain about the noise. The fact that Katty Ann had paid attention to her request was a new twist in the never-ending drama of the household. "My bodice is torn and my clothes are filthy. I fell in the alleyway. Will ye help me?"

Katty Ann nodded and jumped to her feet. Izzy felt a swell of satisfaction. Tommy had not yet come down and she was certain Katty Ann would run into him on the way up. The servants were not allowed to use the front staircase. As long as Angus remained in the print shop below with Master Rabin, then the two lovebirds should have a few moments of peace. If only she could get the same.

Cook had the tea service laid out, along with some biscuits

and jam. Her nephew, Davy, nibbled on a biscuit in his corner by the fireplace with his blue eyes wide at all the excitement. The lad was but nine and made a few coins by running small errands for the household. Izzy spared him a smile as she went to the table to get the service.

"How does the latest victim appear?" Izzy asked as she took the lid off the fine china teapot so Cook could pour the tea inside. She knew Cook could not help peeking into the parlor. Even though she complained about being confined to the kitchen, she seemed to know everything that happened in the house. Izzy often wondered if the woman could see and hear through the walls. She had her ways but they remained a mystery.

"Much more handsome than the last," Cook said. "He appears golden, like an angel," she sighed girlishly. "And both his eyes face in the same direction," she added.

"That should count for something." Izzy grinned. The last one had been cross-eyed to the point that Izzy could never tell if he were coming in or going out. Miss Edina had paraded several suitors through the parlor of the house in the past year. Most were after her considerable dowry as she was the only offspring of Master Rabin and stood to inherit everything he possessed. Whoever married her was guaranteed a successful business that would keep the couple well supplied for years to come, unless she married an idiot. But it appeared that she could find no better. Though Miss Edina was pretty enough, despite being a bit plump, her disposition was not as pleasing. She had a bad habit of shrieking to the eaves when things did not go her way, no matter who was around.

She was also extremely particular about whom she would marry and found many a reason to dismiss her suitors. All were better off for it as far as Izzy was concerned. She wouldn't wish the miss on anyone and thought it fortunate her father had the patience of a saint. If not he would have drowned her long ago.

"Best get on, then," Cook said. "Before she runs this one off with her blethering about Miss Cecilia's new dress." Miss Cecilia was the daughter of Master Fletcher, who owned the shipyards, and the cause of great grief to Edina because she always had the latest fashions and the best of everything. Edina both idolized and hated her and spent most of her time trying to best Cecilia in everything. If Cecilia got a new parasol, then Edina must have one too, only hers must have two sets of ruffles instead of one. The same with hats and dresses and shoes. The problem was that Cecilia could put on a feed sack and look beautiful, while Edina looked ridiculous in ribbons and bows.

That was one thing Izzy was glad she didn't have to worry about. Her wardrobe consisted of the pale green dress she now wore and a few serviceable skirts and shirts for work. Her only desire at the moment was for a new pair of shoes, which she would choose for practicality rather than style. She fastened an apron over her dress and picked up the tray. Izzy took a deep breath and climbed the one flight of stairs to the main level of the house, where Edina and her suitor waited in the parlor for their tea. She heard a deep masculine voice and above it the higher voice of Miss Edina, tinkling with polite laughter. Izzy barely glanced at the pair who stood before the parlor window as she rushed in with her tray. She went straight to the table to arrange the items as Edina spoke.

"Finally, here is the tea," she said somewhat impatiently in her shrill voice. "Where have you been, Isobel?"

"Running errands for your father," Izzy said. She bobbed into a curtsey and lifted her eyes to find herself staring into the bemused face of Captain John Murray. The sun poured through the window behind him and circled his body with a heavenly glow, as if an angel had alighted in the parlor. Except angels in Scotland did not wear red coats.

Izzy blinked.

"What happened to your face?" Edina asked. "You've got a cut and a bruise."

Izzy's hand went to her temple. "It is nothing," she said, her eyes on Captain Murray. "I tripped in my haste."

Please don't say anything. Meeting his eyes, she willed Captain Murray not to mention their meeting. The last thing she needed right now was Edina badgering her about the man who'd come to court her and wanting to know the details of the attack. It would all somehow circle back to Donnie, who was not above begging treats from Cook when he came looking for his sister, and no good would come of it. The less her employers knew about her family, the better. Master Rabin had no idea her father was an outlaw, and Izzy would like to keep it that way. Especially since there was an English soldier now ensconced in the parlor.

"You were lucky that you were not more severely injured," Captain Murray said kindly, and Izzy tried not to smile in relief.

"Yes, I was quite lucky," Izzy said. "A kind gentleman came to my aid and put things right." She bobbed another curtsey. "Enjoy your tea," she said as she hurried from the room before Edina could find something else to question her about.

"Did I not tell you he was handsome?" Cook said when Izzy came back down the stairs. "He has the look of an angel if you ask me."

Izzy shook her head at Cook's fancy. The woman was old enough to be Captain Murray's mother and probably weighed twice as much as the man. Yet she sat with her two chins propped in her hands and her eyes gone all dreamy as if Gabriel himself had just come down and folded his wings into the parlor. "There's got to be more to a man than a pretty face," Izzy said.

"Aye," Cook replied. "But having a pretty face to look at across the table is not a bad thing to wish for in a man."

"I'll just be happy to find one who can provide me with food and shelter," Izzy said as she shook her head at Cook's foolishness. And her own. She was well past the age when a man would consider her for marriage.

The look of an angel indeed.

Chapter Four

What was everyone looking at? The people of Aberdeen, who just seconds earlier had been going about their business, now stopped what they were doing and stared at him. John felt cold, unbearably so, and he briskly rubbed his arms to chase away the chilblains that covered his flesh as he walked down King Street. If only he could get warm. She had a fire. Isobel. If he found her, he would be warm. He had to find her. If only he knew where to look. John stopped at each alley and looked for her, but all he saw were outlaws and bandits waiting to jump him as he walked past. His hand went to his side to pull out his sword but came back empty.

Where was his sword? Before he could look down to see if his scabbard was on his hip, a plump woman with a pile of elaborate dark curls atop her head pointed at him and laughed. What was so funny? The other people on the street joined her until everywhere he looked he saw people pointing at him and laughing.

Then he saw Isobel. And she was laughing too. She walked toward him in her torn dress carrying a tea service on a tray and she laughed so hard that she dropped the tray.

He was naked.

John gasped as he bolted upright from his nap beneath the spreading branches of a Wych elm. He practically sighed in relief when he saw his cloak was still wrapped tightly around his body and his uniform was intact. He had not meant to fall asleep, but he had not slept well the past few nights. A red squirrel looked down at him from the branch above, his tail quivering in silent indignation at the invasion of his territory by the English patrol.

"How typically Scottish," John said, and saw a flash of white belly as the squirrel scampered up the trunk.

John rubbed his temples with his forefinger and thumb, hoping to relieve the headache caused by lack of sleep. Since his day in Aberdeen the vision of Isobel MacDonald had troubled his rest in much the same manner as a rock under his back. No matter which way he turned, there was no way to escape her.

Why?

John looked around the temporary camp. Members of his patrol had gathered under whatever shelter they could find, avoiding the pouring rain that seemed determined to make them as miserable as possible. Waiting was always the hardest part. And who knew if the sheriff and the farmer would even show up? The local sheriff had reported that the farmer had found the remains of a missing sheep near an abandoned campfire. There'd also been talk of bandits in the area, so General Kensington had thought it best to investigate. They were waiting now for the two Scots to appear.

"Did you enjoy your nap?" Rory asked. He handed John a tin cup with what looked like coffee, although the smell indicated something vile and potent. John sniffed at it cautiously. The tin felt warm in his hands and the steam rising from the cup held the promise that whatever it was, it would warm his insides.

"Some of Gordon's poison," Rory assured him as John took a cautious sip. The taste was vile but he felt warmer and somewhat more awake after drinking.

"Why did you let me sleep?" John asked.

"I felt you needed it," Rory said. "You've done nothing but toss and turn since your leave day. Was the future Mrs. Murray that bad?"

John swirled his cup to cool the brew and looked at the dark liquid. It was the same color as Isobel's eyes.

"You've not said a thing about her," Rory continued.

"She's fine," John said. "Exactly as I expected." Edina Rabin had been what he'd expected. She was well endowed in body and wealth, with luscious dark curls around a very pretty face. He didn't care much for her style of dress—it was much to frilly to suit him—and her voice, when she was excited, seemed to rise to an octave that was almost painful to the ears, but all things considered, she would be a good match.

That was his goal, wasn't it? Making a good match? He needed a wife with some wealth and she needed a husband with some intelligence, who could take over her father's business someday. Owning a printing shop would surely provide a good income for a man's family. That was all he could ask for, wasn't it?

John tried his best once again to convince himself that Miss Edina Rabin was a good choice for his future. It was hard to think on her, however, when all he could see in his mind was a cloud of red-gold hair and deep brown eyes. His mind was full of questions about the young lady who'd served tea in Miss Rabin's parlor.

What was she doing in the alley? Why was she accosted? Why would she not allow him to see her safely to the Rabins' if that was where she lived? And why did she not want Edina to know that he'd met her? The look she'd given him had made it clear that she wanted their meeting to remain secret. Just seeing her there had been a shock. Most of the women he knew would have been prostrate after such an attack. They would have retired to their rooms with smelling salts and hot water bottles and attacks of the vapors. But servants were not allowed such luxuries.

When he'd left the Rabins' parlor and gone down the flight of stairs to the street, he had looked into the window of the print shop on the main floor. He'd stood for a moment to calm Sultan, who was not happy about being left out on the main thoroughfare of Aberdeen.

He'd seen her then, her head bent over a table, her nimble fingers arranging the print tray alongside a tall and extremely thin young man. Master Rabin was talking to a customer at the counter while a stout man who appeared to be near John's age seemed more interested in what Isobel was doing than his own work.

She looked up and stared at the stout man until he looked away and then John was surprised to see her dark eyes land on him as he stood beside Sultan with the reins in his hand. John touched the tip of his forefinger to his hat in farewell and she bent back to her work as if she'd never laid eyes on him.

But she had seen him. There was no doubt in his mind as to that. She was a mystery, one that would not leave his mind and seemed ever present in his dreams. Dreams that left him feeling slightly embarrassed because they all seemed to feature his undoing yet left him waking with his rod stiff and throbbing. Luckily for his own peace of mind, Rory had not noticed that part of his agitation. Or if he had, he hadn't commented on it.

John held high hopes that the task of chasing down bandits would be enough of a distraction to remove the girl from his mind and his dreams. Another restless night like the ones just past and he'd be forced to seek out a prostitute, and that prospect did not please him, no matter how pleasurable the outcome.

Such places were not for a man who cared about his reputation. Especially one who was courting an eligible young woman of Aberdeen.

"That bad?" Rory said, and John suddenly realized Rory had asked a question.

"I'm sorry," John said. "I was distracted."

"Obviously," Rory said with a smile. "So either she's very pretty or very rich, but not both, else you would not be so distracted."

"She's both," John assured him. "We are meeting for tea again on my next leave day."

"Good," Rory said. "You'll be married and a father in no time." He grinned. "But just remember, while you are proper and settled, I will still be out finding what destiny has in store for me."

"Isn't that just another way of saying you'll still be chasing whores?" John asked dryly.

"Call it what you like," Rory said. "I prefer to think of it as exploring my options."

"Be careful lest one of your options is a hot needle up your roger," John said, refering to one of the more dreaded cures for the clap.

"Ouch." Rory shifted uncomfortably. "You sure know how to bring a man down, John Murray," he added.

"Better me than the clap," John replied. "Any news?" he asked as he pitched out the brew in his cup. His soldier's eye looked over the men; they seemed as lethargic as he felt. At this rate they would have to spend the night at their temporary camp and it promised to be a miserable one. They needed some sort of shelter, a barn, a cave, or, hope beyond hope, an inn with a nice bed. All of those seemed improbable, given the inhospitable circumstances they found themselves in. John looked over his shoulder at young Private Pearson, who stood by one of the gentler horses. The boy was talking to his mount and John was glad to see that he'd taken his instructions to heart.

John shook his head as he turned back to Rory. "We'd better keep an eye on young Pearson when we move out," he said. "Lest he fall off and lose himself in the heather."

"It looks as if our sheriff has arrived," Rory said, and pointed toward two men riding their way.

"At least now we can find out whether our day will be a total waste," John said as he watched the men ride up.

The sheriff, a portly fellow with a balding pate, dismounted beneath the spreading shelter of the tree and wiped his face with a large square of linen. The other man was short, even on his horse, but seemed to have the thin muscles of someone accustomed to hard work without much food. His eyes shifted from the sheriff, to John, Rory, and the rest of the patrol, who watched the gathering with interest.

"This is the farmer with the dead sheep," the sheriff indicated with a toss of his head, conveying his frustration all in one glance. Obviously the farmer had been unwilling to come and John couldn't say that he blamed him considering the weather.

"Tell us what happened," John said as Sergeant Gordon offered the farmer a tin of his vile coffee. The man seemed grateful for it and sucked it down in spite of its bitter taste. He swiped his sleeve over his mouth and handed the cup back to Gordon.

"When I did me count, I noticed one of me ewes was gone," the farmer said. "I tracked two days up into the hills and found the carcass and the remnants of a fire by a cave. I found some skins too. Hares and such. Like someone's been stayin' there a bit."

"Two days on foot?" Rory asked.

The farmer nodded. "She wandered round a bit, but who-ever kilt her took her straight back to the cave. It would be half a day or more from here on horseback."

"You'll take us there," Rory said.

The farmer looked belligerent at Rory's assumption and John could not say that he blamed him. He looked dubiously at the farmer's horse. The beast looked more appropriate for a stew pot than a long day's ride through the rain.

"This man has lost a ewe and several days' work," John said. "Tell us the direction and give us landmarks, and you can be on your way back home."

The farmer seemed shocked at John's kindness. The sheriff also. Rory merely shook his head and smiled as if he'd just heard a joke.

It was his father's words that guided John. All men de-served respect. No matter what their title, or their riches or their lack of both. It wasn't the way of the world, but it was the way it should be.

Why should this farmer, who had to struggle for every-thing he possessed, continue to suffer because someone had stolen one of his sheep?

"Thank ye, sir," the farmer said, and bobbed his head.

"Gordon, get the directions," John instructed as he mo-tioned the sheriff and Rory aside for news on further rebel activity in the area.

"What is the news, Sheriff?" John asked.

"More of the same," the sheriff said. "He's the only one missing a sheep, but there have been signs of bandits, although I don't think it's more than two from what I can tell. Just a few things missing like clothes and food and such . . . and the sheep, of course."

"Of course," John said. He looked at Rory. "Nothing to do, then, but go see about it."

"I was afraid you were going to say that," Rory sighed. "Sergeant Gordon, tell the patrol to mount up."

They rode out into the downpour, Sergeant Gordon in the lead with Rory by his side. John let them go on, content to ride behind a few paces, enough so that the muck the horses' hooves flung backward did not hit Sultan. The rest of the patrol filed behind them as they moved out on a track that was too narrow for a coach. All of them rode with their heads down against the weather, trusting in the good sense of the horses and Sergeant Gordon's tracking skills to get them safely where they were going.

John let his mind wander, confident that Sultan would follow Rory and Gordon. It was too wet and too foggy to see anything around them and much too miserable a day for the stud to kick up his heels. Too bad Pearson couldn't see more of the country. The lad would more than likely have his fill of Scotland after this trip.

John tried to focus on the task at hand. The patrol. Finding shelter for the night. A search of the cave and the surrounding area when they got there. He did his best to concentrate on procedure.

Instead his mind filled once more with a cloud of red-blonde hair and deep brown eyes. If he was going to think about a woman, why couldn't he think on the pleasingly plump, albeit frilly form of Edina? There was no future thinking about the other. Isobel. She was a servant, nothing more, and a skinny one at that. There was no money, certainly no title, no way she would fit into his carefully made plans for respectability and comfort.

Stop thinking about her, John reminded himself for probably the hundredth time. *Put her out of your mind.*

If only it were that easy.

What if you marry Edina and see Isobel every day? What if you take her for a mistress? A vision of red and gold hair spread on the grass assailed him. Deep brown eyes looked up at him from a sweetly smiling face as arms reached out for him. Would she have him?

John squirmed uncomfortably in his saddle. He took off his hat and let the rain trickle down his neck, grateful for the cooling effect it had on his suddenly heated skin.

What has come over me?

It was almost as if he were bewitched, if one believed in such a thing. The impossible was easy to believe in this country with its stories of monsters who lived in lochs and faeries who stole children and the other tales he'd heard from the common folk.

Bewitched by a skinny servant girl.

Bewitched indeed.

Chapter Five

"It will work, Da," Ewan said. "I know it will."

"Ye think they will just let me walk onto a ship?" Donald Ferguson said. "Willnae the redcoats be watching?"

"They donae watch as they used to," Ewan assured his father. "They will think ye are a dockhand, nothing more. We can get passage to America. I've saved every coin I could and now I have enough for the two of us. Once there, we can start over. No one will know who ye are. We can disappear."

"What of Donnie and your sister?"

"We can send for Donnie later when we have a place."

"And Isobel?"

"She willnae come, Da."

"The lass is as stubborn as her mother." Donald Ferguson ran a hand through the long strands of his silver and gold hair and scratched at the beard that covered his chin as he looked out at the rain that curtained the world.

How small his world had become. Nothing in it but fear and hiding, cold and hunger. For the past twenty-some years he'd lived his life as a fugitive. He'd sacrificed home, family, title, riches, all of it, for Bonnie Prince Charlie, who'd left Scotland never to return. The only thing he had left was his life, his claymore, and an arm that was too weary to use it in battle.

He also had three fine children, one who would follow him to his grave. The other two he was not so sure of.

"She blames me for her mother's death," Donald said. And why shouldn't she? Ellyn had died in childbirth, another daughter with her, while he hid in the caves and waited for word. Would it have been different if he'd been there? Could he have changed Ellyn's fate?

"She doesna remember the way of it, Da," Ewan said. "Ma wouldnae leave you. She would have lived in the caves if you would have allowed it."

Ewan was right about that. Ellyn had followed him when she was nothing more than a lass and he just barely considered a man. She'd run from her family, she'd run from the church where she was promised, she'd followed him to the Highlands, and she would have followed him onto the battlefield at Culloden if she'd not been carrying Isobel in her womb. Her pregnancy and Ewan clinging to her skirts had been all that stopped her.

"Ye all would be better off if I had died at Culloden," Donald said. "Ye could have gone on with your lives." And maybe, just maybe, Ellyn would be alive today instead of dying of worry and hunger and birthing another babe when she should have been done with that part of her life.

"We can go on with our lives in America, Da. We can build a new life."

Donald gripped his son's shoulder. This child, his eldest, was the image of his mother. He had her dark red hair and brown eyes and her chin. Aye, Ewan took after Ellyn, while Donnie, taller than his brother and broader, resembled his father. Then there was Isobel, a mixture of both her parents. A bridge between her brothers. Whether that was good or bad, he'd never had time to determine. There had never been time for his children beyond quick and stolen visits, mostly when they slept. Except for Ewan. Ewan, who seemed to know when he was coming and would stay awake and hang on his every word, only relenting when sleep finally overcame him, or when he was older, he sensed his mother's hunger for her husband.

"Let me think on it," Donald finally said. How could he tell his son that leaving Scotland meant leaving his last connection with Ellyn, even if it was only a narrow grave with a simple stone in the churchyard at Kildrummy? "Ye best get back to town." Ewan had been gone long enough. If he were to keep his job and not arouse suspicion, he must be off, no matter what the weather. "Tell Donnie and Izzy that I love them and hope to see them soon." Donald knew his greeting to Isobel would fall on deaf ears; still, he could hope, couldn't he? When one led a life such as his, hope was all a man had to sustain him.

Ewan nodded. "Da," he said. "Ye can't think too long on it. I have to book passage. Before winter sets in."

"I know, son." Donald squeezed Ewan's shoulder. "Be off with ye now."

Ewan grabbed him in a quick hug and then disappeared into the rain.

Izzy shook the rain off her cloak beneath the small overhang that covered the entry to the shop. Why couldn't Master Rabin send Angus or Tommy out into the rain to make the deliveries? Why did she always have to be the one who made the trips, no matter what the weather?

She knew the answer as well as she knew that she was soaked and they were dry. They were apprentices and she was nothing more than a servant, even though she did the same sort of work in the shop and could read and write as well as the two who stayed warm and dry inside.

If not her, it would be Tommy running about in the rain since he was second to Angus. At least he seemed grateful, giving her a nod and a quick smile when she came in before he turned his attention back to the customer he was working with.

Her shoes were soaked through, along with her stockings.

There was no fire in the brazier since it was high summer, even though there was a damp chill in the air. She'd just have to live with wet feet. Angus waved her to the back of the shop, no doubt to take over his task so he could sneak off for a quick nap.

"Cook said fer ye to come to the kitchen as soon as ye got back," he said gruffly. He looked at her expectantly as if she should tell him why Cook had summoned her.

No chance of that. . . . At least she could hang up her cloak and dry her shoes out a bit by the stove. No doubt Angus would find an excuse to follow her. The shop bell rang as the door opened and Izzy quickly ducked into the back hall so Angus would have to wait on the customer. That should give her enough time to go to see what Cook wanted without Angus snooping around.

"Donnie?" Izzy said as she walked into the kitchen. She walked past him to the back door and hung her cloak on a nail, then turned to look at her brother.

Donnie sat at the table eating a piece of cake while Cook poured milk into a mug and Katty Ann stood wide-eyed and pale by the staircase. Izzy couldn't decide whether the maid wanted to throw herself at Donnie, or faint at the sight of him. Donnie seemed to have that effect on most women and as usual he was enjoying himself immensely. Even Cook was fussing over him. Izzy noticed the towel hanging about his neck, no doubt used to dry his hair, which hung damply around his blue eyes. Donnie's shirt gaped open at the neck, revealing smooth skin and the clear-cut definition of his muscular chest.

No wonder Katty Ann was in such a dither. Izzy shook her head. Donnie was her baby brother. His looks had no effect on her whatsoever.

"He's an angel," Cook said as she looked up from her worship of Donnie's face. "This one is, just like the other."

Izzy stopped, startled at the comparison between her brother and Captain Murray. She had not thought of it when she'd met him, but it was true, they did resemble each other. Both were tall and straight, with wide shoulders and long legs. Both had golden hair and deep blue eyes. But Donnie's face had a softness about it that hinted at the innocence of youth, while there was a manly firmness about Captain Murray's sharply angled jaw and straight nose. It was obvious he was not one to be trifled with. Command would suit him if that was what he desired.

I wonder what he looks like when he laughs.

Now, where did that thought come from? As if Captain Murray would ever be laughing around her. More likely he'd be bossing her around after he married Miss Edina. But he had smiled, briefly, in the alleyway, and then again in the parlor.

"Iz?" Donnie said, and Izzy realized it wasn't the first time he'd spoken. Cook, Katty Ann, and Donnie were all looking at her with puzzled expressions on their faces.

She'd drifted off for a moment. She had to admit it. Thinking of Captain Murray instead of why Donnie was sitting in the kitchen eating cake.

"What is it, Donnie?" she asked. "Why are you here?" The only time he ever came around was when he wanted something from her. "Is it Ewan?" she asked as she suddenly realized that she had not heard whether Ewan was back from his rendezvous with their father.

"Who is Ewan?" Cook asked.

"I have another brother," Izzy said.

"Is he as fine as this one?" Cook asked.

Donnie's gulp of milk sprayed all over the table at Cook's question. If Izzy didn't get her brother away from the woman, and soon, his head would be too big to fit through the door.

"Stop wasting everyone's time, Donnie," Izzy said. She

grabbed his arm and pulled him from the chair as Cook mopped at the table, and threw in a few swipes at Donnie's broad chest for good measure.

"Good day, ladies," Donnie said with a dazzling smile as Izzy led him out on the back step.

"What is it?" Izzy crossed her arms impatiently after she pulled the door shut behind her to shut off Cook's admonishments to come back and visit again. The rain still poured from the heavy clouds above.

"Ewan wants to talk to us."

"Can't it wait?"

"He said to fetch you and bring you to his place. He said it was important."

"And because Ewan said so, what everyone else has to do isnae as important?"

"I think it's about Da, Iz," Donnie said. "Ewan was troubled."

Izzy rolled her eyes impatiently. Ewan was always troubled about Da.

"Ye must come," Donnie urged, and Izzy felt herself relenting, as she always did with Donnie.

"Aye," she said. "I will, but only because you won't leave until I do and I donae think Cook can deal with much more of the sight of ye. And besides that, ye should be working instead of running around in the rain doing as Ewan bids ye."

Donnie smiled, dismissing her worry over his work. "Who is the little maid? The pretty one."

"Her name is Katty Ann and don't ye dare to go near her. Tommy likes her and I'll not have ye turning her head. She will break his heart chasing after ye, and then ye will break hers and leave her crying, and I'll have to do both of their work."

"Get your cloak, Iz," Donnie said. "It's raining and I donae know how long Ewan wants us."

Izzy sighed. She'd have to make up the time tonight. Then there would be Angus to deal with, snooping around in her business. Master Rabin was gone, so she would not have to ask his permission to go . . . just his forgiveness later. She opened the door and grabbed her cloak, which was still damp from her last excursion.

"I donae know when I will be back," she told Cook.

"Take care, both of ye," Cook said through the opening. Izzy swung her cloak over her shoulders and they set off into the rain.

"Where's your coat, Donnie?"

Donnie shrugged as they dashed through the puddles. "The wet doesna bother me," he said.

Donnie had always been the type to be comfortable, no matter where he was or what was happening. He never complained about things the way Ewan did, always going on about the English and how unfair life was for the Scots.

It was a long walk to Ewan's lodgings. Across the Brig of Balgownie and the river Don, then down to the wharves. Donnie took Izzy's arm as they finally turned onto Market Street lest she be run down by one of the wagons loaded high with goods coming from the pier. The smell of low tide assaulted her senses, along with that of the wet slops that were pitched into the street. Izzy covered her nose with a handkerchief as they hurried along. Gulls swooped overhead, wanting to feed on the garbage along the curb and screeching their anger at the pedestrians who kept them from their meal. Donnie held her arm and Izzy let him guide her, content, for the moment, to allow someone else to lead the way. She heard the calls of the whores hanging from a window above and peeked out beneath the hood of her cloak long enough to see Donnie's cheeks turn fiery red.

"Friends of yours?" she asked.

"Some are." Donnie grinned, in spite of his obvious embarrassment. "Handy to have such friends at times," he added.

"Indeed," Izzy agreed although she was innocent of such things. She only knew what she'd glimpsed when her da and ma lay with each other after they thought the children were asleep. She knew that men enjoyed sex: It was all Donnie seemed to think about and Ewan too, although he never let on to Izzy about such things. She recalled that her mother seemed to want it too; Izzy remembered an image of her mother's head thrown back in ecstasy by the light of the fire while her father kissed her throat. Izzy's pale cheeks turned as red as Donnie's when she thought on it.

Izzy stole a glance toward the whores above. She saw plenty of bosom and painted lips as they leaned out the windows and shouted at the men working the wharf. They must enjoy sex also, but for the life of her she didn't know what there was about it that made it so pleasurable. There must be something, however, or men and women would not pursue it so avidly. But for someone who'd never even been kissed . . .

Izzy touched a finger to her lips as the visage of Captain John Murray once more entered her thoughts.

What was it about the man that haunted her so?

She'd better put him out of her mind, once and for all.

Chapter Six

What would happen to Izzy when he and Da left for America? What would she do when Donnie joined them? Would she decide to come? Ewan liked to think so. He wanted them to be together as a family, not living separate lives, each one of them scraping to get by. If only he could have kept them together after Ma died. The only choice they'd had at the time was to come to Aberdeen, because it was the only place they could get work.

Thank you, God, for finding Iz a good place. Ewan crossed himself as he sent up his prayer of thanksgiving. Iz had a roof over her head and three good hot meals a day, even if she did have to put up with that apprentice who had a roving eye. If he ever laid a hand on her . . .

Ewan glanced out his window with a sigh. He was grateful for the window. It was more than the other men had. Most dock workers bunked in rooms with ten others who snored and farted and stole whatever wasn't nailed down. He was especially glad that he had a room to himself when Donnie had too much drink in him. It was a long walk back to the stable where he slept in the loft. For Ewan, the private room was worth the extra he had to pay. He did not need anyone snooping around asking about where he went and who he saw. It was a place where he could even hide Da if need be.

Ewan pressed his forehead to the pane and let the coolness ease the pounding in his head as he counted his blessings just like Ma had taught him to do each day. The four of them were doing fine. They weren't starving and they each had a warm, dry place to sleep in and clothes on their backs. Still, there had to be a better life for them somewhere. Someplace where they could be together as a family. Perhaps a farm where they could live and Donnie could work with the horses and he and Da could raise the food they needed to get by and Izzy could cook for them. Then maybe, someday, a wife for him and Donnie and maybe, just maybe, a husband for Iz before she got too old to be a wife. No matter what happened, he would take care of her. If she would let him.

They would leave for America. Ewan would not even think of the alternative. If only there was some way to convince Izzy that it was the right thing to do. He watched his brother and sister pick their way through the puddles caused by the heavily loaded wagons that constantly moved up and down Market Street. The windowpane was covered with condensation caused by the heat rising from his body and he swiped at it with the shirt he'd removed upon coming in.

Ewan flexed his shoulders. He was exhausted. The long walk to meet Da had been followed by the terror of the trip home where he had to go immediately to work unloading the cargo of a ship that had docked at the same moment he'd arrived at the pier. Ewan wanted nothing more than a hot meal and a long sleep. If only he could.

Food and rest would have to wait. He heard Donnie's footsteps on the stairs and Izzy's lighter tread behind him. Ewan pulled on a dry shirt and answered the door when he heard Donnie's knock.

"Izzy," Ewan said. He didn't get to see enough of his sister. She seemed tired as she swung off her cloak and hung it on the peg beside his coat.

"I'm wet, Ewan, and I'm missing work," Izzy said abruptly. "What is so important that you had to send Donnie to get me and cause both of us to miss work in the middle of the day?"

Ewan rubbed a hand through his wet hair as he turned to look at his siblings. "Da's been taken."

Donnie's face turned ashen, while Izzy slid into the one wooden chair as if her legs no longer worked. "What happened?" she asked.

"The soldiers. Up past Rhynie. It must have happened soon after I left him because they passed me on the road." He would never forget it. The English soldiers on horseback with one on a snowy white stallion in the lead. And Da, his hands tied before him, being led by one of the soldiers as he tried to keep up with the horses. Ewan punched his fist into his hand. "I knew I shouldnae have let him take that sheep. But he was so verra hungry and I didnae bring enough food to get him back to the Highlands."

"Da poached a sheep?" Izzy asked. "It doesna surprise me," she said when Ewan nodded.

"What do ye mean by that?" Ewan asked. "He was hungry. He did what he needed to do to survive."

"As he's always done, no matter what the consequences to anyone else," Izzy said. "As far as he knew, it could hae been the only sheep of a poor family that would starve without it."

Ewan stared at her. How could she sound so heartless? Their father was in the tollbooth.

"Iz—" Donnie started.

Izzy held up her hand to stop him. "It doesnae matter now. The English will see that he is fed and he willnae have to steal for his supper."

"Until they decide to hang him at the Gallowgate," Ewan said. "Or cut off his head." He'd seen enough executions in his lifetime to know the penalty for treason.

Donnie's face turned whiter than before and he placed a hand on the wall to steady himself.

"He knew the penalty when he decided to run all those

years ago," Izzy said. "He could have served his time by now and been a free man."

"Away from his family," Ewan reminded her. "Lost to us in America."

Izzy jumped up from the chair. "Lost to us!" Ewan flinched, surprised at her sudden fury. Her brown eyes flashed as she stood before him with her hands on her hips and her head tilted back so she could look him in the eye. "He's been lost to us our entire lives, Ewan." Her voice rose with her anger. "He chose Prince Charlie and the rebellion over his wife and family. He's never been a father to us beyond putting his seed inside Ma."

"Izzy!"

Ewan could not tell from Donnie's outburst if he was shocked or awed at his sister's outrage. Donnie stood off to the side, his blue eyes wide as he looked at the two of them.

"I'll not have you speak of him that way, Isobel." Ewan used her proper name as their mother always had when trying to soothe Izzy's sudden flairs of temper. "He is our father and is owed our respect."

Izzy looked as if she wanted to say more. Either that or she wanted to hit him. Ewan could not really say which. She stared at him for a long moment, her brown eyes a mirror of his own. Yet Ewan could not really say what was going on in her head. Some days the things she said surprised him. He could not believe that she really hated their father, yet . . .

Finally she turned and walked to the window. Izzy folded her arms over her waist, her palms gripping her elbows. She seemed smaller, somehow, and slight, as if a stiff breeze would blow her away. It was strange to Ewan to see her that way. Izzy was always a force to be reckoned with. She was always strong and sure about everything she did.

"Can we see him?" she asked.

"I havenae asked."

"Do ye think there will be a trial?"

"Not if I have anything to do with it," Ewan said.

"What is that supposed to mean?" Izzy asked. She looked over her shoulder at him, her eyes suspicious. It was funny how she could make him so uncomfortable with just a look. As if she were his conscience.

Ewan quickly dismissed her look and the discomfort it caused him. He knew what he had to do. He had to save his family. Ewan looked at Donnie. "It means we're going to get him out," he said.

"We will," Donnie said.

Izzy stepped between them and stuck her hand on Ewan's chest. "Tell me ye are not serious," she said.

"I am serious," Ewan said. He knew Izzy would protest, but he also knew he needed her help.

"Do ye even know what ye are saying, Ewan? Do you have any idea how ye are to go about it? Without getting killed or captured in the process?"

"I have a plan," Ewan said. "I need ye to help me with it." He had a seal, a Lord's seal, found on the ship he'd just been on, undoubtedly left behind when the man had disembarked. If Izzy would write a proper letter, the seal would make it official. But it had to be done soon.

Izzy jerked her cloak from the hook. "Come on, Donnie. We're leaving."

"No, Iz," Donnie said. "I'm staying. Ewan needs our help." He grabbed her arm. "Da needs our help."

Izzy swung her cloak around her shoulders. Water flecked Ewan as the violence of her movement shook off the raindrops. "How many times have ye even seen Da in your lifetime, Donnie? Ten? Five? Yet ye are willing to sacrifice your future for him."

"He's my father," Donnie said firmly.

Ewan could not help feeling proud. Donnie was just like Da in his convictions. It was a good thing.

"Don't do this, Ewan," Izzy said. "Ye have always been a fool where Da was concerned, but I beg ye, donae drag Donnie into this."

Her eyes seemed fearful as she glanced at Donnie, who moved to stand next to him. She stood there, looking at them, and Ewan could not help thinking of their mother.

Izzy turned without another word and left, the door slamming loudly behind her.

"She's a bit put out with us, Ewan," Donnie said.

"Ye think so?" Ewan replied as they heard their sister storming down the stairs.

Izzy's anger kept her feet going, but she could not say what her destination was. She passed the whores and the dock workers and the wagon drivers without so much as batting an eye. She ignored the rain that plastered her hair down to her head since she had not bothered to raise the hood on her cloak. She ignored the puddles that soaked her shoes and her stockings up to her knees. All of it fell away, as she repeated one phrase over and over in her mind.

"Da's mistakes will cost all of us in the end."

If only she could make Ewan see that. And Donnie. Especially Donnie.

"They'll both wind up dead." Izzy spoke aloud as she walked. Her fear was so real she had to give voice to it. The pain the words caused was so acute, she stopped in her tracks. She blinked and looked around as she sucked in great gulps of cold, damp air and realized that she stood in front of the Mercat Cross. The arched structure soared above her, over three times her height. She looked up to see the pedestal with the royal unicorn upon it glistening in the rain. Around the base were engravings, all featuring the former kings of Scotland.

"How many families were destroyed to keep the lot of ye in power?" Izzy mused as she stared at the medallions. She'd never taken the time to study them before and she wouldn't bother now except that she did not want to look at the toll-booth, nor up the way to Castle Hill where the English soldiers were stationed.

"Oh, Da," she finally sighed when she could no longer see through her tears. Izzy turned and walked smack into a bright red wall. She staggered back a pace and gazed up into the handsome face of Captain John Murray. He was looking down upon her with concern evident in his sky blue eyes.

Without a thought she crumpled into his chest. She wrapped her hands around the lapels of his coat and clutched them to her. She felt a pair of warm and very strong arms come around her, providing comfort and shelter from the rain. If only it could really be this easy.

"There, there, miss," the deep voice said. "I'm sure it will be all right in the end."

But it wouldn't. Donnie, Ewan, and even Da could all be dead at the end, and their sacrifice would all be for nothing except misguided loyalty and Scottish stubbornness.

Love and respect was what Ewan called it. And here she was standing in the middle of Aberdeen crying like a fool in the arms of an English soldier. If that wouldn't add to the mess, nothing would.

Izzy pushed herself away and wiped her tears into the rain that coated her face. Captain Murray moved his hands from her back to her shoulders and gave her a most reassuring squeeze.

Drat the man. He didn't even have the decency to look any

worse for the weather. She knew she must resemble a drowned rat, yet he seemed as shiny as a new coin. He was probably wondering what she was doing blubbering in front of the Mercat Cross instead of working as she very well should be. And the Lord help her if he told Edina about it. If Master Rabin should hear of Da's arrest, she'd be out in the street in no time.

"What troubles you, Miss MacDonald?" Captain Murray asked. "Is there anything I can do for you?"

If only he knew what troubled her. The lot of them would end up in the tollbooth alongside Da.

Izzy blinked back the next set of tears that threatened to burst forth. Da had been taken by an English patrol. Wouldn't it just be beyond belief if it was Captain Murray himself who'd taken him? Wouldn't that be a fine topic of discussion the next time he came to tea with Miss Edina?

"There is something ye can do for me," Izzy said when she finally found the courage to look into his eyes. "Ye can mind your own life and leave mine alone from now on."

Chapter Seven

It took John a moment to realize that his jaw was gaping open as he watched Isobel storm away. If he did not know for a fact that she worked for Rabin, he would be checking to see if she was recently escaped from Woolmanhill. The woman was an enigma, and if many people saw him standing in the pouring rain with his mouth hanging open, he might wind up in the madhouse himself.

He'd realized right off it was Isobel when he'd seen her petite frame sobbing in front of the Mercat Cross. She was all he'd thought about in the ten days since he'd saved her in the alleyway. What strange fate had brought her there, weeping as if there was no hope left in her world?

Obviously, her problem was something she did not want him to know. The only thing he was accomplishing at the moment was getting wetter, if that was possible. It seemed as if the rain would never stop. One gray day followed the other until John could not recall what it felt like to be warm and dry and not surrounded by dreadful smells.

John made his way back to the barracks. He'd been summoned to the tollbooth to give a report on the capture of the prisoner Donald Ferguson. He was not surprised to see there was a long list of charges against the man, dating all the way back to the rebellion. He would likely be executed, or if he was lucky, transported. Either way, the man's fate was none of his concern.

And he had other things to think about besides the strange moods of Isobel MacDonald. Namely a letter from his sister, handed to him on his way out of the barracks. John made his way back to his room, where he could have some privacy to read it. He hung up his coat and ran a towel over his hair before he sat down at the small desk he shared with Rory and lit the lantern against the dark gloom of late afternoon. He had hoped to find a letter from his father enclosed also, but to his dismay all he found was a short note, as if Carrie had been hurried when she wrote it.

Dearest Brother,

I hope all is well with you. I so despise troubling you when you are off doing your best to serve our King and Country, but I feel I have delayed long enough in informing you of our mother's illness. Mother has insisted for months that I not tell you of her troubles, but the doctors have informed me that they have no hope for her continued health and she refuses to spend any more of father's hard-earned coin in searching for a cure that is not to be. We do not expect her to last unto the New Year. If you can get leave at any time soon, I know she would greatly love to see you again.

I also regret to inform you of the death of my fiancé, Lord Frammingham. He died peacefully in his sleep as men of his advanced age are wont to do. I will confess to only you, dearest brother, that I am relieved at his passing. I know Mother had my best interests and the interests of the family at heart and hoped to see me settled in marriage as I am at an age when my prospects are dwindling. Alas, once again, it was not meant to be and I fear that I will not be asked again since this is the third untimely death suffered by men who have proposed to me. I will not complain about my fate but will cheerfully take care of our mother until the time she is taken from us.

I am, as always, your loving sister,
Carrie

"A letter from home?" Rory asked as he came into the room. He quickly removed his coat and hung it next to John's, loosened his stock, and stretched out on his cot with his hands crossed behind his head. He appeared quite content and John knew, without asking, that his friend had recently been with a woman. "Bad news?" Rory asked.

"Yes," John replied. "Full of it."

"Give me the least of it first," Rory said.

"Carrie's latest fiancé has passed."

"How many is that now?" Rory asked. "Three?"

John nodded. "This one expired of old age."

"Tell me, John, how can this be considered bad news? Beyond the obvious lack of income for your sister."

"She has no dowry and now no prospects. Lord Frammingham was a last resort on our mother's part. He had no heirs and no property, but he did have some money and a nice little house in London. It would have been enough to keep Carrie comfortable."

"I suppose now it will all go to some distant relative," Rory concluded.

"Yes," John sighed. He dropped the letter on the desk and stretched out on his own cot. "They call her the Virgin Widow, you know."

"Yes," Rory said. "I've heard."

"It's too bad really," John said. "She would make someone a wonderful wife. She's pretty and intelligent and a most pleasant companion."

"Indeed," Rory agreed.

John looked hopefully at his roommate. "She has a wonderful sense of humor also."

"I know what you are thinking, John. My father would sooner disown me than allow me to marry a woman with no wealth or title, no matter how well he thinks of you. When and if I marry, it will be to enhance the family coffers with coin, land, and titles." Rory looked at John with a wry expression. "Although it might be worth the disownment to watch Carrie pour tea in his lap as she did in mine when I visited your mother last time we were in London."

John had to grin at the memory. What Carrie possessed in beauty, she lacked in grace. She had a dreadful penchant for tripping over her dress hem and knocking over tables and such.

"How is your lovely mother, by the way?" Rory asked.

John sighed. "Not well. Not well at all." He pointed at the letter. "Feel free to read it. I'm not sure I can stand to speak the news aloud at the moment."

Rory quickly read the letter and sat down on his cot to look at John. "I am so sorry, old friend," he said. "What do you plan to do? Ask for leave?"

"I don't feel as if I can at the moment," John said. "Even though I know the general will allow it because of his friendship with my father. I don't want anyone thinking I am taking advantage of that friendship and asking for special privileges, especially since we have only recently come to this post."

"I'm sure no one would think that, under the circumstances."

"Oh, but someone will," John said. "It would come out, sooner or later. There is some time. I think it would be better to wait until . . . later."

"It would give her something to look forward to," Rory added.

"Indeed."

"What about your father?" Rory asked. "Do you think he knows?"

"I doubt that he does." John rubbed his hands over his face as the seriousness of the situation settled upon him. "If Carrie sent Father a letter at the same time she sent mine, then it is weeks away from delivery, and that is only if Father is at his post. The last I heard from him, he was on the Western Frontier, in a place called Pennsylvania, fighting the savages." John continued. "It could be months before Carrie's letter finds him and then more months before he can get home. What are the chances that Mother will still be alive if and when he gets here?"

Rory reached out and laid a comforting hand on John's shoulder. "There is only so much you can do from here. Write Carrie and tell her you will ask for leave this fall and that your prayers are with her and your mother. Then write your mother and tell her you look forward to seeing her soon, but make no mention of her illness. I have found in my own experience that mothers like to think they are in charge and can make everything right just by wishing it so."

"It is the same with mine," John said.

"Then she will appreciate your subterfuge," Rory said. "I will leave you in peace for a bit to write your letters." With that, he stood and stretched his arms over his head as if waking from a nap. "I suddenly find that I am starving and will have to go raid the mess lest I expire before mealtime arrives."

John sat for a moment and listened to Rory's footsteps as they faded down the staircase before he moved to the small desk the men shared. He scribbled a quick note to Carrie, then stared at the paper for a long while as another realization hit him.

What would become of his sister once their mother was gone? Father would continue to support her, of course, but he would not live forever. The colonies were a dangerous place, savage and wild. Carrie would receive his pension should something happen to him, but it would not be enough to support her into her old age. Her prospects for marriage were now as slim as her prospects for employment.

"You shall have to support her," John said to the paper as he envisioned his sister's lovely face. "Support her and yourself and hopefully a wife and a family." Of course, if he married well that would not be much of an issue. Surely he could persuade his future wife to accommodate his dear sister.

"I shall mention Carrie to Edina when next I visit her," John said to the paper before him, as if he were talking to an actual person. "Let her know how dear Carrie is to me." He tried to picture the conversation in his mind, even rehearsed the words he would say. The only problem was the fact that instead of Edina's pretty face, all he could see was Isobel crying in the rain.

John cursed. His life was complicated enough. He would be happy to stay out of Isobel's life. If only she would return the favor and stay out of his mind.

Chapter Eight

She was suffocating. Izzy fought against the overwhelming darkness that pressed down upon her. It pinned her to her narrow cot, so she kicked out and was satisfied when her foot connected with something solid and she heard the sound of a pained "Oof!"

"What are ye doing in my room, Angus?" Izzy demanded as soon as she blinked to awareness and realized that the apprentice was doubled over with his arms across his stomach in a vain attempt to catch his breath. She hoped he choked, although it would be better if he did not do it in her room. She pulled the sheet up to her neck as she quickly sat up.

"I heard ye call out," Angus huffed out as he finally sucked in air. "I thought ye might need help."

"I'm fine, but thank ye all the same," Izzy said. "It was only a dream." She looked directly into his huge round face. She could not show any fear. She knew Angus well enough to know that if he sensed her fear he would use it against her. She looked toward her door. It was closed. She knew he'd closed it intentionally. Had she cried out? Or had Angus just said that as an excuse to be in her room. "Ye can go now," she said as she stared pointedly at the door.

Where is Tommy? Close, she hoped. It was Sunday morning, wasn't it? Her mind was still dazed by the dream and the shock of finding Angus in her room.

"Leave," Izzy said again, this time more forcibly. Fortunately, there was no tremor in her voice.

"Izzy!" Tommy's voice was urgent.

"Now," Izzy said as Tommy pounded on her door.

"Get up, Iz," Tommy said. "Edina wants you."

Angus looked at the door and then back at Izzy, and a sly grin revealed his uneven teeth. Izzy eyed the candlestick on the small table next to her cot. How much damage could she do to him with that bit of brass? She knew what he was thinking. She was compromised.

But not if she had anything to say about it. "Come in, Tommy," she yelled out. "Since a closed door means nothing to anyone else around here."

"What?" Tommy asked as he opened her door.

"Angus has been drinking," she said.

"I have not," Angus declared.

"Why else would ye come into my room unbidden?" Izzy asked.

"Ye know how Master Rabin feels about such things," Tommy said quickly. "Especially on a Sunday."

Angus sputtered as Tommy held the door wide open for him to leave. Izzy would have kissed him if not for the fact that the look on Angus's face showed he would get even for her small victory.

"What happened?" Tommy asked after Angus lumbered away.

"I donae know," Izzy said. "I woke up and he was here. He said I called out."

Tommy inspected the latch on her door. "The lock is broken," he said. "He probably did it when ye were out."

"Pig," Izzy spat out. Her head was still swimming from being awakened so abruptly. She tried to recall the dream that had troubled her so but could not. Too much had happened since she woke.

"I will fix it before nightfall," Tommy promised. "Miss Edina is calling for you."

Izzy threw back the blanket and stretched wearily. "Why?" she asked with a yawn.

"Captain Murray is accompanying her to church. And Katty Ann cannae get her hair to suit her."

"So the world must stop for Miss Edina?" Izzy asked.

"Aye." Tommy pulled Izzy's good dress from its peg. "She wants you to go with her also. As her chaperone."

"Her what?" Izzy sputtered.

Tommy's face turned a deep shade of red. "She said it isnae proper for her to be seen out on the arm of Captain Murray without a proper chaperone, and since ye are older . . . and unmarried . . ." Tommy's voice trailed off as Izzy glared at him. He put his hand out in helpless surrender. "Katty Ann is under the staircase again."

Izzy took the dress from Tommy. "I suppose this all came up because Miss Cecilia now has a chaperone following her around. And she expects me to go to a Protestant church? Does she nay ken I am Catholic?"

"I donae think she cares," Tommy said.

"Get out so I can dress," Izzy sighed. "But stay close. . . ." She looked toward Angus's room. It would not do for him to catch her alone again, especially since she was dressing. At least Tommy would make sure her door would lock from now on. Then he could spend the day with Katty Ann. A thought flashed through her mind. Had Katty Ann intentionally ruined Edina's hair so she would not have to trail after her this day? Izzy doubted the girl was so calculating.

In either case, her Sunday was ruined now and there was nothing she could do about it. She had hoped to see Ewan today and to talk sense into him before he did something foolish about Da. Maybe it was better this way. Ewan would expect her to visit Da. She wasn't sure if she was ready for that step yet. Better the devil she knew, Edina, than the devil she would sooner not know at all.

Luckily she had bathed the night before and her laundry was done thanks to an unusually sunny and breezy Saturday. Her hair also seemed to be cooperative for once. Instead of tying it back, she let it hang loose. Izzy quickly put on her shoes and stockings and grabbed her hat before leaving her room.

Tommy waited for her, bless him, and walked down the flight of stairs to where Edina's shrieks could be heard blending in with Katty Ann's wails.

"Thank you, Izzy," Master Rabin said as Izzy stepped through the door that separated the servants' quarters from the rest of the house. "She's in a rare mood this morning, and will not get into Captain Murray's good graces like this."

Izzy bit back what she was thinking as she gave Master Rabin a swift curtsey and knocked on Edina's door.

"Come in," Edina called shrilly. She sat at her dressing table in her undergarments with a brush in her hand and her hair in total disarray. A gown was laid out on her bed, a hideous concoction of bright pink and wide green stripes, with bows ranging from dark to light green attached to every conceivable surface that wasn't covered with ruffles. A tall hat sat on a chair, covered in green ruffles and pink bows and what Izzy could only guess was a bird's nest with a huge purple feather springing from the side.

"God help us," Izzy said, and crossed herself as she entered the room.

"God help us all." John whispered the prayer as Edina came down the front steps of her house followed by Isobel. He desperately wanted to look at Isobel, but he could not tear his eyes away from Edina. She looked like a ship under full sail with all her skirts, ruffles, and bows. Her dress was a riot of color, every shade of green and pink possible. But the hat . . . John took a firm hold of Sultan's reins.

The hat was like a monument to some long and perhaps luckily dead peacock, complete with a long purple feather that almost poked Isobel, who jumped back a pace when Edina turned her head to say something to her father. Master Rabin seemed to be bolting down the street in his haste to escape his daughter, who smiled up at him from her perch on the bottom step. A boy sat by the step and looked up at Edina with his jaw gaping wide open.

Sultan chose to show his distaste for Edina's milliner. He reared on his hind legs and lashed out with a hoof, luckily striking the hitching post instead of the dreadful concoction, which seemed in danger of falling off as she daintily jumped up a step.

"I thought we could walk to church," she suggested.

"I am sure that would be a pleasant undertaking," John said as he turned to calm Sultan. He needed the moment to collect his thoughts and make sure that his face did not betray his absolute amazement at Edina's couture. He was also taken aback. He had thought to ride alongside the Rabins' carriage. Sultan would not be pleased to be tied up all day.

"I can send Davy to see to your mount," Isobel suggested as if reading his mind. "My brother works at the smithy and has a fine hand with horses," she added. The boy, Davy, jumped to his feet upon hearing his name.

"Yes, that is an excellent idea," Edina chirped. "I was so hoping to take in the gardens after the service. I do hope the weather holds," she added as she placed a firm hand upon her hat and looked up at the partly cloudy skies.

Perhaps Sultan felt John's despair at the thought of walking through the public gardens of Aberdeen beside Edina. The horse lashed out with his hind legs. A carriage passed by at that exact moment and John slammed his body into the side of the stud so that his kick missed it.

"Perhaps the sooner the better?" John said hopefully as he eyed Davy and wondered if the lad would be able to handle the stud.

"Davy, take him the back way so he will not be distracted by the traffic," Isobel said. Davy yanked on his forelock and slid the coin John handed him in his pocket before he took a firm hold of the reins. "He helps my brother sometimes," Isobel added with an indulgent smile.

With her smile, the day seemed suddenly much brighter. Sultan settled down immediately and let Davy lead him away down the alley. Edina stepped from the porch and slipped her hand through his arm. "I hope you don't mind," she trilled. "I've asked Isobel to serve as our chaperone." The clouds above parted on her words and the sun dazzled down upon them as they began their journey.

John looked over his shoulder as they walked toward the church. Isobel swatted at the feather that struck out at a dangerous angle from Edina's hat and smiled innocently in his direction. Her reddish hair seemed shot with gold threads as the sunlight danced upon the curls that swung about her shoulders. A straw hat dangled from her fingertips. She timed her steps so as not to step on the trailing frippery of Edina's hem. Her dress was plain and serviceable, a lovely pale shade of green that brought to mind the grass in winter. She wore no frills or furbelows, just a bit of lace around her cuffs and at her neck, along with a white linen scarf that was thrown casually about her shoulders. She seemed totally at ease with her dress and her place.

John, on the other hand, felt as if all the eyes of Aberdeen were upon them. It wasn't as if anyone could miss them. He wore the bright red of his dress uniform and he could not think of any color that would look worse beside it than pink and green. The people gathering at the entrance to the church all looked in their direction.

"Oh, there's Cecilia," Edina said. "Cecilia! Hello!" she called to a beautiful young woman with golden hair and a trim figure. She was dressed in a pale blue gown and wore a small hat at a pert angle. The young woman reminded John of Carrie. She was with a gentleman of some means, if his clothing was any indication. John nodded politely to the couple and noticed an older woman trailing after them. Cecilia's chaperone, no doubt.

John stole another look at Isobel as they climbed the steps that led into the church. She had covered her head with the scarf, and her dark eyes darted about as if she'd never set foot inside the doors.

She was Catholic. She genuflected and crossed herself as they passed the rows of pews. That would certainly set all the gossips atwitter with news. Edina seemed not to notice. She moved on, nodding and smiling at everyone while keeping a hold on his arm that was almost painful. John nodded at her father as they slid into a pew. The man sat in the side rows reserved for the elders of the church. A wise move on his part. Everyone in their vicinity was in danger of being gouged by the feather. John found his thigh smothered beneath layers of fabric as Edina's dress expanded when she sat down. He moved as far away as he could without being rude, then had to readjust again as Isobel slid cautiously into the last few inches of available space beside him and crossed herself.

John inclined his head so he could speak quietly into her ear. "You don't have to do that here," he said. He was close enough to her that she did not have to lean toward him to catch the sound of his voice. Indeed, he was so close that their thighs were touching.

"Yes, I do," she quickly replied as he felt the muscle of his thigh clench at the proximity of hers.

"This is a Presbyterian church," he added as he willed his leg to relax. She was so close; he could feel the heat of her through all the layers of fabric that separated them, which was considerably less than the fabric that overflowed upon his left side.

"Aye. I ken," she said as she smoothed the skirt of her dress over her legs. Just the sight of her hands moving in a gentle caress over the fabric felt like a punch in the gut. If the sermon did not start soon, he would be unmanned before both of them. "I'm asking God to forgive me for being here," Isobel added.

That was enough to distract his body from its sudden rebellion. John covered his laughter with a cough and quickly bowed his head. Edina turned to look at him, and a parishioner behind them gasped as the feather sliced through the air.

Since his head was bowed, John decided he might as well pray. He prayed that his shoulders would quit shaking with the effort not to laugh and his rod would not spring up at attention as it seemed wont to do whenever Isobel MacDonald was in his presence. He prayed for his mother, and for his sister and for his father. His list of needs was long and he realized his sins were many. Since he was so distracted by the women on either side of him, he decided to pray for patience. It looked as if that was something he would need a great deal of to get through the day.

Ewan tore his eyes from the seal in his hand to the horse as Davy led the white stallion into the stable. His eyes narrowed in recognition and speculation. Donnie, as usual, was immediately drawn to the fine quality of the stud and rubbed its arched neck as he took the reins.

"Miss Izzy says to watch him while Captain Murray escorts Miss Edina to church," Davy quickly reported before taking off as if shot out of a cannon.

"Did she say how long?" Donnie called after the boy, who stopped in his tracks and shrugged before taking off at a run again. "He must be after his breakfast," Donnie said as he led the horse into a stall.

"Did he say Captain Murray?" Ewan asked as he leaned over the side of the stall.

"Aye," Donnie replied. He quickly lifted the saddle off the horse and rubbed the animal's back with a cloth. "According to Cook he is Edina's latest beau."

"He's also the one who captured Da," Ewan said.

"How do ye know that?" Donnie asked as he paused in midrub.

"How many horses like this are there in all of Aberdeen?"

The horse's ears flicked back and forth as they talked. Then he stretched out his neck as Donnie continued rubbing. "This stallion is one of a kind," he admitted as he moved the cloth over its withers and down its legs. "And he is well cared for."

"Make sure he likes you," Ewan said. "We may have use of him."

"They all like me," Donnie said. "Women, horses, and dogs," he added with a grin. "But I will give this one the attention he deserves," he whispered close to the horse's ear. "We shall become the best of friends, shan't we?"

Ewan nodded in approval.

Chapter Nine

The rafters of the church had not caved in upon her. Izzy considered that to be a blessing. The day was lovely and she had to admit, at home she most likely would have missed the beauty of it worrying over Donnie, Ewan, and Da.

It was nice to have time when she could just *be*. She had never indulged in such a thing in all her life. Since being a chaperone consisted of nothing more than trailing after Captain Murray and Miss Edina and making sure he did nothing inappropriate, her task was relatively simple. He was the perfect example of propriety. He paid courtly attention to every silly word out of Edina's mouth and kept his arm properly stiff so that her hand touched nothing more than his sleeve.

The gardens were lovely. They were on the grounds of a long-abandoned abbey built on the banks of the Dee and the monks who had lived there at one time had made exquisite plantings. Now it was in the care of the parish and treated with the same care the monks once used. Everything seemed fresh and clean after the recent rain, and the heady perfume of the roses was heavenly, especially when one was used to the rank smells from the twisted backstreets she often ran through while running her errands for Master Rabin. Several of Aberdeen's affluent citizens walked among the flowers, stopping occasionally to speak to each other. Edina seemed especially anxious that everyone notice her and her handsome escort. How could they not? Izzy was sure they could be seen from miles away. If ever there were a finer pair of peacocks . . .

It suddenly occurred to her that Captain Murray must

have the patience of a saint. She wondered if he was after Edina for her money. Surely that was the assumption everyone who had seen the couple that day would make.

But Izzy knew him in her own way. If you could call two brief interludes knowing someone. He had seen her at her worst both times and shown nothing but kindness and compassion. And there was no reason for him to show either to her. She was nothing more than a servant. A servant with a lot of problems as far as Captain Murray was concerned.

She was drawn to him. She had to admit it. Why else would she foolishly throw herself into his arms as she had when he'd found her weeping in front of the Mercat Cross? Why else was she imagining herself walking the gardens with Captain Murray instead of Edina?

Izzy let her mind go as she trailed after the couple. It was much better than dwelling on how nice Captain Murray's muscular backside looked in his breeches or the long line of his calves in his stockings. If Cook could see the view, she would positively faint on the spot. She imagined herself in a beautiful blue dress trimmed with lace and a pert little hat with a bow on top of her perfectly arranged hair. She would wear gloves because she wanted to, not because her fingers were stained with ink. And Captain Murray would be wearing a fine suit instead of a uniform. She could see it all in her mind. She could even see Captain Murray, or John, as she would call him, plucking one of the soft pink roses from a bush and handing it to her to inhale the dazzling scent. As long as she was at it, she might as well imagine that Da was a proper gentleman with plenty of money and Ewan and Donnie were both married with lands of their own and lots of little children about to call her aunt.

"Oh, look, Cecilia is on the river," Edina exclaimed. Izzy came out of her dream and looked out across the water.

Sunlight dazzled off the ripples made by the dips of the oars as small dinghies floated about the inlet made by the curve of the river. Izzy rolled her eyes at what she knew was coming next.

"Would you like to go out?" Captain Murray asked, forestalling his companion's demand.

"Oh yes," Edina said. "That would be simply lovely."

Were they not hungry? Izzy had missed breakfast and it was long past time for the noon meal. Davy had instructions to meet them with a basket from Cook near the grounds by the cemetery. She placed a hand over her stomach to stop its protests as Captain Murray procured a boat from a man along the riverbank.

"Surely all of Aberdeen has seen her by now," she muttered with an impatient tap of her foot. Izzy raised a doubtful eyebrow as Edina settled into the boat with her skirts safely folded around her. They heaped up in her lap as if bolts of fabric had fallen from the shelves of the dressmaker. Edina opened her parasol and posed prettily as Captain Murray extended his hand to Isobel.

"Perhaps I should stay ashore," Izzy said. "I'm sure I can see enough to maintain propriety from here," she added.

"Please come," he said quietly. His voice seemed strange and Izzy looked up into his bright blue eyes and saw a desperate yearning in them that took her breath away. She placed her hand against her stomach again as the sudden emptiness she felt inside threatened to overwhelm her. A hunger of a different kind took her. One she'd never felt before.

All she could do was nod as he gently took her hand and helped her into the boat. She sat behind Edina in the back and looked out across the water as Captain Murray got into the front facing Edina. The boatman pushed them off and

Captain Murray drew the oars through the water with one smooth stroke that carried them out into the current.

Izzy watched the river. She did not dare look at Captain Murray.

She heard the dip of the oars, she knew Edina was chattering away, she felt the heat of the sun beating down through the straw of her hat and the sleeves of her gown, and she ignored it all as she tried to make sense of the rush of feelings that swirled through her insides.

Was she imagining it? Why had he looked at her like that? As if she were his entire world. He certainly had not looked at Edina in that manner.

It was the same look her father had given her mother, conveying the same desperate longing. She knew it well. She'd watched her mother light up as soon as he came round and she'd known the not-so-quiet noises would follow that night when the children were supposed to be sleeping.

She knew what it meant. Even though she'd never known a man's touch, she knew what was supposed to happen.

For the first time in her life she wanted it to happen.

She felt her skin flush, from her cheeks down to her neckline. Izzy dipped a hand in the water and brought the coolness to her cheek.

His attention no doubt caught by her hand in the water, Captain Murray leaned out so he could see around Edina. Edina chose that very moment to rise and wave at Cecilia's boat, which was making slow progress in their direction.

Captain Murray quickly sat back to level the boat, which had tipped precariously in the water. Edina realized her mistake and plopped down but missed her seat and landed on the side. Captain Murray quickly grabbed her arm and pulled her to safety as the boat lurched and Izzy was pitched into the water.

It happened so quickly that she did not have time to think about it. One minute she was in the boat and the next she was sinking toward the bottom of the river. She felt the current pull at her as she fought to right herself. She looked up and saw the sunlight through the cloud of her hair and realized, foolishly, that she'd lost her hat. Her legs were tangled in the skirts of her gown and she felt one of her shoes fall off and float away from her.

Let yourself sink. Her brain took over as the cold water surrounded her. *Touch bottom and then push up.* She knew how to swim. Any girl who grew up close to the lochs with two brothers learned how to swim at an early age.

She felt chilled to the bone and desperate for air, but she would have trouble swimming in her long skirts. She needed to push off the bottom. Her toes touched something solid and she bent her knees, ready to kick off.

She was stuck. Something held her fast. She threw out an arm and realized a tree was snagged on the riverbed and she was trapped in its branches. She kicked and her skirts tangled more as her foot slid down and stuck in the mud.

She could not move. She looked up at the surface and saw the white moon of Edina's face gazing down at her, quite out of her reach.

Izzy's lungs burned. She needed air, yet she dared not breathe. She was drowning. *I willnae die. . . .*

Her head swam as dark points spun before her eyes. She reached down, hoping to free her foot, but she could not find her way through her skirts. The darkness overcame her and then it turned to a light so bright that she could not stand it.

I willnae die. . . .

It happened so fast, he could not believe it. One minute he was steadying the boat, and the next Isobel was thrown overboard. She was so light that it didn't take much motion to do it. Edina's sudden lurch and the tipping of the boat had unseated her.

The water was murky. A trail of bubbles broke the surface as the boat moved downstream without the guidance of the oars. Where was she?

John tore off his coat and kicked off his shoes. "Take an oar and hold on," he barked out to Edina, who looked ready to faint. He did not have time for her hysterics. He wanted to dive in but feared the sudden motion would upset the boat. Instead he stepped over the side and let his body sink.

The water was about three feet deeper than he was tall. Which meant it was well over Isobel's head.

Where was she? He tried to see through the murkiness. The water stung his eyes, but he refused to blink; instead he turned his head every which way, hoping beyond hope to catch a glimpse of her.

There . . . something . . . gold. It was her hair. John moved toward her with bold strokes, swimming against the current. He saw her arms moving as if she were trying to swim, but she wasn't rising from the bottom. As he got closer, she grew still and he realized she was caught.

His lungs burned with the effort it took to reach her. She stood in the water like a statue, swaying gently in the current with her hair and gown swirling about her. Finally, finally, he reached her. He desperately needed to breathe, but he could not take the time to go up for air. Her face was still and her eyes vacant. They closed as he touched her.

John pushed his way down. Her foot was snagged in a branch and her petticoat was twisted about her leg. Her foot was bent in an awkward position from her struggles. He pulled it out and wrapped his arm around her waist as she floated free.

He reached for the surface with a long stroke. His legs ached and his eyes bulged from the effort it took to pull Isobel with him, even though she was as light as a feather.

Finally he broke through the surface and sucked in a great breath of air. Beside him, Isobel gasped and struck out with her arms.

"Isobel!" he exclaimed, turning her to face him as he treaded water. He saw Edina's boat upstream and her friend Cecilia's boat next to it. Her companion was struggling to get both boats in to shore. The boatman ran down the bank of the river toward the two boats. People were gathered along the bank, all of them watching with their hands shielding their eyes from the glare of the sun.

Isobel looked up at him with her deep brown eyes and swiped a hand across her face to push her hair back.

"Izzy," she said as she grabbed on to his shoulder. She kicked with her feet, a good sign. She might be slight, but she was strong. She breathed deeply as if she could not get enough of the air.

"What?" he asked. Was she confused?

"No one calls me Isobel," she gasped out as she caught her breath. "They all call me Izzy."

John wrapped his arm tightly about her waist and she placed her other hand on his shoulder so that he was looking into her face. They floated in the water, their bodies intimately pressed against each other. His skin burned despite the wetness of his clothes and he wondered if she felt it. "I thought I'd lost you, Izzy."

She did not look at him. "Ye seem to be making a habit of saving me."

John looked over her shoulder at the boat. Edina called out and waved cheerfully.

"Under the circumstances, it seemed like the thing to do,"

he said. He felt perfectly content to stay in the water, as long as he could hold on to Izzy.

Izzy looked over her shoulder. "If only her dress had been ruined instead of mine," she said. She made a face as she turned back. "Forgie me for saying so," she said. "It seems that nearly dying has caused me to forget myself." She looked up at him through lowered lashes.

"It would have been a favor for all of us," John agreed.

She managed a trembling smile.

"Let's get out of the water before they decide to help us," he said, and she nodded.

"More than likely their help would be the death of us," she said. "And your effort would be wasted."

"Never," he said as he struck out for the shore. She seemed content to hold on and let him do the work. His feet found the bottom and he held her in his arms as he waded through the water to the riverbank.

"I've lost my shoe," she said. "And my hat."

John turned with her still in his arms and surveyed the river. "Should I go back for them?" Edina waved from her boat once more and a surge of protectiveness toward Izzy swelled up inside him. She had almost drowned and Edina was smiling and waving as if the incident were all a lark of some kind.

Izzy's arms tightened around his neck. "No," she sighed. "They are not worth much, certainly not your life."

"I will buy you new shoes," he said. "And a hat. Anything, as long as Edina does not pick it out."

"A hat I can do without," she said quietly. John looked down at her face. She had her cheek pressed against his shoulder and her eyes were half closed so he could not tell what she was thinking. She dropped a hand to her stomach as if it pained her. Did it? Could she have swallowed water? She would certainly be sick if she had. Maybe she was embarrassed. John hoped he had not insulted her about buying her shoes. The one that remained on her foot did not seem like much to lose, but if it was all she had, she would be in dire straits.

He slogged on toward shore. Davy jumped up and down beside a huge picnic hamper and a plainly dressed woman waited there with a blanket. She wrapped it round Izzy as soon as he staggered onto dry land.

"Poor thing," she crooned as she rubbed Izzy's arm. "You're near to frozen."

Izzy shivered in his arms. She needed warming, but he did not feel inclined to put her down yet. *Not ever. . . .* He was tired of fighting this strange attraction. Or maybe it wasn't so strange at all. Whoever said you could choose where your heart loved? He'd tried for many years to be practical. Why couldn't he just this once let his heart lead him instead of his mind? John looked at the small boathouse that sat by the pier. "Can we take her inside?" he asked the woman.

"Yes, indeed," she said. "I'll have a fire going in no time."

"Ye shouldnae go to so much trouble," Izzy said, but she allowed him to continue carrying her; indeed, she held on tighter as he carried her to the boathouse. Davy followed along, dragging the basket after him.

Izzy was still trembling. The woman threw some sticks into a small stove and slid a chair up before it. The house was tiny and held nothing more than the stove, a few chairs, and a table. It was nothing more than a place to while away the time while the boats were in use and to take shelter from the weather. John sat down before the stove with Izzy still in his arms.

She pulled the blanket close around her and the woman threw another blanket over John's shoulders.

"Thank you," John said just as his stomach emitted a loud growl.

Izzy burst into laughter.

"What is so funny?" he asked as she shook in his arms. He meant to apologize, but it was so strange to see her laughing, especially after almost dying. But people reacted to danger in strange ways.

"I've been wondering . . . all this while . . ." she finally got out. "Which is worse . . . drowning or starving."

John shook his head, smiling at her observations. "And which is it?"

"Drowning is certainly quicker," she said. "So I ken that it has its advantages."

"Davy," John said. "The basket if you please. It seems that we've worked up an appetite."

Davy placed the basket on an empty chair and opened it with a flourish. Izzy immediately took a soft roll from a folded cloth, and its scent filled the room.

"It seems, Captain Murray, that you have saved my life once more." She took a bite of the roll.

John took a bite from his own roll as they heard Edina call out and the sounds of many footsteps approaching.

"I think, Miss MacDonald, that you may have saved mine." He inclined his head toward the door as Edina burst through. He dropped his mouth to her ear. "I shall never be able to repay you for that kindness, but be assured, I will certainly try my best to do so."

Chapter Ten

"I'm fine, Donnie," Izzy said for the hundredth time. "Go back to work." She pulled the blanket that slipped from her shoulders into place and sipped the tea Cook had prepared for her.

If only Donnie had not been present when Captain Murray carried her in. Her first fear upon seeing him had been that John would find out her last name was Ferguson, but in all the confusion Donnie only mentioned that he worked at the stable.

Luckily, Cecilia's companion offered the use of his carriage to bring everyone home. Izzy wished she could have just slipped out and crept up the back staircase. Instead Captain Murray had carried her into the kitchen right in front of Donnie, who seemed more puzzled than protective.

Now she felt as trapped as she had in the water. Cook had her injured ankle soaking in warm water and Katty Ann had taken her clothes to be washed and dried. She wore nothing but a shift, a towel around her head and the blanket. At least she had pleasant company. Angus was nowhere to be seen and Tommy was up working on her lock to make sure she was not disturbed.

As soon as Captain Murray had handed her over to Cook's gentle care, Edina had fainted dead away. It took both Captain Murray and Donnie to carry her up to her room, where Katty Ann and her father were left to deal with her. Captain Murray, being a soldier, knew when to retreat and he did so.

There was no doubt in anyone's mind that Edina's hysterics were an act. But they all cosetted her nonetheless.

At the present time Izzy was more concerned over the loss of her shoes than the state of her ankle. Somehow she had managed to lose the second one and had no way of getting another pair until she was able to go out. Which would be impossible because her ankle was injured and she was now barefoot.

She worried about her shoes because it was simpler than worrying about everything else that had happened.

What exactly were Captain Murray's intentions toward her?

Could she have mistaken the things he'd said to her? The look he'd given her? The feelings that swelled up inside her own body when he'd carried her from the water? She placed a hand over her heart and pushed at the pain she felt at the base of her breast. It felt as if her heart might burst. It was something new, a feeling she'd never had before. Izzy knew the pain in her chest had nothing to do with her near drowning. She knew because she'd felt it before, when John had looked at her, and asked her to go with them out on the river. It was as if her heart had never really been alive until that exact moment.

It terrified her.

"Are you in pain?" Donnie asked. He knelt before her with concern plainly showing on his handsome face. "Should I send for a doctor?"

"No." Izzy moved her hand from her breast and placed it on his cheek. "I am fine. I just want to sleep, I think."

"Should I send for Ewan?" Donnie suggested.

"No," Izzy said. "I would like to lie down, but my room is four stories up."

"You can sleep in my room until you can walk again," Cook said. "I'll set up a cot for you. Take her on back so she can get some rest," she said to Donnie.

He scooped her up in his arms as if she weighed next to

nothing. It felt strange being cared for by the one who had always depended on her. She had to admit he was a man now. He no longer needed her mothering. What would she do when and if he found a wife?

"Stop it, Iz," he said as he lowered her to Cook's bed.

"Stop what?"

"Worrying over me. I can tell by the look on your face what ye are thinking."

She shook her head. "I was thinking how ye've become a man right before my eyes. A strong, fine man."

He dropped a kiss on her forehead. "All because of you." He wrapped her blanket tighter about her and tucked it up under her chin. "Get some rest. I'll be back later to see how you fare."

Izzy snuggled down beneath the blanket and let the sounds of the house wash over her. She heard Donnie's deep voice and Cook's higher one as he teased her, followed by her girlish laughter. She heard Davy pipe up and the clatter of the pots. She heard heavy footsteps on the floor above her and knew that Master Rabin must be on his way down from Edina's room. Poor Katty Ann was probably trapped up there for the rest of the day. She wondered briefly where Angus was and realized that for once she did not have to worry about his sneaking about. She was safe.

Safe . . . safe as she had been in the arms of Captain John Murray of His Majesty's army. It all seemed like a dream. The moment he'd handed her into the boat, the look in his eyes. She had not imagined it. Not after what he did, what he said, how he held her in his arms as if he never wanted to let her go.

It was as Cook said. He was an angel. A beautiful guardian angel who'd come to her rescue yet again. Would he come back to call on her? Would he rescue her from the everyday drudgery that awaited her for the rest of her life? For once, Izzy went against her practical nature and decided to let her dreams carry her away as she fell into a deep, contented sleep with his name lingering on her lips.

Two days later Izzy sat upon a stool in the shop with her ankle wrapped in bandages and one of Edina's cast-off slippers upon her other foot. She sat close to the door that led back into the kitchen so the Cook could keep an eye on her. The woman felt she should not be back at work so soon. Izzy had argued that point because she could not stand to be idle, and Master Rabin did need her in the shop.

The bell over the door rang, but she ignored it as she continued to proof the pages Master Rabin had handed her before he went off to meet with one of his best customers. She could sense the resentment oozing out of Angus as he lumbered over to the counter. Tommy was off making deliveries. If only Master Rabin would send Angus off instead, Izzy would not have to worry about the older apprentice constantly looming over her. She could not easily escape him with her injured ankle.

"I have a delivery for Miss Isobel MacDonald," a voice piped up.

Izzy nearly fell off her stool. She gripped the table edge firmly as she looked at the young woman standing in front of the counter. The only person who knew her by that name was John.

"There is no one here by that name," Angus said.

"I'll take it," Izzy said.

Angus drew his brows down at her. "I thought yer name was—"

"MacDonald is my mother's name," Izzy said sweetly, although her body trembled. She did not need Angus asking questions or poking his nose in her affairs. "I cannae walk, miss. Would you mind bringing it around?" Izzy knew Angus was curious about what was in the parcel. So was she.

"Compliments of Captain Murray, miss," the girl said as she handed over the package and hurried away.

Izzy could have done without that bit of news. Especially in front of Angus. He looked at her speculatively as she placed the parcel on the table before her.

"Are ye going to open it?" he asked.

Izzy sighed. She'd love to open it. In private. Away from his prying eyes. But she also knew that he would not give up until he knew what was inside.

It couldn't be anything too personal, could it? There was nothing she could do but open the package. She picked up a knife to cut the length of string that held the thick paper wrapped around her parcel.

There were three shoes inside. Her old one, its sole worn through to nothing, and beneath it, a brand-new pair, obviously made to size. The leather was soft and creamy, the finest available. They were flat and practical but also beautifully made. She was sure they'd cost more than she would ever dream of spending on a pair of shoes.

"Why would Captain Murray be buying you a pair of shoes?" Angus asked.

"Because he is a kind man," Izzy said. "And I lost my other in the river Sunday."

Angus shrugged. "Seems like a waste to me," he said.

"I shall buy you a new pair," John had said and he'd done it. *"I shall never be able to repay you for that kindness, but be assured, I will certainly try my best to do so."* How would he repay her? With the shoes? If only she knew what he'd meant. If only she could be sure of his intentions.

Ye are a nothing more than a foolish girl, Izzy Ferguson. A foolish girl with a brand-new pair of shoes. She slid a shoe onto her uninjured foot. It fit perfectly.

"It seems to me that Miss Edina might not approve of this," Angus said. He had moved uncomfortably close while Izzy was trying on her shoe. "And why does the man think yer name is MacDonald?"

"What business is it of yours?" Izzy snapped. She was tired of Angus sticking his nose in where it did not belong.

Angus shrugged. "I'm just saying."

"Ye are not saying anything, because there is nothing to say," Izzy said. She wrapped her new shoes back up and placed the bundle safely beneath the counter where it was protected by her skirts. "Captain Murray is a kind man and knew that I was in need. If only everyone were as kind as Captain Murray, think of what a wonderful world this would be." She stared directly into his eyes and dared him to say otherwise.

"Why does he think your name is MacDonald?" Angus demanded. He was obviously not intimidated by her directness and even had the audacity to move a step closer. He knew she was trapped.

Then as if in answer to a prayer, the shop bell rang and in walked Captain John Murray himself. Izzy's heart leapt up into her throat as the shop seemed to fill with light from his presence. She knew she was being ridiculous, but it was all she could do to keep her seat and not foolishly throw herself into his arms.

She was smitten and she didn't quite know what to do about it.

"Good day," he said, and the shop brightened even more with his smile. Izzy could not help smiling back and felt some satisfaction at the fact that Angus stepped away from her as Captain Murray came closer. "I have come to see how you fare after Sunday," he continued.

"I am quite well, thank you," Izzy said. "And I am most grateful for your kindness in sending me the shoes."

He stood at the end of the table where she worked. Close enough that she could reach out a hand and touch him. But not as close as Angus had been a few moments earlier. Not close enough as far as she was concerned.

Izzy felt her face flush as that thought entered her head. Captain John Murray smiled at her. A light danced in his sky blue eyes and she wondered what caused it. Could it possibly be the company? It was as if they were alone, even though Angus watched them circumspectly from the other side of the shop.

"It was my pleasure," he said. "I hope they are to your satisfaction."

"They are," Izzy said. "They are quite practical and beautifully made. I am sure they will last me for many years."

"Practical," he said. "Is that something you look for in shoes?"

"Oh yes," Izzy said. "If shoes can't be practical, then what good are they?"

"Indeed," he agreed.

It was the most bizarre conversation she'd ever had, talking about shoes with a man, but still it seemed better than grinning at him like an idiot.

"What are you working on?" he asked politely.

"I am reading proofs for a book," Izzy explained. "Master Rabin hopes to run them later today when he gets back from his meetings."

"Ah," John said, and shook his head. "Is this the type of thing you do every day?"

"I do a bit of everything," Izzy explained. "Usually I make the deliveries since there are two apprentices and I am just an employee."

"Yet it seems that Master Rabin trusts you with the same work as the apprentices."

"He does," Izzy said, "but since I am a woman, I cannot be an apprentice."

"It does not seem as if life is quite fair most of the time," he said in a low voice.

"What do you mean by that?" She noticed Angus was straining to hear their conversation.

"My father was illegitimate," he explained as if apologizing. "It was no fault of his, yet he has borne the stigma his entire life. Our place in society often depends on accidents of birth."

"It has always been that way," Izzy said. "And probably always will be. Those who have, want to keep their superiority. Those that don't, must work for a living. It isnae right. It is just the way it is."

"Then there are those that just try to steal what they want," John added, and his eyes flicked toward Angus.

"Which leaves the rest of us to be ever vigilant," Izzy replied. She heard a creak by the door that led into the kitchen, but no one came through. She was afraid Edina would swoop in and take Captain Murray away.

"Do you think your ankle will be better by next Saturday?" he asked.

"I imagine so," she answered. "I can put my weight on it now although I have not attempted the stairs yet."

"I have heard that the fair will be in town," he said. "I was wondering if you would like to accompany me."

"Yes, I would," Izzy said. "I would like that very much."

The door creaked again but she ignored it. She was going to the fair with Captain Murray.

"What about Miss Edina?" she asked.

"I will speak to her," John said. "I will tell her that I should not waste any more of her time as I find my attentions are drawn elsewhere." His eyes were steady upon her face and Izzy felt a slow burn begin inside her. She wanted to fling herself into his arms but did not dare. Not in front of Angus.

What has come over me?

"Perhaps to spare her feelings, we should arrange to meet somewhere else?" she suggested. "The stables?" If she was going to be seen with a soldier, she might as well get her brothers used to it. Or one of them at least. Maybe Donnie could convince Ewan to be agreeable.

His smile dazzled her. "That would be wonderful," he said. "I will be counting the minutes."

Izzy smiled back. *So will I. . . .*

Donnie crept on silent feet back to the kitchen, where Cook was waiting for him with two thick sandwiches and a glass of milk.

"Stubborn lass," she said, "your sister."

"She comes by it naturally," Donnie answered as he chewed. "She's more like Ewan than she will admit."

"When will I meet this brother of yours?" Cook asked. "I did not even know he existed until just recently."

"He and Iz don't always get along," Donnie said. "Neither has my own sweet nature."

"Always at it?" she asked.

"Since I can remember." Donnie swallowed the last of the first sandwich and downed the milk. "Tell Iz I stopped by," he said as he wrapped up the second in a bit of paper Cook provided.

"Did you not talk to her?"

"Nay, she was with a customer," he called out as he went through the back door to the street.

Donnie hated cutting Cook off. But he was in a hurry. He

had news for Ewan. News that concerned all of them. News that might help them get Da out of the tollbooth and on the ship that was leaving for the colonies come Sunday.

"She's what?" Ewan asked when Donnie relayed his startling information. They stood in the doorway of the stable while Ewan ate the sandwich Donnie had brought.

"She's going to the fair with the soldier next Saturday. I heard him ask her and she said yes."

"The same soldier who pulled her from the river?"

"Aye, 'tis him."

Ewan thought on it as he chewed. Izzy was seeing a soldier. An English soldier. He could almost be happy for her. But Da would not be pleased about the soldier bit.

If Iz was at the fair with the soldier, then his horse would be in Donnie's stable all day. But they needed more.

"We need to get his coat," Ewan said. "And we need a letter. The seal will open the gate, but the letter has to give the orders."

"Iz could write a letter," Donnie suggested. "She would know how to make it official."

"She won't."

"Maybe ye should ask her," Donnie suggested.

"I will," Ewan said. "But donae tell her of the plan."

"Iz would never betray us," Donnie insisted.

"She would if she thought you might get hurt," Ewan countered.

Donnie shrugged the danger off. "What could happen? They would never shoot one of their own."

Chapter Eleven

There was nothing to do but get the conversation over with. He could not take Izzy to the fair if he still was courting Edina, nor could he let Edina know his intentions toward her servant. Izzy would likely wind up on the street.

What exactly are your intentions toward Izzy?

John paused on the stoop in front of the Rabins' door and took a deep breath. What were his intentions? He could no longer deny the strange attraction he'd felt toward Izzy since the first time he saw her. So his intention was to find out why. Why did he feel this way? Why her? What was it exactly about her that consumed his every waking moment and haunted his dreams as no woman had ever done before?

She has nothing to offer you. . . . John shook his head at the thought. There had to be more to life than position and money. There just had to be. What about love? His mother and father were proof of it. Love could not put a roof over your head or food in your belly, but it could make every day worth living. Love was something worth having.

Do you love her? There was plenty of time to think on it. An entire day coming when he would figure it out. A day with Izzy. But first, he must tell Edina.

John rapped on the door.

The maid, Katty Ann, opened it as if she'd been standing on the other side just waiting for him to knock. She dipped into a quick curtsey and showed him into the parlor, where Edina lounged upon what he hoped was a sofa. It was hard to tell what was beneath her with all the frills and frippery upon her dress. A tray of sweetmeats sat beside her on a small table. Katty Ann picked up a large fan and went back to her job of cooling Edina's flushed cheeks.

"I saw your horse below," Edina said. "Were you perhaps looking for my father?" she asked hopefully

My God . . . she thinks I mean to propose. . . . John's stomach sank at the prospect of Edina going into hysterics as she'd done this Sunday past after Izzy's rescue.

"Katty Ann, go tell Cook to serve tea please," Edina said, and Katty Ann scurried from the room.

John settled himself uncomfortably on the edge of a chair and then jumped up to walk over to the fireplace when Edina smiled sweetly at him.

"Oh my," she said. "Is there perhaps something pressing upon your mind?" Her voice trilled.

"Yes, Miss Rabin, there is," John said. He looked at her reflection in the ornate gold-framed mirror that hung above the mantelpiece. She was busy arranging her dress while he was turned away and John averted his eyes, focusing on the mantel, which was covered with all kinds of knick knacks and a lace scarf. The display was too fussy for his taste. He liked things simple. Like Izzy.

There is more to her than meets the eye. . . . As there undoubtedly was to Edina also. But that would be up to a different man to find out. Perhaps one who went for frills and lace. But not him.

A shadow caught his eye as it moved across the mirror, and John realized that Angus stood on the front stoop. If the man had business with Edina, why did he not come up the back staircase? John turned and looked toward the window just as Angus moved out of his view.

Was he listening at the door, as he'd been trying to listen downstairs? There was something about the man that disturbed him. He did not like the way the fellow looked at Izzy.

"Cook said the tea will be ready in a moment," Katty Ann said with a quick curtsey at the door.

"Thank you," John said before Edina could summon the maid back in to continue her fanning. Katty Ann bobbed her head and with a grateful little smile disappeared.

"I must apologize to you, Miss Rabin," John began.

"Must you call me Miss Rabin, John?" Edina interrupted. "Especially after the intimacy we shared this Sunday past?"

Intimacy?

"I am afraid I do not understand what you mean."

"You were in my bedroom, were you not?"

John rubbed his mouth to cover his smile. Yes, he had been in her bedroom. Along with her father, Izzy's brother, and the maid. And Edina was supposedly in a dead faint at the time. He'd also been the first one to leave it.

"Why, no," he said, calling her bluff. "Whatever gave you that idea? As I recall, you had fainted and I did help get you to the top of the stairs. But your father and Donnie took care of you from there."

"Oh," Edina said. "I was certain I saw you . . . when I was coming around."

"It must have been Donnie," John said. "It seems that we resemble each other."

"Indeed you do," Edina said as she studied his face. "But you are much more handsome in my opinion."

"Thank you,' John said. There was no harm in being polite. But he also needed to turn the conversation back to his purpose. "As I said, I must apologize." He held up his hand to stop her protests. "It seems that I have wasted your time and for that I am most sorry."

"Whatever do you mean?" Edina asked.

"I mean that I will not continue to waste it," John said hastily. "I fear that as our . . . er . . . tastes . . . do not run the same, I . . . er . . . you . . . should find someone else to share your . . . er, tastes in the future. Therefore I will not be calling on you again."

"Oh," was all she said.

"Good day, Miss Rabin," John said. "I shall see myself out."

Her screech hit the rafters at the same time that he closed the front door behind him. It was a pity that Katty Ann would have to deal with the aftermath. But at least he'd been honest with Edina. Their tastes really were not the same and he'd found out Sunday that his patience wore a bit thin where Edina was concerned.

Angus stood at the bottom of the steps.

"I could tell her, you know," he said as John came down.

"Tell who what?" John asked. He went to Sultan, who tossed his head impatiently.

"Tell Miss Edina why you won't see her anymore."

"And what would you tell her?" Sultan's impatience became his own.

"That you're seeing Izzy instead."

It sounded so dirty when Angus said it. John leapt from the curb and grabbed Angus by the collar. He slammed him up against the wall in the corner next to the steps. The man was as tall as he and outweighed him, but John did not care. He would not speak of Izzy that way. Not ever.

"You will not speak of her." He had clenched his jaw so tight it hurt. Angus's eyes were wide in his head. "To anyone." He let go of Angus's shirt and stepped back. "Do you understand me?"

Angus nodded, his eyes darting about as if he were seeking

escape. John took another step back and Angus jumped away from him.

"Her name is not MacDonald," Angus called back as he took off down the street. John watched him go and then noticed that someone was watching him. He was a tall, lean man with dark red hair. He stared at John for a moment, then turned and walked off in the same direction Angus had taken.

John took a deep breath. He never lost control. Never. He prided himself on his control. Had he just made things worse for Izzy? Would Edina listen to Angus? Was she vindictive enough that she would put Izzy out on the street?

There was nothing he could do to change the situation now. What was done was done. John went to Sultan, who had been amazingly quiet throughout the exchange.

"Her name is not MacDonald. . . ."

What exactly did that mean? And what difference did it make?

Ewan kept his eyes on Angus as the man lumbered down King Street. If he was any judge of character and Angus's lack thereof, then the apprentice would turn into one of the taverns close to the waterfront. He would need a pint to fortify himself after the redcoat's attack.

I wonder what that was all about. Did it have anything to do with Iz?

Izzy had not been happy to see him. That did not surprise him. What did surprise him was the fact that Angus had left willingly when he'd walked into the shop from the kitchen and told him he was Izzy's brother and they needed a bit of privacy.

"What do you want?" Izzy had asked in a dither. If she had not been confined to the stool, she probably would have thrown him out bodily.

"Donnie told me of your accident. I came to see how you fare."

"I fare quite well, thank ye," Izzy retorted. "And ye knew that since Donnie tells ye everything. This is the first time in all the years we've been here that ye have shown your face at the Rabins'. What is it ye want?"

Ewan took the seal from his pocket. "I want a letter asking for Da's release," he said. "Sealed with this to make it official."

"Are ye crazy, Ewan?" Izzy spat out. "Are ye going to march up to the tollbooth and demand Da's release?"

"The letter will do it for us."

"And they'll just hand him over to a dockworker and a stable hand?"

"I have a way around that too," Ewan told her. He was not about to explain that part of his plan to her.

"No," Izzy said. "I willnae do it. And ye will give up this madness before ye both wind up in the tollbooth with Da."

"Iz—" Ewan began.

"No." He recognized the set of her shoulders, the tilt of her chin. She would not do it. He'd have to find another way.

That other way had just walked into the Blue Boar.

Chapter Twelve

"Always proper," Izzy said as she looked John over from his carefully arranged hair to the perfectly polished toes of his boots. A mischievous thought took hold. She bit her lip to keep from laughing, reached up with both hands, and thoroughly mussed John's golden blond hair. Locks pulled loose from his queue and fell around his handsome face, softening the angular line of his jaw.

"That was time I wasted," he said with a smile.

"Think of all the things you could have been doing," Izzy agreed. She was afraid at first that he might be angry and felt relieved to see that he wasn't.

"Time I could have spent with you?" John asked with an arched eyebrow.

"Indeed," Izzy agreed. She looked at his coat. The sunlight was streaming down upon them and it wasn't even noon. "It's terribly warm, don't you think?"

"It is." John took off his red coat and with a mischievous grin, flung it over Sultan's saddle. He pulled loose his stock and stuffed it inside a pocket of his coat and rolled up his shirtsleeves. Then he loosened Sultan's bit and handed the reins to the stableboy, who led the horse inside.

"You're sure he'll be safe here?" John asked.

"Donnie will take good care of him." Izzy looked around. Where could Donnie be?

"Donnie lives here," Izzy added. "In a corner of the loft. So he can check on Sultan from time to time." Though she doubted Donnie would be in the loft today. Not with the fair in town and lovely girls to be chased and possibly caught. Izzy chewed on her lip as she imagined just what being caught by Captain John Murray might lead to. She felt her cheeks warm with a flush and quickly covered them with her hands.

"Is your ankle strong enough for a wall?" John asked.

Izzy did a slow pirouette. "Like new," she replied.

"Shall we go?" He offered her an arm.

"Iz! Wait!" Izzy turned and saw Donnie trotting up with a small basket under his arm. Izzy chewed her lip as she wondered just what mischief Donnie was up to. "Cook sent this," he said. "She said you forgot it."

Izzy took the basket. She did not recall Cook saying anything about packing a lunch for them. And what was Donnie doing at the house this morning?

"I thought to have myself a good breakfast," he explained as if he'd read her mind. "And she sent the basket with me."

It made sense. Cook adored Donnie and he wasn't above begging a free meal. John took the basket from her and opened it.

"I will be sure to tell her we appreciate her kindness," he said as he pulled out a bottle of wine. Izzy's eyes widened at the sight. It had obviously been opened. Had it come from Master Rabin's supply? Why was Cook giving them Master Rabin's wine?

"Have a wonderful day, Iz," Donnie said, and dropped a kiss on top of her head. Izzy looked up at him in puzzlement. He touched a knuckle to her cheek. "I love you," he mouthed, and walked into the stable without another word.

Izzy looked after Donnie, her mouth practically hanging open at what he'd whispered. How many years had it been since either of them had bothered to say those words? The last time she could recall she'd been tucking him into bed when he was nothing more than a lad. Then she looked at

John, realizing that her brother had not even acknowledged he was there. "I'm sorry," she said. "He's been acting a bit strange of late."

"I think I know what's troubling him," John said as he extended his arm again. "I have a sister too. Let me tell you about her."

Izzy soon forgot all about Donnie's strange behavior as they walked toward the south of town where the fair was set up in the fields below the ruins of Dunnottar Castle. She laughed over John's stories of his sister and her many disastrous escapades, along with her bad luck at finding a suitor who would live long enough to marry her.

"I fear ye are spinning tales to me, John Murray," she said as they came upon the fair.

"I promise you, I do not lie," he said in return. "Have I not told you my deepest, darkest secret?" He took her hand in his and his eyes seemed to sparkle with some hidden secret as he looked down at her and gave her fingers a gentle squeeze.

"Ye have," Izzy said. Yet she had not shared hers.

I should tell him. . . . But not here, surrounded by the Gypsies and townspeople, all drawn together to celebrate summer solstice. Not now when the sun was high in the sky and she felt beautiful and free for the first time in her life. She would tell him her secret later. Surely there would be a later for them.

John held her hand tightly and they wandered through the crowd. They watched jugglers, acrobats, and magicians perform tricks. They looked at wares set out by vendors, but when John tried to buy Izzy a small chain she refused.

"You have bought me the shoes," she said. "That is enough."

They moved on to where musicians were playing a lively tune. John set the picnic basket down and spun Izzy into a dance that had her feet flying and her lips grinning. She leaned back into the arm he held around her waist and looked up at the sky as he twirled her around. She was so happy she felt as if she could fly off into the sky.

He was too. She could tell by the smile that broadened his face and the merriment in his eyes. Gone was the Captain John Murray who'd escorted Miss Edina to church this Sunday past. In his stead stood John. John of the angel face and smiling eyes who chose her . . . Isobel . . . plain and simple Izzy, a servant, over a wealthy heiress.

They stopped their spinning and staggered over to where the basket waited. John scooped it up and gave her an inquiring look and Izzy nodded. They were hungry, they were thirsty, and without a word they knew it was time to move on.

Why suddenly was she so blessed? Why had he chosen her? From the first time they'd met in the alley, he'd been there for her, her hero, her conqueror, her savior.

I love him. . . . Izzy nearly stopped in her tracks, but John's hand around hers kept her moving. She barely knew him. She could count on one hand how many times she'd seen him or talked to him, yet she knew without a doubt that she loved him.

The realization stunned her. She wasn't ready for love. It was never something she'd considered or even wanted. Love made people do foolish, foolish things. She'd seen it destroy her mother. She did not want to be like her mother, a woman who sacrificed everything for the love of a man.

They moved past the Gypsy wagons and John snagged a blanket from a clothesline before they started the climb up to the ruins of Dunnottar Castle.

"I promise to return it," he said as Izzy laughed at his mischievous grin.

She felt like laughing and crying at the same time. She felt like screaming for joy and throwing herself off the cliffs.

What was wrong with her? Or maybe it was something so very right. Yet she was not sure how he felt. Did he love her as much as she loved him?

Her insides were a churning mass of confusion. Izzy placed a hand against her stomach as if she had a stitch in her side from the hard climb. It was no stitch that plagued her, just that vulnerable feeling of uncertainty as she realized that her entire life had just changed in the blink of an eye. John held her future in his hands. What would he do with it?

"I've always wanted to explore this place," John said as they climbed the broken steps that led to the keep. "It's history is fascinating."

"Really?" Izzy said. "I only ken than it's supposed to be haunted and no one has lived here for over sixty years."

"The last lord abandoned it because he was a Jacobite," John said. "He should have stayed and made the army rout him out. It's easily one of the most defensible positions I've ever seen."

A Jacobite . . . like my father. She should tell him, but not now, not when they were talking, just getting to know each other. Izzy looked around the ruins and tried to see them through a soldier's eye. "Aye," she agreed. "I can see. With the sea on one side, there's only the one way in and out."

"The ghosts you have heard of are most likely the ones who died in the Whigs' Vault," John said.

"Aye," Izzy agreed. "I have heard their tale." Close to two hundred men and women had been imprisoned in the dungeon because they refused to acknowledge the king's supremacy over their spiritual lives. "I wonder if the survivors who were banished felt as if they would have been better off dead."

"At least they were alive," John said.

"To some, it would be better to be dead than to be separated from the people and the land you love." She was thinking of her father and what was in store for him. Would he be hanged? Or merely deported? For a few dizzy moments while she'd been transported by happiness, she'd forgotten his plight. Now worry swept over her again.

"Indeed," John said as he spread the blanket. "I will agree that if you are forced to leave a place and the people you love, it is painful. But some people freely make that choice every day."

"You are talking about you and the fact that you are a soldier," Izzy said as he took her hand so she could sit gracefully upon the blanket. The grass was thick and high. It made a soft cushion beneath her.

John sat down beside her and spread his long legs out so that his boots were buried in the deep grass. "Actually I was thinking of my father," he said. "He is in the colonies and has been for many years."

"Did he choose to go there?" Izzy asked. "Or was he sent?"

"He chose to be a soldier," John said. "And therefore knew he would be sent to far-off places."

"But I wonder if he really did choose to be a soldier," Izzy said. "With his background, how else could he earn his living?"

"True," John said. He looked up at the sky and Izzy could not help doing the same. It was a remarkable day. The sky was as blue as she'd ever seen it and a few fluffy white clouds drifted by. The tall grass helped to keep the bite of the wind from their skin, and the sun felt warm and comforting. John stretched out on his back and folded his arms behind his head as a pillow. She heard the sound of the sea crashing against the cliffs and a gull cried out as it circled overhead. Sheltered in the grass, they seemed to be the only two people in the world.

"I think he did choose to be a soldier," John continued. "His father would have given him whatever he needed to make a good start in life. But my father wanted to prove himself, just as I do."

"Is that why you are in the army?"

"Yes," John said. "And so I'll be able to provide for my sister if necessary, though it is my mother's last wish that Carrie marry well."

"Your mother's last wish?"

"She is dying," John said. "Or so the doctors say. I'm sure Mother has a different opinion on the subject."

"Oh," Izzy said. She was not sure what she should say. "Will it be soon?"

"Carrie thinks not. Mother is a fighter. I can't ask for leave yet, not when I am so recently posted. At Christmas, however . . ."

"It must be hard."

"It's a part of life," John said. "It's funny, I always thought it would be Father going first, since he's a soldier. . . ." His voice trailed off for a moment. "I am more concerned about Carrie. I don't know what will become of her once Mother is gone."

"Ye sound like me, worrying over Donnie," Izzy said. She leaned her chin on her knees. "I've cared for him since he was a wee lad. 'Tis hard for me to look at him now and realized he's a man grown."

"So you were orphaned at a young age?"

"Our mother died in childbirth . . . and our da . . ." *Tell him.* "He wasnae around much." Why couldn't she tell him about Da? That he was a rebel and in prison awaiting trial? Why wouldn't the words come?

Because you love the man and you are afraid if he knows the truth, he'll walk away. I will tell him later. When I know . . . when I know for sure that he loves me.

"Let's open the basket, shall we?" John said, and Izzy fell gratefully to the task.

I will tell him about Da later.

She handed John the bottle of wine and unpacked the rest of the lunch. Cook had outdone herself. Izzy smiled at John as he exclaimed over the feast set before them on the blanket.

Later. . . .

Chapter Thirteen

A man could drown in those eyes. John lay on his side with his head propped up in his hand and stared at Izzy, who was stretched out on the blanket beside him. Her eyes were closed now, but a moment before when they were open and looking down at him he would have sworn he was drowning. They were so dark and deep, fathomless . . .

But now she lay on her back with her arm thrown over her face as if the sun hurt her eyes. It might just be so. It was suddenly too bright, and the sky too blue and the ground beneath him too soft as if he might sink down into it and become a part of the earth himself.

It must be the wine. He kicked at the bottle that lay near his feet. It was empty. They'd drunk it all as they talked about mundane things and ate the bounteous lunch and enjoyed the warmth of the day. It had to be late afternoon, time to return, to begin the long walk back to Aberdeen and the stables and the Rabins' house.

He didn't want to move. He couldn't move. Moving would mean leaving Izzy's side and there was no place else he wanted to be.

"Izzy?" he said as he watched her chest slowly rise and fall as if she were sleeping.

She moved her arm a bit and turned her head to look at him and once more he was drowning. He could not help himself, nor could he stop. He felt as if his entire life hinged upon the next moment, the next breath, the next heartbeat. John slowly lowered his head and kissed her.

Her lips parted with a sharp intake of breath and her arm fell away from her face, only to creep slowly around his neck as he deepened the kiss. He took advantage of her parted lips to slip his tongue inside her mouth, leading her in a sensual dance that set his body on edge.

He framed her face with his hands and kissed her until they both had to take a breath.

"God . . ." he gasped. "Izzy."

She pulled his face down with her hand on the back of his neck and they kissed again, only now he pulled her on her side and into his arms. She tasted of the wine and fresh-baked bread and sharp cheese and the exquisite lemon tarts that had been in the basket. She smelled like fresh grass and sunshine and she felt so wonderfully right in his arms. John placed a leg over her hip and she squirmed up against him as he wrapped it around her and pinned her to him.

He stroked his hand down her back and pressed against the curve of her behind and she moved against him. John felt a jolt of pleasure in his groin and he groaned as his member sprang to life, hard and throbbing against the constraints of his breeches.

Somewhere in his mind he knew what was happening was wrong. He knew it was too fast, too furious, too soon for the feelings that had burst into life. He needed to think, he needed to step back, he needed to take a breath, but his body would not let him; nor would Izzy's. She was as caught up in the moment as he was.

John felt as if he were outside himself. He watched as he pushed aside the soft cloud of her hair and rained kisses down her neck until he reached the line of her bodice and the swell of her breasts. He was surprised when he placed his hand inside and tore the fabric, freeing her breasts from her shift. He felt the softness of her skin as he kissed them and moved his hand over them as he pushed Izzy over on her back.

She wrapped her hands in his hair and arched upward when his mouth closed over the taut peak.

He wanted to feel all of her. He wanted to touch all of her. He felt clumsy and out of control next to her gentle grace. How could he be so wild when his entire life was about control? Everything he had ever done he'd studied before he ever attempted it. Yet now he fumbled about in the grass like an ignorant schoolboy. It was Izzy who removed his shirt and trailed her hands over the skin of his chest until he was gasping for breath. It was Izzy who sat up and turned her back so he could unfasten her dress and cast it aside along with her petticoats and shift, her stockings, and her new shoes, which he tossed carelessly into the grass as they both laughed. It was Izzy who reached for the lacings of his breeches and with her nimble fingers freed him as he toed off his boots and stockings and she pushed the breeches down and away over his hips so that they both lay naked in the sun with his body covering hers.

Skin to skin, mouth to mouth, with his hands tangled in her hair.

"I love you, Iz," he said, and she laughed joyfully.

"Aye, I love ye too, John Murray," she replied and once more he found himself drowning in the dark brown depths of her eyes.

Drowning . . . he was drowning. He felt the water close over his head and knew the only way he could survive was to possess her, body and soul. He wanted to touch every inch of her and so he did, with his hands, with his mouth, until she lay quivering and gasping beneath him.

The part of him that knew this was not the time rushed back inside his mind as he slid inside her parted thighs and broke through the barrier that said there had been no one before him. "Izzy," he cried out as her legs folded around his waist and he buried himself deeper inside her. "Izzy," he breathed as she joined him in the familiar rhythm, pulling him closer. Their lips met and the tumultuous sensations carried him away.

He felt her tense, knew that her storm was gathering. He wondered if she'd ever felt it before and knew that she hadn't, that he was the first, the only, and he would be the only one. No other would touch her. No other would give her this. She stilled and her eyes widened and then they shut as she shuddered in his arms and he caught her cry in his mouth with another kiss. He knew she had peaked, but he had not and he could not stop. She moaned beneath him and her legs tightened and held him close as he jerked and thrust until he felt the explosion coming.

The world spun until her eyes were the sun and he was burning up inside her. He threw his head back and groaned as the sun consumed him. Then his strength gave way and he collapsed into her arms.

"I'll make it right by you, Iz," he said when he could speak again. "I promise."

"I know ye will," she said. "Because ye love me."

"I do." He rolled her over into his arms so that they lay side by side. "I do love you. And I will marry you as soon as we can get it done."

"I'm sure I would like that," she said. Her voice sounded slurred and far away, but he felt her in his arms and he knew everything would be fine. It was the last thought on his mind as he drifted into sleep, content with Izzy beside him.

Ewan looked at his brother. The coat fit Donnie perfectly and with his hair tied back in a neat queue, it was hard to tell the difference between him and Captain John Murray unless you personally knew the man. And Ewan was betting that there were few who knew the captain at the tollbooth. Murray had only been in Aberdeen a few weeks and from what Ewan could find out in the taverns, most of the soldiers were not yet familiar with him.

"Ye've got the orders?" Ewan asked.

"Aye," Donnie said, and patted his chest, where the papers were stashed inside his coat.

"We'd best go, then," Ewan said. "The ship sails on the evening tide and if we time it right, we can be aboard before they even know he's missing."

"I left a letter for Iz with Cook," Donnie said as he mounted the snowy white stud that belonged to Murray.

"We'll be gone before she reads it," Ewan said as he mounted a horse on "loan" from the stable. He grabbed the reins of another.

"Good thing, because she will most likely want to kill us."

"Aye," Ewan said. "We can send for her when we are settled."

Donnie grabbed Ewan's arm before they left the stable. "Ye are sure the wormwood will not harm her?"

"The Gypsy said they would fall asleep after a bit," he said.

"And wake up without any trouble?"

"Aye," Ewan said as he urged his horse forward. "Ye need to take the lead, Donnie," he instructed.

Donnie kicked his mount ahead. The stud was not cooperating, but Ewan was sure Donnie could handle it.

Ewan spared a look toward the south where the torches from the fair lit up the sky. Izzy and Captain Murray had been gone for hours.

The Gypsies said the wormwood added to the wine would make whoever drank it fall in love and act on that love, then sleep long and deep. If Captain Murray was an honorable man, then Iz would be well cared for during the rest of her life. Ewan was betting he was an honorable man and Iz would be happy.

It was all he could do for her. Make sure she was cared for and happy.

"Sorry, Iz," Ewan said as he followed Donnie.

It was the cold that woke her. She felt the air chill her nude body and Izzy woke with a start to find herself enfolded in John's arms with her face pressed against the smooth expanse of his chest. Shock coursed through her body as she realized what they had done. She had never been this close to a man before, never, and here she was lying naked in the grass like a whore.

"Oh God," she whispered as shame overtook her. She had to get away, she had to hide, and she wanted to die on the spot. She wiggled out from beneath John's arm and tried to find her shift in the moonlight. John flopped over on his back and the silvery light of the full moon touched the lines and angles of his body.

He was beautiful. His face was relaxed and his golden hair tousled. His limbs were long, smooth, and strong with muscle. His chest was broad and tapered down to a trim waist and narrow hips. She reached out a hand to touch him but then pulled it back.

Like an angel . . .

Izzy touched her fingers to her lips. They felt swollen and bruised from his kisses. Her thighs ached and between them she felt . . . empty. She crossed her arms over her stomach to hold back the sobs that threatened to erupt as she turned once more to find her shift. She could not be here when he awakened. She could not bear to see the condemnation in his eyes.

A hand touched her back, trailed up her spine, then grasped

her shoulder. She trembled. She was afraid, so very afraid to look at him, afraid of what she would see. Afraid he would brand her a whore.

"I'm sorry," he said, and his arms came around her and pulled her back against his chest. "I will make it right."

The tears came, overflowing, she could not stop them. "How can ye say that?" she sobbed. "How can ye want to? Ye must think I'm a—"

"Shh," he said, and turned her so that she faced him. She looked up at the angles and planes of his face, which were lit by the moon. His eyes were dark shadows and she longed to gaze into them, but they were lost beneath the fall of his hair. "I love you, Izzy." He must be speaking the truth. Why else would he say it? He could condemn her now and leave her without a second glance. "I have from the first day I met you. It was my fault. Mine . . . and the wine."

Izzy jerked her head. "The wine?"

"Yes, sweet. The wine. It was very potent."

Donnie had given them the wine. He couldn't have. He wouldn't have . . . but Ewan . . .

"It is not an excuse," John continued. "I swear, I am not normally a seducer of women."

"Yes." Izzy's mind whirled. Had Ewan put something in the wine?

"But I have to admit when I am with you, I seem to lose all sense of propriety."

Izzy felt a strange hysteria threaten to rise to the surface. She did not dare look at him.

"I meant what I said, Iz," he continued. With a finger he tilted her chin up. "Marry me?"

Her mind tumbled. How could she marry John if Ewan had drugged the wine?

But he said he loved me from the first day he met me. So what did it matter? Would they not have come to the same realization eventually? Maybe the wine just hurried matters along a bit. She didn't even know for sure that it was drugged.

"Please?"

Izzy nodded. "Yes," she said.

"We can marry on my next leave day," John said. "I will have to find quarters for us, of course."

"Yes," Izzy said again. She felt strange. Outside herself. Outside her body and mind, as if she watched the scene from a cloud hovering somewhere above.

"You can leave the Rabins', you know."

The thought had not even occurred to her. "I can?"

"Izzy," John said with a smile and a shake of his head. He bent to kiss her, and all the things that had troubled her seemed to melt away as he pulled her into his lap. If only she could stay in this moment forever. This moment when she felt as if they were the only two people in the entire world.

"You're trembling," he said. "Are you cold?" He pulled the ends of the blanket around them as Izzy nestled in closer to him.

"Nay," she said. "I think I'm a bit overwhelmed."

"As I am," he said. "by you."

"Truly?"

"Truly."

"'Tis not something I expected to happen," Izzy confessed. "I never imagined ye could love me."

"I must confess I did not expect it either," John said. "You were most definitely a surprise." He kissed her again. "A very nice surprise."

"I am certain that is the first time anyone has said such a thing about me."

"I will say it every day for the rest of our lives."

Izzy laid her head against his shoulder and tried to let everything that had happened sink in. She should be deliriously happy. But she still could not shake her worries about Ewan and the wine.

"I must talk to your brother since you have no parents," John said as if coming to a decision.

Izzy sighed. She would have to tell him. "I have a fa—" she began.

John turned his head toward the sounds of voices. They heard a woman screech, followed by the deep laughter of a man.

"We should go," he said, and reached for his breeches. "I would hate to further compromise you." Izzy nodded as he began the task of dressing. He found her shift and handed it to her, then helped her dress quickly.

Izzy put her shoes on, and then scooped up the basket. John kicked the wine bottle into the deep grass along with the remnants of their lunch as he grabbed up the blanket. He took her hand and they set out through the grass, away from the voices, away from the fair, and along the beach, north toward Aberdeen.

Chapter Fourteen

He'd torn her dress. Add that to his long list of sins. As they approached the lights of Aberdeen, John placed the blanket over her shoulders.

"Ye promised to return it," Izzy said. Her teeth chattered as she clasped the blanket in her hand to cover her dishabille. Why was she cold? The air had turned crisp with nightfall, but his body was warm and the sea breeze felt good against his chest where his shirt hung open. The sky was peppered with stars that seemed close enough to touch.

If only he could gather a handful to give to Izzy . . . Would it make up for the dishonor he'd put her through? It was not like him to lose control. He was the one who was always in control. He never drank too much, he never talked too loud, he was always proper, always a gentleman. Had his feelings for Izzy taken over?

"I will," he said, "after I see you safely home."

He'd meant everything he'd said today. He would marry her and spend the rest of his life taking care of her. It wasn't what he'd planned, nor expected. It was better than that. He'd never planned on falling in love. He'd hoped for it at one time when he was young and foolish. Lately he would have settled for companionship in marriage. But now that he'd met Izzy, he knew life without her would be a disappointment.

He took her free hand and helped her climb the rocks that littered the sand of the beach and the road above. The stink of the wharves soon overpowered the freshness of the North

Sea's waves. A reminder that the dream of this perfect day was now over and it was time to think on practical matters. Like talking to her brother.

"Do you think Donnie will be at the stables?" he asked.

"I hope so," Izzy said. She sounded distracted.

John stopped and pulled her to his side. "Do you doubt what I said? Do you need your brother to avenge your honor?" She did not meet his gaze, so he tipped her chin up with his finger. Her hair was wild about her head, either from the breeze or their earlier passion. He took a moment to smooth it down with his fingers as he tried to look into her eyes.

"Nay," she said finally. "I trust you."

John kissed her forehead and she leaned into him, suddenly wrapping her arms around him as if she were desperate to hold on to him. She placed her cheek against his chest and it felt damp. Was she crying?

"There are things I need to tell ye," she said against his chest. "Things ye should know about my family before ye decide."

"Nothing will change how I feel about you." John wrapped his arms around her. "We'll talk when we get to the stable."

Izzy nodded against his chest and then they moved on past the docks, where a ship was making ready to sail on the turn of the tide. The whorehouses on the wharf were brightly lit and spilled laughter and squeals from the women. John spared a glance at the windows and thought of Rory until he remembered his friend was on duty tonight. They did not speak another word until they came upon the street where the stable was located.

It was Sultan barreling down the street that brought them out of their silence. He was saddled and his reins trailed after him as he ran by, wide-eyed with fear. John was so startled, he could do nothing but turn and watch him go by. It was then that he noticed the dark splotches on the stallion's hindquarters.

"He's hurt!" John yelled. He turned to run after his horse but instead went after Izzy, who dropped the blanket and took off toward the stable with her skirts bunched in her hands. It took him but a second to decide to follow Izzy. He knew Sultan would head back to the stable at the post. And if he was hurt, someone there would take care of him.

Something is horribly wrong. He could not shake the feeling as he ran after Izzy.

He caught up with her just as she ran through the stable door. She cried out and went into the stall where they had left Sultan earlier in the day.

"It would have worked, Iz," declared a man wearing a private's uniform. It was the same man he'd seen on the street the day he attacked Angus. Suddenly John realized he and Izzy were related. Was he another brother? In his arms lay Donnie. He wore a red coat, and he was bleeding from a wound in his gut. He held both hands pressed against it.

John had seen wounds like that before. He knew what the outcome was. Death would be here soon. A very painful death.

"Donnie!" Izzy sank to her knees beside her brother as she cried out his name.

"His friend is what done it," the other brother said, and pointed his chin toward John. "We would have had Da now if he had not showed up."

"Ewan," Izzy cried out. "What hae ye done?" She took Donnie from Ewan and settled him against her. She wrapped her arms around his chest and pulled him close. She kissed the top of his head and pushed his damp hair back from his face.

"I shot him," Donnie said with a groan. "I think I killed him." He grabbed at Izzy's hand. "Will God forgie me, Iz?"

"He shot you first," Ewan said. "God forgives a man defending himself."

"What do ye know about it?" Izzy cried. "Ye don't listen to God, ye don't listen to anyone but Da. Why did ye do this?"

"The plan was sound," Ewan said. "We had the letter, we had the seal, and we had the way to get in, thanks to your man."

"What?" John felt his heart turn in his chest. "Who did you shoot?"

"We have to get to the ship before it sails." Ewan strode around the stall impatiently. "We'll put Donnie on the back of a horse."

"What is he talking about?" John looked at Izzy, who rocked Donnie back and forth as if he were a babe. Donnie's eyes were clenched shut and his face contorted in pain.

"Don't ye see?" she cried. "They needed ye out of the way so they could use your horse and coat." She looked up at him with eyes full of tears. "To break our father out of the tollbooth."

"Help me get him to the ship," Ewan said.

"He's dying," John said. "He's not going anywhere."

"Find me a priest," Donnie ground out between his clenched teeth. "I need to confess."

"The wine was drugged," Izzy said. She looked up at him with those damned eyes.

"No," John said.

"Our father is Donald Ferguson," she said, and John felt the world tilt beneath him. *Her name is not MacDonald.*

"The outlaw?" Was that his voice? It sounded so strange, so far away. "The one I just captured?" He heard the sound of horses and a shout of command and knew that the king's army had arrived.

"Please," Donnie gasped. He gripped Izzy's arm and she sobbed. She looked up at him again with eyes full of pain.

"We need to go." Ewan moved toward the back of the stable. John let him go. He knew the stable was already surrounded.

"Can ye find him a priest?" she whispered. Tears ran down her face and into the torn neck of her dress. The dress he'd torn in his passion.

They needed ye out of the way. And she was the lure. The wine was drugged. He'd fallen into their trap. Her trap.

John shook his head. *No.* He placed his hand inside his shirt, over his heart. How did you keep a heart from shattering like glass? "No." He turned and found himself face-to-face with General Kensington.

"Captain Murray," he said. "Do you know these people?" John snapped to attention. "Yes, sir."

"Then you are under arrest for collusion in the escape attempt of Donald Ferguson." Sergeant Gordon stepped forward and pulled John's hands behind his back to bind them. "And as an accessory in the death of Captain Rory Beauchamp."

"Rory is dead?" John gasped. *Not Rory . . . they killed Rory. . . .* He lunged for Ewan. He wanted to kill him with his bare hands. Gordon pulled him back and bound his hands. "You killed Rory?"

"He knew it wasnae you on the horse," Ewan said helplessly as two soldiers bound his arms and patted him down for weapons.

"What about him?" Kensington's nephew asked.

Kensington walked into the stall and toed Donnie's leg with his boot. There was no response. Then he crouched down in the straw beside Izzy. "Did you know of the plan, miss?" he asked.

Izzy closed Donnie's vacant eyes with her hand.

"Aye." Her voice was so quiet, he barely heard her. "I knew."

She knew . . .

"Bring her too," Kensington said.

"No," Izzy cried out. "I cannae leave him."

John turned away. Away from her. Away from her secret brother. Away from the death in the stall.

"It's over," Kensington said. "He's dead."

Yes . . . I am.

Chapter Fifteen

"It is only out of respect for your father that I give you this opportunity to explain yourself," Kensington said. He leaned back in the chair behind his desk.

John stared at the fire. He felt so cold. Was it just an hour ago that he was warm? He sat across from Kensington, his shirt still open, his hair still wild from the afternoon. He was not as he should be. He was not in control. He'd lost his control the day he'd met Izzy.

Isobel Ferguson . . .

It was all a lie. Every bit of it. John leaned forward and ran his hands through his hair. How had she slipped beneath his defenses? When had she decided to use him? Did she plan every bit of it? Not the attack in the alley, but the rest? Did she fall in the river deliberately so he would save her? Had she waited in front of the Mercat Cross for him to make an appearance? That was after her father was taken.

I am a fool. . . .

"You are not the first man to fall victim to a woman's manipulations," Kensington said gently.

"I should have known better," John said. "I should have known the wine was drugged."

"Were you compromised?"

John looked at the fire as it crackled and popped. He saw Izzy beneath him. Her brown eyes were deep pools that claimed him. Her hair a cloud around her lovely face. Her mouth swollen from his kisses. Her body twisted beneath his in passion.

"Yes." He said the word as a sigh. As if all the air left his body. There were better words for it than *compromised*. *Betrayed* came to mind. Used. Manipulated. Deceived.

She was a virgin. . . . A virgin given up as a sacrifice to save her father.

Damn the Scots. Damn the Highlanders. They were a vicious breed. They could not be trusted. They were a deceitful lot and would use any means possible to achieve their end. It was why they lost the rebellion.

Let it be a lesson to you . . . they cannot be trusted.

"I cannot let this transgression go unpunished," Kensington said. "No matter what my feelings for your family. A man was killed."

Rory . . . "Yes, sir." John focused on the bookshelf to the right of the general's head. He could not look him in the eye. He was afraid of what the man might see in his gaze.

"You will not be charged with collusion, or as an accessory."

Does it matter? "Thank you, sir."

"The charge is dereliction of duty with extenuating circumstances."

Another way of saying I was a fool. "Yes, sir."

"Your sentence is twenty-five lashes to be carried out day after tomorrow."

His stomach turned violently and he gripped the arms of the chair. "Yes, sir."

"Tomorrow there will be a service for Captain Beauchamp."

Rory's family . . . his father and mother . . . how would he ever face them knowing he was responsible?

"As you will be confined to a cell, you will not be attending," Kensington continued. "I think it best under the circumstances."

He almost sighed in relief. He would not have to face them

when they came to claim their son's body. "Yes, sir." He would not have to face anyone on the post until . . .

He's giving me time to think about it . . . to dread it . . .

"How fares your mother, John?"

John's eyes snapped to the general's face with the question. "Not well, sir."

"So I have heard from a mutual acquaintance." There was a knock on the door. "I will give you time to recover and then I am sending you to her until . . ." Kensington cleared his throat. "Afterward you will be posted in the colonies. With your father. It's the least I can do for him."

"Yes, sir," John said. "Thank you, sir." He was not sure if the orders were a blessing or not. He was to be banished from England. Word would get around of what had happened. About his circumstances and Rory's death. His reputation was ruined. Kensington was giving him another chance. But only under the guidance of his father.

Better if it had been me that died instead of Rory. How would he face his family? How could he face his father? Kensington would tell him. Or else the gossip would filter down to him. While England's arm was long, her borders were small. Word would get around.

Concentrate on Mother now . . . on home . . . put this behind you. He still had the lashing to get through. Maybe that would kill him. If he was lucky.

Her dress was torn. Shamefully so. Izzy held the torn piece up over her exposed skin with her bound hands. She kept her eyes downcast on the blood that stained her skirts. Donnie's blood. It was better to look at that than the faces of the soldiers who blamed her for the death of their comrade.

If only she knew what they'd done with Donnie's body. Somebody needed to tend him. Wash him. Prepare him. It should be her, not some stranger who didn't know him or care for him. Someone who knew that his second toe curled under the other and when he was a babe she had pulled on it endlessly so it would be as straight as the others. If only there had been a priest to hear his confession. Would he go straight to hell because he had not confessed? Would they put him in the churchyard? In holy ground? Or would he wind up in the paupers' cemetery?

"God, please take care of him," she prayed silently. "He didnae mean it. He did it out of love for Da and Ewan."

"You may enter," the voice behind the door said. The guard who'd brought her to the general's quarters pulled on her upper arm and she stumbled after him. He shoved her through the door and she found herself facing the general, who stood behind his desk. Before the desk, in a straight-backed chair sat John, who quickly turned away from her shocked gaze.

"I will give you leave to say your piece, John." The general strode past his desk and stopped to look at her. Izzy could not meet his gaze. She felt his contempt as he moved on, taking the guard with him. She heard the door shut firmly behind them and knew the guard was stationed right outside the door.

Did they expect her to run? Where would she go? There was no one she could go to. The Rabins would cast her out without a second thought. Cook, Tommy, and Katty Ann would show her kindness, she was sure, but there was no need for them to jeopardize their jobs for her. *I'm not worth it.*

She'd run if she could. If it meant not having to face John. If it meant they'd kill her so she'd never have to see the hurt in his eyes again.

Maybe he wouldn't look at her. Maybe he wouldn't speak to her. Maybe the floor would open up and the earth would swallow her and take her down to the depths of hell so Donnie would not be there alone.

She should have known . . . she would have stopped it . . . if only she could have. If only she had not been so selfish, grabbing for something that she knew she could not and should not have.

One day of complete happiness to carry her through whatever was left of her wretched life.

John stood suddenly and Izzy flinched. She knew it was coming. The cursing, the accusations, the condemnation. Whatever he said, she would take it. She deserved every bit of it. She squared her shoulders. She braced herself. She raised her chin. She blinked back her tears and willed her body to quit shaking.

John walked to her. Izzy stared at his chest where his shirt hung open. The skin was so smooth. She could still feel it beneath her hands, along with the strength that lay beneath. If only he would fold her into his arms and hold her in that safe haven and tell her that everything was going to be fine. That it was all a horrible nightmare. That the day would start over again and everything would be as it should be.

"I have decided—" he began, and Izzy tore her eyes from his chest and looked up at his face. His eyes were upon her. Instead of the lovely blue of the sky, they were dark and stormy. They were full of hatred and contempt.

He stumbled over his words, cleared his throat, and started again. "I have decided never to think of you again."

"I am so sorry," Izzy murmured, but John threw his hand up to stop her.

"I will never think of you again because it hurts too much. What I will remember is how you betrayed me. How you took what I offered and threw it in my face. Damn you and damn your family, Isobel Ferguson. I have learned my lesson. I will never again let my heart rule my head."

She felt her heart shatter as he quietly left. She did not hear the door close, nor did she hear it open again. The guard came and jerked her arm so that she fell in step beside him. She could not hear anything but John's words echoing in her head.

"I will never think of you again."

Chapter Sixteen

Izzy gulped in great breaths of the cool clean air. It was if she had been suffocating and finally realized that she was once more allowed to breathe. She didn't want to breathe. Not really. Breathing meant she was still alive. Breathing meant that Donnie was dead and Ewan and Da imprisoned and John hated her with the same passion he'd shown her when he'd made love to her. She'd rather be dead.

The mist in the predawn hour chilled her quickly. The gloom made it hard to see, but there were shapes moving about. She blinked. She felt as if she'd been underground for years, hidden away or even thrown away. What did it matter? She was out of her body, not living, just existing, and even that was more than she wanted.

How many days since she'd lain in the grass overlooking the sea and felt John's lips on her bare skin? How many nights since Donnie lay dying in her arms and the soldiers arrested all of them? How many breaths had she taken since John's eyes turned on her with hatred? Even though she had not known of Ewan's plan, she was a part of it. A most willing part of it. She would pay the price for the rest of her life. There was nothing anyone could do to her that could hurt any worse than the pain in John's eyes.

The gloom grew a little lighter. Now there was no doubting what the post in the middle of the yard was for. Did they mean to lash her?

The soldier who'd led her from her cell pulled on her arm. Her hands were tied in front of her and her feet tangled in her skirts. She almost fell . . . almost. He caught her as she tripped and kept her from landing face-first in the mud. Her new shoes pulled at her feet as she stumbled along. She tried to hold her skirts up, tried to cover the torn neckline of her dress, but it was no use. What difference did it make? Her dress would be in tatters after the lashing. And if she survived it, they could carry her back in and she would die in whatever deep, deep hole they chose to throw her into. She simply did not care.

Yet she could not help being relieved when she was led past the post to a small platform on the opposite side of the yard. Her body shook violently, from the cold, from the wet, from relief as she climbed the stairs. She was told to stand and wait.

Wait . . . for what . . . she was too terrified even to think of it.

Izzy stood with her hands tied before her and her head down. She felt her hair flatten against her head. She felt the misty spray wash down her bodice and trickle down her breasts. She felt the cold damp wind at her back. If only she could dissolve into the wind and blow away.

She was conscious of men moving around. Soldiers filed from the barracks and formed a line on either side of the platform. She faced the doors that led to the cells.

General Kensington stepped onto the platform next to her, along with his aide. She felt small and insignificant next to him.

"Good morning, Miss Ferguson," he said. "It is Miss Ferguson, is it not?"

"Aye . . . Aye, sir," Izzy said.

"At one time it was rumored to be Miss MacDonald?" His pale blue eyes pierced through her, saw her lies and treachery. There was no hiding it. Why should she try?

Izzy bit her lip as she nodded. She had lied. But not for the reason they thought. Never for that. But what did it matter? She had lied.

"Let's get started, shall we?" General Kensington said in a voice that sounded as if he were inviting her to tea. Izzy stared out over the grounds, wide-eyed. What was going to happen?

The soldiers stood at attention, but she could tell they were restless. Who wouldn't be with the wet and the wind and the misery of the morning? All eyes were turned toward the cell doors.

Izzy gasped as Ewan was led forth. Had his cell been close to hers? Was he with Da? Da was behind Ewan and he was led out and placed next to a soldier by the doorway.

She choked back a sob as her brother was led to the post. She saw his brown eyes light on her for a quick moment; then he lowered his head and looked at the ground, even when his arms were stretched mercilessly above him and tied and his shirt ripped from his back.

The sentence was read. Twenty lashes. She heard the whiny, nasal voice of the general's aide as he read the charges.

"Oh God, oh God, oh God." Izzy whispered the prayer over and over again. Ewan faced her with his cheek pressed against the post, but he would not look up. She clenched her fingers into her palms. She felt the nails pressing into her skin. She felt the pain come and saw the whip curl and she jumped at the first stroke just as Ewan moved when the lash hit him.

"Dear God . . ." she cried.

"How are you feeling, Miss Ferguson?" General Kensington asked her.

Izzy shook her head as she bent over and emptied what was left in her stomach onto the platform. There wasn't much there, just a nasty taste that burned her throat and mouth as she wiped it away with the sleeve of her dress. She turned her face up toward the sky and the mist as the next blow landed.

"I would appreciate it if you would watch this, Miss Ferguson," General Kensington said. "You may count along if you like."

He knew. He knew that she would rather take the beating herself than watch her brother suffer. And Da? Was he next? How did he feel, knowing all this was because of him? Because of Ewan's foolish devotion. Donnie was dead and his family arrested so they could not even pray over him and see him properly buried.

"Three," the aide said, and Izzy whispered the word along with him.

Ewan choked back a cry. He kept his cheek tight against the post. Every muscle in his body strained against it. How much more could he stand? How much more could she stand?

"Four."

"Holy Mother, full of grace," Izzy began. She counted the rosary off on her fingers, her shoulders flinching with each stroke. She heard Ewan groan, and then he screamed as if the sound was ripped from his throat with the whip.

It was. She kept her eyes on him, terrified that if she moved them, the general would extend the lashing. She counted off her prayer and watched as Ewan collapsed against the post.

Then it was over. Finally, over. Her knees trembled with the effort to remain upright. Would Da be led to the post now? She looked over to where he stood, tall and proud, without a sign on his face of what had just happened, or any fear of what might happen.

Had he looked the same that day at Culloden? Tall and proud and strong even though he knew he would likely die?

Wouldn't they all be better off if he had? Would not Donnie be alive?

Izzy tried to work up the hate in her heart, but it wouldn't come. Instead she watched as Ewan was dragged to him. Da took him in his arms and half carried his son back down to the cells.

Izzy looked up expectantly at the general. Would they take her back now? What did they plan for her?

The general seemed to be studying her carefully. Then he motioned toward the cells with his hand.

Izzy watched with her breath caught in her throat, not daring to let it out, afraid of what horror would come at her next.

John. She looked at the post, at the blood, Ewan's blood, as it puddled in the damp mud. Surely not. He was an officer, he was one of them, English. He was the victim, and her brothers had used him. He was going to be whipped? She looked up at the general, who watched John intently as he stood in the doorway, his eyes searching the grounds. Izzy turned back and felt his eyes upon her, piercing and so blue. She felt them cut through her like a sword.

She squared her shoulders, she raised her chin. She was a Ferguson. A Highlander. Damn him. Damn the English. If he chose to believe she'd betrayed him after what they had shared . . .

They were drugged . . . Ewan had admitted it. He'd put the wormwood in the wine . . . still . . . John had said he loved her . . . before the wine. How could he love her and then hate her?

Bastard. Son of a bastard. And she'd become his whore . . .

John stepped out into the yard, into the mist, with an old, grizzled soldier by his side. The old soldier seemed to be talking to him, maybe consoling him; she could tell John was listening to the man, yet his eyes never left her face.

Too soon they stood before the post and the old soldier attached the hook to the bonds around John's wrists. The old soldier nodded to a younger man, who jerked on a rope attached to a pulley. John's arms were stretched above his head and he was pulled against the post. Izzy watched as his boots sank into the muck and the young soldier pulled again so that he was stretched up onto his toes.

The older soldier said something to the younger and Izzy almost sighed in relief as the young man lessened his hold on the rope and John was able to place his feet on each side of the post.

The older soldier talked to John for a bit, and then he slipped a piece of wood in John's mouth. John nodded as he placed his cheek against the post. The old soldier stepped behind him and ripped away his shirt. The older man spoke again, this time directly into John's ear. What did he say to him? What could he say to make this any more bearable?

Izzy watched as John blinked the rain off his eyelashes and looked toward General Kensington. She heard the sentence being read by Kensington's aide once more. Twenty-five lashes. Five more than what Ewan had received. Why? Why were there more for John?

"Do you understand your sentence?" the aide asked.

John looked at the general and nodded. The general raised his hand. His face looked sad and Izzy wondered why. If he hated this so much, then why was he doing it?

Think on something else. . . . She knew the lash was coming. She saw it coiling and gathering. She heard it whistle through the air.

John looked at her. It was her fault. He had trusted her with his life, with his soul, with his heart, and she'd betrayed him.

She felt the sting of the lash as if it struck her. Her back burned as John was slammed against the post.

"One," the aide said.

Please, God . . .

The next one came from the opposite direction. She could not see his back, but she knew the stripes crossed it both ways.

"Two."

The third one landed straight across. She didn't hear it, but she knew John let out a hiss as he kept his eyes on her. Her own eyes felt huge in her face.

"Three."

How could he stand it? How could she stand it? She wanted to scream, she wanted to cry, she wanted to die, but all she could do was stand there like a fool, like a betrayer, like the sinner she was and watch.

Hail, Mary, full of grace. . . .

The next blow struck straight down his spine. The man with the whip seemed determined to flay every inch of skin off John's back. Did he enjoy his job that much? How could he? She raised her hands to her mouth as John pushed against the post, his body automatically seeking escape from the next blow.

"Four."

Hail, Mary, full of grace. . . .

Izzy heard the whistle of the lash once again. She saw John's flesh tear. She saw the blood pour down his sides. She heard him groan and saw his jaw tighten as he clenched his teeth in the wood.

"Five."

Twenty to go. How could she stand it? She had to. Crying wouldn't stop it. Begging wouldn't stop it. Screaming her anger and apologies at the heavens would not stop the lashing any more than it would stop the rain that now poured down upon them all.

John just kept staring at her, blinking in the rain. It was her fault. All her fault. Every bit of it.

John, I am sorry. So sorry. John . . . John . . .

She heard the count, she watched him flinch, watched him struggle against his bonds as his instincts took over when his courage finally failed him and he cried out. She knew the count was twenty when she finally slid to the platform and laid her face against the cool dampness of the wood. She felt her tears run off, taken by the rain. The general let her lie there as the count finished. She finally closed her eyes when they cut John down and carried him away.

Then the general bent over her and spoke into her ear.

"You, Miss Ferguson, will be taken to the tollbooth, where you will await transport to the colonies sometime in the spring. You will never, God willing, set foot on this ground again. You will have a long, cold winter to think about your transgressions and what your treachery has cost a very fine soldier. I am certain he will never forget you or your lies. His back will be a reminder for the rest of his life."

Izzy let out a soft sob.

"May God have mercy on your soul," he added. "Because I have none to give you."

Chapter Seventeen

It was snowing. Flakes mixed with shards of ice that stung her skin through the thin fabric of her dress as she stood waiting to climb into the back of the transport that would take her to God only knew where. Izzy kept her head down as if she could ignore the snow and ice that only added to the misery. She stood shivering until her turn finally came and the soldiers heaved her bulk up into the cage.

"Damn," a voice snapped out, biting at her like a lash. "It's the Englishman's bastard." Izzy recognized the voice and looked up to see her father and brother sitting on the floor of the cage with their legs shackled and their backs pressed against the bars. Their imprisonment had taken a toll on them, just as it had on her. Both had hair down past their shoulders and long beards, with deep shadows under their eyes and pale skin. Izzy could only imagine how horrible she must look.

"Aye, Da, 'tis John's," Izzy said as she settled into the space Ewan made for her on the floor between them. "As if I had a choice in the matter."

"Ye didn't have to do the deed to help our cause," Da spat out with disgust. Izzy felt as if he'd slapped her. Fortunately for her own peace of mind, she'd learned a long time ago not to take his admonishments to heart.

No, she hadn't been compelled to make love with John. But she'd wanted to, even without the effects of the drug Ewan had added to the wine. When looking back upon it, upon the warmth and splendor of the day, of that sweet instant when she'd finally let her guard down and let her heart and her body carry her away on the tide that John's kisses and touch had created within her . . .

Izzy sighed. "Ye have Ewan to thank for that. He took the matter out of my hands." It was easier to blame Ewan and the wine than her own foolishness for trusting a man, and an English one at that.

The wagon lurched into motion, the wheels jerking free of the muck and the mud and finally rolling forward. The prisoners all swayed forward and back, moving with the wagon, their eyes downcast, not wanting to see their own desperation reflected on each other's faces. Izzy was grateful. At least she had her father and her brother with her. They weren't much of a family, but at least they were blood. She was not alone like the other poor souls surrounding them.

"Ye should get rid of it," Da said as Aberdeen faded behind them. He looked pointedly at the swell of her belly and Izzy's hands instinctively went to cover it, as if she could shield the babe inside from his harsh words.

"Da," Izzy gasped. "'Tis God's will that this child come into the world and I will set its fate in his hands."

"From what ye said, 'tis Ewan's will," Da snorted. "Chances are it willnae survive the journey to come." He folded his arms across his chest and closed his eyes. "Ye'd be better off without it." He tilted his head back against the cage and closed his mouth as if he were done talking. Thank the good Lord for small blessings.

"Settle back, lassie," Ewan said. He placed a comforting arm around her shoulder. "'Tis a long trip to London, so we may as well make the best of it."

"Oh, Ewan," Izzy said. "What is to become of us?"

"I donae ken, sweet," Ewan said. His mouth moved against her filthy hair. "I am so verra sorry for dragging you into this mess. I should hae listened to ye from the start. Can ye ever forgive me?"

Izzy let her body melt against Ewan. Angry as she was with him, she could feel his sorrow and regret. It did no good to hang on to her anger. No good at all. Just as her anger at Da had not changed a thing. It was best to let it go. Forgive and forget.

Unfortunately, the babe she carried would never let her forget. She felt it moving inside her. Izzy placed a hand over her side, where a foot, or a hand, she could not tell which, stretched the skin. Ewan looked down at the movement and his eyes widened in amazement.

"Can I touch it?" he whispered.

"Aye, ye can feel it moving about if ye are patient," Izzy whispered back. Ewan placed his large hand where she showed him and a smile split his beard. "Does it move often?" he asked.

"Often enough that it keeps me awake," Izzy said.

"Do ye think it's a boy or a girl?" Ewan asked.

Izzy curled her fingers around his wrist as he followed the movement with his fingers. "I hae not thought on it much."

"Did ye love him, Iz?" Ewan asked.

Izzy closed her eyes as John's face appeared in her mind. *Aye. I did.*

"What difference does it make?" she asked, and looked at her brother. "I'll never lay eyes on him again."

"If I could change it all, I would. Gladly."

"I know, Ewan." She suddenly felt so tired. She closed her eyes and let the swaying of the cart take her away as she settled against Ewan.

"Sleep, sweet," he said. "I will watch over ye."

Dear Ewan . . . I fear it is too little too late.

★ ★ ★

"The snow makes it pretty, don't you think?" Carrie said. She linked her arm with his so she would not slip in the snow trampled by the mourners who'd come to say good-bye to their mother. The snow still fell, thick flakes tumbling from the sky in a fury, as if each one was resolved to do its bit to cover up the dreariness of the last week in December. The hood of Carrie's cloak was covered with snow, along with her shoulders.

John blinked the frost from his lashes as he looked around the small cemetery. They had decided to bury their mother in Bremhill by the small church that held the remains of her family. One of her distant cousins led the parish there. It was nice to know that she would be looked after, that someone would come and place an occasional flower on her grave.

Her children would be hard pressed to do so from the colonies.

"Yes, it does," he agreed.

John rolled his shoulders beneath his heavy coat. Even though the lash wounds were long healed, they still pained him terribly. He woke nearly every night, in agony, with his back burning from the strokes of the whip. In his dreams it was Isobel who used it on him. She whipped him mercilessly, night after night after night.

"I have decided never to think of you again." If only it were that easy. If only his dreams could be controlled by his will.

"We don't have to stay, you know," Carrie said as the grave diggers lowered the coffin into the damp hole in the ground. "We can go in now."

John knew she was worried about him. He looked toward the parish house, where he knew a cheery fire roared and a nice meal was laid out for them.

"Go on," he said. "I'll stay."

"John." His sister looked up at him with serious blue eyes.

"I truly believe Mother is better off now. Her suffering is over. She's in a better place." She stood on tiptoe and kissed his cheek. "Maybe now you can rest. You don't have to worry about her anymore."

John smiled at his sister's misdirected concern. It wasn't worry for their mother that caused his sleepless nights. But there was also no reason for her to know the real cause of his distress.

Carrie walked away, carefully placing her booted feet along the slick path. She let out a small "eek!" as she slipped and fortunately caught herself before she fell into a bank of snow that had drifted up around a tombstone. The last thing he needed at the moment was Carrie diving headfirst into a snow drift. As it was he'd have to spend every waking moment during their ocean passage making sure she didn't fall overboard.

When she was safely inside the parish house, John turned back to watch the grave diggers at work. The mound of dirt was frozen solid and they used picks to break it into chunks before they pitched the earth down upon the coffin with hollow thunks. John nudged a chunk in with the toe of his boot, wanting to participate in some way.

John knew that to the casual observer he looked as if he was bidding his mother good-bye. They would say he was a good son. He'd stayed there until the end. But when they talked about him, as they surely would, would they also say it was a shame about the fiasco in Aberdeen? He could practically hear it now. The whispers, the knowing looks, the growing legend of his stupidity at being seduced by the penniless daughter of a Scottish outlaw.

How did Isobel fare in prison?

"Dammit!" The curse exploded from his lips, unbidden, and most certainly inappropriate. The grave diggers kept at their task, mostly ignoring him as he quickly walked away from the hole that held the earthly remains of his mother.

If only he could stop thinking about Isobel. She was like a disease that had spread throughout his system much in the same way his mother's disease had spread through hers.

John walked away from the parish, churning through the snow, leaving a trail that was quickly filled as the heavy flakes swirled behind him. Even though it was barely noon, the daylight was so dim that it felt as if dusk was settling around him. He made his way to a stand of thick yews that guarded the cemetery on the western side. The boughs were weighted with the heavy snow, dragging against the ground.

John jammed his hands into the pockets of his cloak and with legs spread wide, tilted his head back so the snow struck his face. The minute crystals stung as they hit his flesh and melted against the warmth of his skin.

Where was she? Was she still sitting in her cell in her pretty green dress? He should have asked Kensington about her sentence, but he was afraid the man would see any inquiry as further weakness on his part.

Further weakness . . . It was Izzy's life and he was worried about appearances.

"I will never think of you again." John repeated the last words he'd said to her. Another lesson hard learned. Saying something did not make it so. He could scream to the heavens that he did not love her and that he would never think of her, yet that was all he did.

Would time and distance make the love and the resulting pain of her betrayal go away?

God, I hope so.

The smells of the harbor were familiar. They stirred Ewan from the deep lethargy that had been his constant companion since they were loaded into the wagon back in Aberdeen. Izzy's head rocked against his chest as the wagon pitched over the deep ruts caused by the recent snowmelt. It was unseasonably warm for January; at least he thought it was January. He'd lost count of the days sometime around Christmas.

"Wake up, sweet," he said to his sister. "We are here."

Da was awake already; Ewan often wondered if he ever actually slept. It seemed as if he was always alert and always ready for whatever life might bring them.

If only he could have seen what life had in store for him. He would have done things differently. Izzy and Donnie were the ones who'd suffered for his actions. In a roundabout way he'd got what he wanted. His family was together, what was left of it and they were going to the colonies.

"Where is here?" Izzy mumbled against his chest.

"The docks," he said against the top of her head. "At the ship."

She sat up and blinked like an owl as she looked around. "Which one do you suppose it is?" she asked.

Ewan pointed toward a large ship with a gangplank against the wharf. "I would say that one, as it is being loaded." They watched a net being swung over the side from a pulley system that hung over the deck of the ship. "It looks as if they will put some livestock aboard."

"The animals will probably have better quarters than us," Da said. "And better food."

"Da," Ewan said in disgust. He had always seen his father as some kind of hero. But being in close quarters with him all these months had led Ewan to see things in a different light. Izzy needed to be reminded of the good things in life, not the bad. As long as there was life, there was hope. He would not let her give up. He owed her that much and more.

"Get out," the guard commanded as he swung open the

door to the wagon. They were all weak and half starved, filthy too, but grateful to get out of the wagon. Ewan helped Izzy down and their group was herded over to the side where another group waited. There were two women among them, and Ewan almost sighed in relief. Surely they would care for his sister.

The men were chained together in pairs, he with Da. They left Izzy alone, since the two women were already together.

"Ye can't go far in your condition," the guard said as he looked her over. "From yer looks, we shouldn't even waste the time of putting ye on the ship."

Ewan jerked at his chain to move Da and stepped boldly in between Izzy and the guard. "Let her be," he said. The man carried a club, but Ewan did not care. The guard would not abuse Izzy.

"Carrying your bastard, is she?"

"She's my sister," Ewan said.

"And my daughter," Da snarled "Keep your hands off her."

Da did not hold his claymore, but the look on his face was enough to make the guard back down.

"She'll be at the bottom of the ocean before you make port," the man snarled as he walked to the head of the line of prisoners.

"Donae listen to him, Iz," Ewan said. He turned to comfort her, but her attention was not on him. Instead she was looking toward the ship. A snowy white horse was in the sling, crying out in fear or fury, he could not tell which, as it was lifted from the wharf and swung out to the deck of the ship. On board a tall blond man wearing the red coat of His Majesty's army followed the progress of the horse as it was lowered into the belly of the ship.

" 'Tis John," Izzy said quietly.

"How can it be?" Ewan asked.

"Who else?" Izzy said. "I ken it is him." She placed a hand over the hump of her belly. "So does the babe." She looked at Ewan. Her face was pale, her eyes huge, and she grabbed his arms. "He must not know, Ewan. Ye must promise me. Ye must hide me. I couldnae stand to see him again. I cannae stand to see the look in his eyes." Tears ran down her face as if her heart were breaking in two.

"Hush, my sweet," Ewan said, and pulled her to his chest as best he could with his hands bound by chains. "We will protect ye, I promise." He looked at Da, who nodded in agreement. It would be a small victory over the English. They would take any they could get.

Chapter Eighteen

How much more? How much more of the cold that never went away, the hunger that gnawed at her insides, and the pain in her back that made her feel as if a chain were wrapped around her and pulled tight against her stomach. How much more could she stand before she simply just gave in to it?

Donnie was the lucky one. Donnie was dead. If only she could have the same sweet peace instead of this never-ending misery that her life had become. The constant movement of the ship. The hard planks of the floor that slammed against her bones as the ship lifted and dipped in the waves. The straw that jabbed and stabbed instead of cushioning. The incessant smell and noise of the other prisoners.

The babe weighed heavy on her. No matter which way Izzy turned on the straw, no matter whether she lay or stood or sat, she felt it pressing upon her, a burden she had not asked for, any more than she'd asked for the circumstances that brought her to this misery.

You wanted him. Aye, she did. She had to admit it. Would she have done it anyway? If Ewan had not drugged the wine and she had been in full control of her mind, would she have done it?

An image flashed before her. One of golden warmth and smooth skin and John's handsome face smiling down at her with eyes as blue as the summer sky.

She still wanted him. Even though he'd cursed her as a traitor, she longed for him with an ache in her heart.

Izzy wiped her eyes with the heel of her hand and pushed

her tortured body up to find some relief. Janet sighed as if missing her warmth and snuggled deeper beneath the blanket the three women shared. Ruthie sat up with her and placed a hand on Izzy's arm. "Is it time?" she asked.

"No. It's too soon," Izzy said. "I must use the pail; that's all." She struggled to her feet and placed her hand in the small of her back. If only the pain there would stop, she might be able to stand the rest of it. She spared a look at the cell across the way. The men all seemed asleep, scattered on the floor or leaning against the wall of their cell, some even snored until those closest jabbed them with an elbow. The lantern, turned down to a dull glow, swung on its hook, an accompaniment to the never-ending movement of the ship.

It was as much privacy as she'd ever have under these circumstances. Izzy gathered up the worn skirts of her dress. She was much too big and too sore to squat, so she spread her legs over the pail and hoped for the best.

Her bladder emptied in a whoosh and liquid splattered in the pail. The noise was so loud that Ruthie and Janet both rose on their elbows to look at her.

"Is there blood in the pail?" Ruthie asked.

"What?" Izzy asked, aghast that Ruthie would suggest such a thing.

Ruthie got to her feet and gently pulled Izzy away from the pail. "There's blood," she said. "Yer water just broke."

"It's too soon," Izzy protested. "I shouldnae have the babe for at least a month."

"It's coming," Ruthie said simply. "Does your back hurt?"

Izzy placed both hands in the middle of her back. "It has for days," she said.

"It's coming, then," Ruthie said again.

"What do I do?" Izzy asked. She simply could not believe what Ruthie said. The babe could not come. She had counted off the months, the weeks, the days on her hands over and over again. The babe should not arrive until March. They should be in the colonies by then. She couldn't have it here. In a cell. In the middle of the Atlantic.

"Will it live?" Izzy felt dizzy as she realized what was about to happen. The babe would be too little. How could it survive? Especially here and now. She looked over at the other cell where the men were stirring to life, distracted by the drama unfolding in her cell.

Da would get his wish. He said she'd be better off without her babe.

Janet and Ruthie grabbed her arms before she slid to the floor in a faint. "Ye must stay strong," Ruthie said. " 'Twill be a while before the babe arrives."

"It will still be too soon," Izzy gasped.

"What is it?" Ewan stood at the edge of the cell with his hands wrapped around the bars. "Izzy?"

"The babe is coming, Ewan." Izzy looked across the way at him. If only he could be with her. She could use his comfort.

Was it wrong to long for your brother when your lover was so close at hand? She stared across at Ewan and at Da, who had joined him.

"*No.*" She mouthed it. She would not say it. John must not know. He could not. He hated her and he would hate her more, knowing that she bore his bastard child. A bastard child for the child of a bastard.

A pain gripped her. It moved from her back and around her sides. The chain she had so often imagined tightened around her as if it would squeeze the life from her.

Her baby's life.

"Donae tell him, Ewan," Izzy said. "Swear to me."

"Izzy." Ewan reached through the bars. Izzy shook off Ruthie and Janet and moved slowly to the edge of her cell.

She stretched her hand through so that her fingertips brushed against Ewan's.

"Swear to me." She looked him in the eye and hated the fact that his face was lost in the shadows. "Da. Ye both must swear it. He must never know."

"What if ye die?" Da said. "And the babe lives?"

Leave it to Da to be practical. For the first time ever.

"I'm already dead to him, Da," Izzy said. "It willnae matter."

"Donae speak of such things, Da," Ewan said. "Look at me, Iz. We willnae tell him. Do ye ken?"

Izzy tried to see. She had to be sure. Ewan stretched his arm out farther, until he could grasp her fingers. He gave them a reassuring squeeze. "Ye will have the babe and ye both will survive. And we will all somehow be together in the end. A family."

Izzy nodded. She believed him. And she knew Ewan would make sure Da respected her wishes. He owed her now. He knew it and Da knew it.

"Come, dear," Ruthie said. "Ye must save your strength for later."

Another pain gripped her as Ruthie led her away from the bars. Janet scraped all the straw together into the corner and they both lowered Izzy to the floor.

"Now what?" Izzy asked.

"We wait," Ruthie said simply.

The hours passed, somehow. Izzy knew they passed because the pains occurred with more frequency and Ruthie wiped her brow with frigid water.

If only she could have a warm bed and clean sheets and some measure of comfort. She clung to Ruthie's and Janet's hands and listened to Ewan as he tried his best to encourage her.

She was so very tired.

"I think something is wrong," Ruthie said. Izzy heard her

voice, but it seemed so distant. "It does not seem as if the baby is in the right place." Izzy realized that Ruthie had her dress pushed up and her legs spread. Janet held the lantern and they both peered between her legs. "We should see the head," Ruthie said, "But it's not there."

"What should we do?" Janet asked.

"Get her up. She needs to walk."

Izzy protested as the women pulled her upright. She didn't want to walk. She didn't want to have a baby. She just wanted to lie down and sleep. If she couldn't sleep, then she would die.

"Let me die," she said as she staggered between the two women.

"Hush, child," Ruthie said.

"Be strong, Iz," Ewan said. She heard other voices behind him. The men were all offering encouragement.

For what?

"I want to die," Izzy repeated. She did. There was no reason to live. All that stretched before her was a lifetime of servitude. Donnie was dead. John hated her. Ewan and Da were both destined for bondage, as was she. Ewan believed they could be together, but she knew they wouldn't.

And the babe was going to die. There was no reason for her to try. No reason to survive. There was nothing to hold on to. She could leave this world and be with Ma and Donnie in heaven. Or hell for her sins. Could hell be any worse than living?

"Please, God, forgive me and let me die."

Janet and Ruthie dragged her across the cell, then back.

"Walk, Izzy," Ruthie said.

"It hurts," Izzy cried.

"Of course it does," Janet said. "It's a baby fighting its way into the world."

"Too much fighting," Izzy gasped as they turned again.

"You cannae die, Iz." She heard Ewan's voice in the distance. All she could see was blackness and all she felt was pain and despair.

"She needs a priest," Da said.

Aye. She did. She would confess her sins and receive the blessing and then she would die. If only they would let her be.

"She needs a doctor," Janet said.

Ewan's yell went through her, splitting her head the way the pains split her body. She tried to see him, blinked her eyes, and realized he was using the water bucket from his cell to pound on the bars. The rest of the men started the chant.

They would all die. They would be thrown overboard.

What would it feel like to sink to the bottom of the sea? Would the cold hurt more than giving birth?

"Put me down," Izzy begged. She could not get her feet to work and there was no break between the pains, just a never-ending burning that shot through her back and down her legs.

Janet and Ruthie dragged her to the corner and placed her on the straw.

A sailor opened the door that separated their cells from the rest of the hold. Another stood behind him holding a musket in his hand.

"Shut up, the lot of you, or I'll have you whipped!" the sailor yelled.

"We need a doctor," Ewan said, and pointed toward Izzy. "Please. She's dying."

"Move aside," the sailor said to Janet and Ruthie. They stepped back and Izzy looked up at the man with tears in her eyes as he opened their cell.

"What is it?" he asked Ruthie.

"It's her time," Ruthie said, and knelt once more beside Izzy.

"She's having a baby?" he asked, dumbfounded.

"Are ye daft, man?" Ewan yelled. "Can ye not see that she's having a baby?"

"Is there a doctor?" Janet asked.

The man nodded, white faced. "I must tell the captain."

"Tell someone," Ewan yelled again. "Get her some help!"

The sailor holding the gun jabbed it toward Ewan. He jumped back as the stock bounced off the iron bars of the cell. Izzy saw it all as if from a dream. She heard the shouts and the clanging of their cell door as the sailor rushed out.

"Stay put!" he yelled over his shoulder.

Izzy laughed, then groaned. "Where could we go?"

"There, there," Ruthie said. "Help will be here soon."

She'd be dead before soon. Dead and grateful for it. If only the feeling of her body ripping in half would end.

"Make it stop. . . ."

"Hang on, Izzy."

"John . . . please make it stop . . . John."

Izzy felt her body sliding into a long dark hole. She opened her mouth to scream, but nothing came out as she continued to fall. It was hell. She was sure of it. When she hit the bottom, there would be fire and torment and the devil himself jabbing her with a hot iron. She could feel it even now, through the blackness.

She could feel him coming. The devil. Lucifer. The one the priests warned against.

He was so beautiful. He was a fallen angel after all. That was what she'd been told. Lucifer led a revolt against God and was banished from heaven. And now he stood before her with his golden hair and eyes as blue as the summer sky.

"John," she said.

"Wake up, Izzy," he said. "You have to push."

"I don't want to."

She felt her body moving. Hands probed her and pushed on her stomach. She felt a horrible tearing, more wretched than any pain she'd felt before. If she was dead, then how could she feel such pain?

Izzy blinked as icy cold water hit her face and slid down her neck. A man knelt between her legs with his hand spread across her belly. Janet and Ruthie supported her in a sitting position.

"You've got to push now, Izzy," the strange man said. He reeked of whiskey and the smell roused her. She didn't want to push. She didn't want to do anything. But her body seemed to have other plans and the urge to push was strong.

"Push, Iz!" she heard Ewan call out.

She took a deep breath, and was surprised that she was able to do that much. She concentrated every part of her being on expelling the creature that would surely tear her in half as it came out. She screamed.

"It's coming," the man said. "The head is out. One more time, Izzy."

"One more, Izzy," Ewan cried out.

Izzy panted, certain she could do no more. But she had to. The baby had to come out. She screamed again as she bore down with all her might and felt the baby finally slip from her body. Izzy fell back on the straw and lay panting. The pain was blessedly gone.

"It's a girl," the man said.

"A girl," Ewan laughed. Or was he crying? Izzy could not be sure of what was real and what was a figment of her imagination.

"Does she live?" she asked. The man held the small form propped in his hand and stuck his finger in the baby's mouth. Izzy saw the wee arms stretch out as the baby jerked and a thin wail came forth.

"She's alive," he said. He laid the baby into her outstretched arms and Izzy pulled her close as Ruthie assisted him with the afterbirth. Janet sheltered the two of them as best she could. The baby felt cold and Izzy rubbed her hands over the tiny arms and legs as the baby cried softly. She sounded very weak. Izzy could not say that she blamed her.

"Where's that hot water?" the man yelled. "And blankets?" He flung the afterbirth into the straw and muttered, "This woman should be in a bed. And out of this filth. . . ."

"Are you a doctor?" Izzy asked.

"I am when necessary," he said. "Although the circumstances that surround us are deplorable and I humbly apologize." He dipped his hands in the water bucket to wash off the mess.

Izzy could not help smiling. "I try to make do with what I've been given, sir."

"I see ye are back to your old sass, girl," Da said from across the way.

"Which of you men are responsible for this girl?" the doctor asked.

"I am," Ewan said. "I am her brother. And this is her father. Our name is Ferguson."

"I am George Keats," the doctor said.

"Thank ye, sir," Ewan said. "For saving her. And the babe."

"Do not thank me yet," Dr. Keats said. "The danger is not over. I need to move her to a cabin."

"Nay," Izzy said. "I will stay here with my family." If she moved above deck, there was a chance that John would see her. She could not take that risk. "I am sure the captain would not hear of it anyway," she added.

"You are most likely correct," Dr. Keats said. "At least the water and blankets are here." Two sailors handed off the steaming bucket of water, some blankets, and a stack of rags to

Janet and Ruthie. "Get her some clean straw to make a decent bed," Dr. Keats bellowed after the men. "Take it from that stud in there if you have to," he added to their retreating backs. "It's a sorry state of affairs when animals are treated better than people."

Janet took the baby to clean and Ruthie dipped one of the rags in the bucket and went to work on Izzy. She was beyond embarrassment. She knew everyone had seen her at her worst and she did not care. She was alive and so was the baby.

And that made all the difference in the world.

Chapter Nineteen

"I do not understand why you would not let me help Dr. Keats," Carrie said once again as she and John strolled across the deck. Their dinner with the captain, Dr. Keats, and the other passengers had been interrupted by the announcement that one of the prisoners below was giving birth. The screams soon thereafter had quickly put an end to the enjoyment of the meal and they had departed the captain's table with quiet apologies to their host.

"It isn't proper for an unmarried woman to see such things," John said again. "And for another, Keats is a drunkard. The woman below will be lucky if he doesn't kill them both."

"He seemed to sober up quick enough when he realized someone needed his help," Carrie snapped.

The air was bitterly cold above deck. Ice hung on the riggings where the spray had frozen. He would have to make sure to place an extra blanket over Sultan tonight. It would be easy for the horse to get sick with the forced inactivity. If only there was some way he could walk the stud above deck. Or at least have more room in the hold to turn him about.

"I am well past the age to worry about such things as whether or not helping someone is proper just because I am unmarried," Carrie continued. "And as my chances of marriage are slim at best, I see no cause to observe the rules of propriety. Especially while we are in the middle of the Atlantic." She pulled her cloak tight around her and grasped it with a gloved hand at her neck to keep the wind from pouring down the opening.

"All it would take is for one of our fellow passengers to mention it and your reputation would be ruined as soon as we reached the colonies," John reminded her. "At least you will have a fresh start when we get there. We cannot do anything to jeopardize that."

"Honestly, John, you worry too much about what other people say and think about you." Carrie sighed. "And me," she added.

"Behaving properly is what differentiates us from the prisoners belowdecks. It is obvious that they did not care a thing about obeying the rules of society or they would not have broken the law," John replied sternly. Of course he worried about his respectability. His reputation was all he had. He had almost lost it and as a result, he could never return to Scotland or possibly even England. At least he had a chance to start over again in America, just as Carrie did. He only hoped his one lapse in judgment would not follow him there.

"Perhaps they are just victims of bad judgment," Carrie said as if she was reading his thoughts. "Did you ever think of that? People make mistakes. Bad mistakes. Sometimes they have to pay for them with the loss of life and freedom. But that does not make all of them bad people. And just because you wear a uniform, that does not make you the judge and jury to condemn them. You don't even know them."

"Carrie," John explained patiently. "The hold is full of rebels and thieves and possibly murderers. All have been sentenced to transport and bondage to repay their debts to the king."

"And one of them is having a baby," she snapped back at him.

His sister was in a fine temper tonight. John took a step away in case she decided to kick his shins, something she was still wont to do when her temper got the best of her.

"I wonder what her crime could possibly be," Carrie said as she walked to the ship's rail and looked out to sea.

John merely shrugged as he followed her. It was not his concern.

"Of course someone as perfect as you wouldn't know about such things," Carrie said angrily. "I swear, John, I do not know what happened to you in Scotland, but I do know I do not like it." She turned to face him and concern showed on her face. "I cannot even remember the last time I saw you smile."

"Our mother just died, Carrie. I find no reason to smile at the present."

"Aren't you excited, John?" Carrie asked. "We're going to a new country. A country like nothing we've ever seen before. I, for one, cannot wait to see it. To explore it. To experience it."

"You can't be serious, Caroline," John said, using her full name as he usually did when she tried his patience. How could she even consider traipsing through the wilderness? Did she have no understanding of where they were going? "It's dangerous. It's full of savages who will kill you for your scalp. There is no possibility of your exploring. I absolutely forbid it."

"You forbid it?" Carrie stomped her foot. "You forbid it? I do not recall enlisting in the army, nor do I recall that you command me." She jabbed a gloved finger in his chest. "Lest you forget, I am your sister, not your soldier." She whirled away in the direction of their cabin.

John rubbed his chest. Even with the padding of his coat and cloak, she had jabbed him hard. John turned back to the rail and looked out to sea.

The sky was dark and gray. The pristine blue of the day showed only to the west, where it was streaked with purples and pinks as the sun set. The ship followed the sun, toward America, his father, his future, and possibly now his home. Was there any reason to go back to England?

None that he could think of.

Except . . .

Izzy. Perhaps he should have inquired about her fate. She could have died for all he knew.

He cared. He had to admit it. After all these months he still cared. Even after the betrayal and the death of Rory and the lashing and the official reprimand.

He cared. He would never see her again. But he hoped she was alive and well.

The sun dipped below the horizon. There were no sounds except the creak of the ship timbers and the slap of the waves against the prow. Carrie would likely not talk to him the rest of the night.

He'd better see to Sultan.

It was warmer belowdecks, but not much. Sultan pawed at the loose straw in his stall as John came down the narrow ladder. He spared a look toward the door that barred the prisoners from the rest of the hold before he walked back to the stud.

He hoped the birth had gone well. It would be tragic to see a baby buried at sea. Tragic indeed.

John checked the nets that surrounded Sultan's stall, placed there so the horse would not crash into anything hard in the event of rough seas. Thick straw covered the floor and the horse's legs were wrapped to protect them. Another large blanket covered his back and was wrapped around his chest to protect him from the cold of their early spring passage.

John unlatched the stall and led Sultan out to walk back and forth in the hold for a small bit of exercise. The horse seemed resigned to his confinement but occasionally let loose with an exasperated huff as he walked back and forth.

John took his time, letting his footsteps fall into rhythm with Sultan's. Forward toward the blocked door and the cells. Back toward the stall. Over and over again he walked Sultan to make sure the blood kept flowing in the stud's legs. Once he heard the weak cry of a baby and then the soft sound of a lullaby and he paused to listen, placing a quieting hand over Sultan's muzzle as the horse swung his ears forward and back at the strange sound.

Footsteps on the staircase sounded and John moved Sultan away as Dr. Keats came down with his arms full of what appeared to be a woman's petticoat. Behind him was a sailor with a bucket of coal.

"Your sister was generous enough to donate some cloth for diapers," Keats informed him as John placed Sultan in his stall and measured out a portion of oats.

"Carrie has a most generous nature," John assured him. "If propriety allowed, she would have assisted at the birth."

Keats shrugged his shoulders. "There was nothing she could do really. The poor babe was coming out backward. Once I intervened, the birth proceeded normally."

John concentrated on Sultan. He wasn't sure if he wanted, or needed, to hear the intimate details of the baby's birth.

"So all was well in the end?"

"Yes," Keats said. "Of course, it's a good thing they sent for me when they did. The mother was nearly done in. She's a tiny little thing, not much bigger than the baby and half starved. I told the captain if he didn't want to lose both mother and child, he'd better do something to keep them warm, fed, and clean." He motioned through the open door to the cells, where John could see a sailor placing coal in a brazier. "Those poor souls haven't even had a fire to keep them warm, and only one meal a day from what I've seen. They won't bring in much money if they're dead before we get there."

"That does make sense," John agreed as he finished up with Sultan. "I'd better go check on Carrie," he said.

"Please thank her once again," Keats said as he went off to check on his patient. John heard the doctor's booming voice as he moved up the stairs. "Have you settled on a name yet, lass?"

John stopped to listen, but the answering voice was so soft and weak that he didn't hear a reply, and he realized that he did not know if the baby was a boy or a girl.

John shrugged. He would ask Keats tomorrow at dinner. Or perhaps Carrie knew the details. Maybe she would talk to him now instead of being angry.

"Ellyn," Donald Ferguson repeated as he heard his daughter say his granddaughter's name. She'd gone and named the babe after her mother. "Ellyn Marie MacDonald Ferguson." It should be Ellyn Marie Murray if the English bastard above decks was an honorable man.

No matter the circumstances of the child's conception, or the deceit behind it. A man should be responsible for his off-spring, desired or not.

Donald shook his head as the memories of Isobel's birth flooded his mind. He was a fine one to talk about the responsibility of siring children. He'd heard he had a daughter while hiding in a cave in the Highlands. Snow covered the moors and crags when word finally arrived that Ellyn had gifted him with a daughter some three weeks past. It was Christmas before he was able to sneak down and visit his wee daughter and wife, along with Ewan, to whom he gave a wooden horse he'd carved during the long afternoons of his exile.

He'd only been able to stay with them for one day. In all of Izzy's twenty-eight years of life, he'd spent no more than a handful of days with her.

Living alone, thinking only of himself, was a habit he'd

acquired a long time ago. His chances of making up those lost years to his children were long past.

"It's a fine name, Izzy," Ewan said.

"Would you like to see her?" Izzy asked from her pallet.

"Aye," Ewan said. "If it is possible."

She handed the baby to Dr. Keats, who carried her into the opening between the two cells. A cheery fire now burned in the brazier and the men in the cell gathered toward the end where the heat was strongest. A few of them stood behind Donald and Ewan as the two men stared down at the tiny face that showed above the wee blanket that had been cut from a larger one. Donald was pleased to see the babe had Izzy's face and her curls held a golden hue, more the color of Donnie's hair than Izzy's. Her wee mouth had the look of a rosebud, and dark crescent lashes touched her rounded cheeks.

"She is beautiful," Ewan said. He looked as if he'd been struck aside the head. He was a good brother to Izzy. Too bad he would nay have the chance to be a good uncle as well.

"I thank ye, sir," Donald said to Keats as he looked down at his granddaughter. "For taking care of them." He stuck out a finger to touch the soft cheek but withdrew it when he saw the dirt on his hand.

"I see no need for a child to suffer for her parents' crimes," Keats said. "Although I am sure the long arm of the English law sees it differently," he added.

Baby Ellyn blinked at the man's rough words and her bright blue eyes stared up at the two men who pressed their faces to the bars. She had her father's eyes. Just as quickly they closed again and the rosebud lips moved in and out as if already tasting the feast waiting at her mother's breast.

"The sins of the father," Donald said softly as Keats took the baby back to Izzy.

A feeling of contentment settled over the cells. For the first time in days they were warm and the pinch of constant hunger had been relieved. The men settled on the floor and talked quietly among themselves or watched Izzy, who lay curled on her side with Ellyn safe in the crook of her arm. Janet and Ruthie shielded the two when she nursed, but now all lay contentedly on their well-padded floor.

Ewan sat in the corner farthest away from the fire. He had his head turned away from the group. Donald watched as he wiped his eyes.

He was hurting for his sister. Donald gave him a moment before he sat down. "Wee Elly looks healthy," he said after a moment.

Ewan swallowed. "Aye," he said. "By the grace of God and the good Dr. Keats."

Donald nodded in agreement. "We were fortunate the man was on board."

Ewan lowered his chin and placed his hand over his face. "I thought she was going to die," he managed to choke out.

"But she didnae."

"Nay," Ewan agreed. "But if she had, it would hae been my fault. It's my fault she is here. It is my fault she had the child."

"Nay, Ewan, 'tis not your fault she had wee Elly. It takes two to make a baby and Izzy had feelings for the soldier, whether she will admit it or not."

"He hurt her, Da."

"No more than she hurt him. He thought her guilty of betraying him, even though she had no part in it."

"I used her, Da. I used her to get you out and now Donnie is dead and Izzy's life is wasted."

"Ye made a mistake, Ewan. Ye did it because ye wanted your family to be together. I cannae condemn what ye did."

"I will gladly pay for my sins, Da, but Izzy . . . This should-nae have happened to her."

Donald laid a hand on his son's shoulder. "Ye are a good man, Ewan. Ye love your family. Ye did what ye thought was best. Ye have done more to keep this family together than I ever did."

Ewan looked at him. He had the look of Ellyn's family about him. Donald well recalled the hurt in Ellyn's father's eyes when she declared she would not go to the church but marry him instead. The same look was in Ewan's eyes.

"I am proud to call ye son, Ewan," Donald said. "I know not what the future holds for any of us, but I know ye and Isobel are strong. Ye will survive it."

Ewan nodded.

"Best get some sleep while ye can. I have a feeling wee Elly will be crying for food soon and keeping all of us awake."

"She is a beautiful baby," Ewan said.

"Aye. She is."

Chapter Twenty

Izzy held Elly tight against her chest as they made their way down the gangplank. She kept her head lowered and focused her eyes on the back of Da's neck. Gulls swooped overhead as if looking for handouts. Ewan walked behind her, close on her heels, as if he could protect her. They all had their hands bound except for Izzy. She carried a blanket across her chest, tied up as a sling with diapers for Elly inside. One of the female passengers on the ship had generously offered up her flannel petticoat for that use. Izzy wondered if it was the woman she'd seen on the wharf with John. The woman who must be his sister, the one he'd spoken of. They had the same golden hair and the same blue eyes.

The Fergusons were last off the ship. Even the horse, Sultan, had been off-loaded before them. They had listened to his fury as he was lifted from the cargo hold and finally placed on the deck before being led down the wide gangplank.

"He's gone," Ewan said behind her. "They got in a carriage and a groom took the horse."

She let out a sigh of relief as her feet touched the wharf.

"Where are we?" she asked.

"Virginia is all I know," Ewan said as they were herded toward a large building.

"What will become of us?"

"We're to be sold," Da said.

"Together?" Suddenly the thought of losing her father and brother was more than she could stand. "We're a family."

Izzy's voice trembled. "Will they separate us? What about Elly? Will they sell her away?"

Once inside the building, they were told to line up before a table. A man sat at the table with a quill and parchment; two guards stood beside him. The Fergusons were at the end of the line and they watched as the men were told to remove their shirts and then open their mouths as if they were horses being inspected for sale. After the inspection at the table, they were taken off to the side, where slaves flung buckets of water on them. They were told to wash up as best they could with a sliver of soap; then more water was flung on them to rinse them off.

Izzy felt relatively clean, thanks to Dr. Keats, who'd insisted on fresh water for drinking, and enough warm water so the women could bathe and wash out Elly's diapers. Still she felt nervous. What would she do with Elly if they decided to throw water on her?

Janet and Ruthie were led behind a screen where slave women waited. It seemed as if they were required to strip, because Izzy saw their clothes thrown over the screen.

Da was next, then Ewan. The months of incarceration had not been kind to them. Their skin was pasty and pale and their bones showed through their skin. Izzy turned away when the light from the high windows fell across Ewan's back and she saw the scars that crossed his skin from the whipping.

She still remembered the day as if it had just happened. The pain that showed on his face. The grunts and cries that he could not help letting out. The sound of the blows as the rain pounded.

Then there was John. He had received five more lashes than Ewan. Izzy knew because she'd counted every one.

Did his back resemble Ewan's? Or had he received more tender care than a prisoner? She would never know.

"Name," the man at the desk demanded.

"Isobel Ferguson."

"Are you related to these men?"

"Yes. My father and my brother."

The man nodded. "Then we can sell you separate."

"But . . ."

The man pointed his quill at her. "We try to keep husband and wife together if we can. Do you have a husband?"

"No." *Not likely to ever have one now.*

"Age?"

"I just turned twenty-eight." *Too old for anyone to want.*

"Show me your teeth."

Izzy clenched her teeth together to show him she had all her teeth. Her family was blessed with strong teeth and her mother had taught them to take care of them. She opened her mouth as instructed and one of the men grabbed her lower jaw and peered inside with an approving nod.

"Child's age?"

"Three weeks."

"Born on the ship, was it?" the man asked as he made notations with his quill. "Child's name?"

"Ellyn Ferguson." Izzy watched as he wrote a big F next to Ellyn's name. "What will happen to my baby?" she asked.

"The child will be sold with the mother for the service of twelve years. Unless you have a relative you would like to give her to."

Izzy looked at Da and Ewan, who were being doused with water. "There is no one," she said.

"You may go," the man directed, and pointed her toward the screen.

Izzy did not realize she was trembling until she got to the screen. She had been so afraid that Elly was going to be ripped from her arms and she would never see her again. Instead the child was to serve the same sentence that she'd been given. Twelve years of indenture. Which was worse? For her child to be a slave or an orphan? A bastard orphan.

"I am so sorry, my sweet," she said to the babe, who was just now beginning to stir in her arms. Elly would be hungry. Would she be allowed a moment to feed her?

"Looky here," one of the slave women said when Izzy rounded the screen. "Look at that bitty baby." The woman fussed over Elly, who looked up at her with bright-eyed attention. "Look at dem pretty blue eyes." The woman took Elly from Izzy's arms without asking permission. "She must have got dem from her daddy," the woman continued as she held Elly close. "I'll take care of dis baby while you wash up."

Izzy looked helplessly after Ruthie and Janet, who were being led into another room by the other slave woman.

"Go ahaid," the woman said. "She be fine wid me."

Izzy had no choice but to obey as the woman sat down on a stool and talked nonsense to Elly.

Her dress was nothing more than tatters and her petticoat much the same. It was hard to believe that it used to be her best. The green was faded away to brown and the lace and trim were long gone. Izzy stripped down to her shift. There was a bar of soap, along with a washcloth and towel and she put them to good use.

"You got to do your hair too," the woman said. "They want to make sure ye ain't got no critters crawling in there."

Izzy's breasts were swollen with milk and she heard the sounds of Elly fretting to be fed, but the chance to wash her hair was a luxury she'd never thought she'd have. Izzy doused her hair with a pitcher of water and lathered it up with the coarse soap.

It felt shameful to put her old clothes back on once she felt clean, but she had no choice. She combed out her hair, tied it back with a scrap of ribbon, and took Elly, who sucked noisily on her fist, from the slave woman. Then she followed Janet and Ruthie into the other room.

Inside were cots and a table, and miraculously a meal of stew and coarse bread.

"They said they want us to appear healthy when they put us on the block," Janet explained. Izzy didn't care. She sat down at the table, put Elly to her breast, and ate as if she had never eaten before. Who knew when she'd get a chance to eat again?

Izzy woke in the predawn hours to a fretful Elly nuzzling at her breast. She quickly obliged before the baby cried out and woke Janet and Ruthie. She enjoyed the moment as best she could, just like the meal the night before. She felt warm from the heat put out by the small stove and comfortable on her cot with its sheet and blanket. Since her imprisonment she had longed for small treasures such as these. Izzy dropped a kiss on the top of Elly's fuzzy head of golden curls. What would the next day hold for them?

When Elly was done with her breakfast, Izzy changed her and rinsed out the diaper. She didn't know what to do with it when she was done. Should she hang it to dry? Would she be here that long? No one had told them when or where they were to be sold. All she knew was that she was locked in a small room with her comrades from the ship. She did not know if Ewan and Da were close or if they'd been taken away already. She did not know if she would ever see them again.

Izzy put Elly on the cot and wrapped up the blankets to form a bolster around her. She took a chair from the small table and placed it beneath the high window so she could stand on it and look out.

The window faced north. Off to the right she could see tall masts and riggings as the sky turned pink with dawn. She heard the creak of the ships against the piers and a few calls of the sailors as they began their morning chores.

Smells assaulted her nostrils. The familiar smell of the ocean along with the stink of low tide, and the waste of animals that had been left in the rutted lanes that ran by her prison. She also smelled ham or bacon frying and the yeasty tang of an alehouse. A slave dressed in drab linen walked by with a small cask on his shoulder and Izzy watched his progression toward the west until he disappeared from sight.

"What do ye see?" Janet asked. The woman rubbed her eyes and stretched.

" 'Twas good to sleep in a bed for a change," Ruthie said as she sat up on her cot.

"Not much of anything," Izzy replied. She suddenly felt cold and stepped down from the stool, briskly rubbing her upper arms against a chill that did not have much to do with the weather.

All three women looked at the door in apprehension when they heard footsteps approach and then the rattle of a key. Izzy scooped up Elly and grabbed her blanket and diapers when she saw the two armed men at the door.

The women were led out into the street. They walked away from the wharves toward what must be the center of town. Izzy looked around with Elly tightly clutched in her arms.

"I don't even know what city this is," she murmured to Elly. How would she ever find Da and Ewan again if she didn't know where they'd been sold?

The men were in a holding area, gathered behind a fence. The women were put in with them and Ewan wrapped his arms around Izzy and Elly as they came through the gate.

"What's to become of us?" she asked against his chest. She was trembling and she tried to quiet herself so Elly would not feel it. She had to be strong for her baby's sake.

"Do not worry, Iz," Ewan said. "Wherever I am taken, I will escape and find you."

"And live our lives here as we did in Scotland? We'd be outlaws, just like Da. Always hiding and scraping by and almost starving?" Izzy said. She pushed away from Ewan's embrace. "I'll not have it for Elly." Izzy wiped her tears away and adjusted her hold on her daughter as she looked up into Ewan's brown eyes. "I ken ye would change it if ye could, Ewan. I ken ye would never have done the things ye did that day if ye had any idea how it would all end up for us." She looked over at Da, who was watching the proceedings outside the fence.

A prisoner from the ship had been led onto a platform. He was a few years older than Ewan and of good build with thinning hair. He stood with his hands tied before him as a man dressed in silk poked and prodded him with a crop. He was forced to open his mouth to show his teeth and the man in silk nodded as he stepped down from the platform.

The bidding began.

"Donae do anything foolish, Ewan," Izzy continued. "Serve your time and I will serve mine. Then we will see where life leads us."

Ewan nodded. "I've made so many mistakes, Iz," he said. "I'm sorry you got caught up in it."

Izzy looked over at her father. "We all got caught up in it." Da turned their way and came toward them. "We were victims of his mistakes. I won't have Elly become the victim of mine."

"Let me hold her one time," Ewan said. "So she will remember me."

"I will make sure she does," Izzy said as she placed the baby in Ewan's arms. Ewan pulled Elly up under his chin and kissed her forehead. He quietly sang an old lullaby to her, one

Izzy remembered their mother singing as he swayed back and forth, gently rocking her in his arms.

If only he'd had the chance to be a father, instead of wasting his youth on his sire. His life was nearly as tragic as Donnie's.

She would have a different future for her child.

"The buyers are mostly planters and such," Da said. "Looking for strong backs to work in their fields alongside the slaves." The three of them watched as the first man was led away and another one put on the platform.

"Even the women?" Izzy asked. Janet and Ruthie huddled together in the back of the pen, watching the auction unfold around them. Their faces were pale in the fresh morning light.

"I cannae say," Da said. "They willnae want me," Da said. "Just young men, like Ewan."

"So ye think we will be sold separately," Ewan said. Izzy knew he'd been hoping the two of them would be bought together.

Da shrugged. "Our fate is no longer in our hands."

Even now, Da was as pragmatic as always. Izzy wanted to scream at him, hit him, kick him, something to make him realize how much Ewan loved him. How Ewan had wasted his entire life worshiping him. If not for Da . . .

She shook her head. There was no changing Da, any more than there was any changing the fate that awaited them.

"Ye best give her back, Ewan," she said, and held out her arms for Elly.

"Isobel," Da said. "I ken ye are used to having your own way," he said. "I ken it will be difficult for ye, having no say in how you live your life. More so than for Ewan." Izzy stopped fussing over Elly as she took in what Da was saying. He laid a hand on her shoulder and gave it a squeeze before gently touching Elly's cheek. "Ye are just like your mother, ye ken? Stubborn and prideful and strong and sure of what ye want." He gave her a wistful smile. "Ye will be fine, my daughter. I am sure of it."

Izzy blinked back the tears. "Thank ye, Da."

"Think kindly on me, Iz," he said. "There is only one thing I've done right in this world and it was to love your mother with all my heart." He turned and walked away, positioning himself so he would be the next one to go.

Ewan put his arm around her as she fought to control her emotions. "Ye think he would have a word for you," she said. She felt angry at Da for making her cry, yet sad that he had waited all this time to say he loved her in his own strange way.

"He did," Ewan said. "He said his piece to me the night Elly was born." They watched as he was taken to the platform. Donald Ferguson stood tall and proud and Izzy imagined, for one brief moment, how he must have looked standing on the field at Culloden, with his long golden hair blowing in the wind and his claymore in his hand. Someone else must have seen his strength and pride too, because the man who called out a bid spoke with the brogue of the Highlands. Izzy watched as Da looked out over the crowd, and then his eyes seemed to narrow as he was led from the platform.

"Can ye see?" Izzy asked. "Do ye ken who bought him?"

"I cannae see a thing," Ewan replied as he stretched up on his toes to look over the gathering. "He is gone."

Chapter Twenty-one

She was last. Ewan had fetched a high price, but she was so small, she couldn't see who had bought him.

"Please, God. Bless Ewan and his new master. Make him kind." She shifted Elly on her arm. "Please, if it is your will, let me see him again. And Da too. Amen." She crossed herself as best she could. It was her turn.

She was terrified as she climbed the steps to the platform with Elly in her arms. The comments during Ruthie's and Janet's auctions had not been kind and Izzy wondered what kind of service they would have to provide for their new masters.

What would her owner expect her to do? But more important, what would become of Elly? How could she work and care for her baby too? Would Elly be taken from her?

The auctioneer pointed to the middle of the platform and Izzy went where he indicated.

"She's too skinny!" someone yelled out from the crowd, and the group laughed uproariously. Elly started to fret and Izzy bounced her in her arms.

"Isobel Ferguson, age twenty-eight and daughter, age three weeks," the auctioneer said as he read his list. "Do I have a bid?"

Maybe whoever bought Ewan will buy me. Izzy dared to hope as she kept her eyes down. She heard a small bid come from the back of the crowd. It was a man's voice and she quickly looked up, hoping she would see Da or Ewan beside the bidder.

There were too many people. The crowd filled the open

area and spilled over into the spaces between the buildings. People hung out of windows and stood on crates and wagons to watch. It seemed as if all the eyes of the colonials were upon her.

None belonged to any faces she held dear. None belonged to her family. None was John.

Izzy shook her head at her nonsense. He did not even know she was here.

There was another bid, and then the first voice piped up again with a higher offer. Izzy tried to see who it was as she bounced Elly, who sucked noisily on her fist. The baby needed to be fed and it was only a matter of minutes before she would get tired of her fist and show just how hungry she was.

"Do I hear another bid?" the auctioneer asked hopefully. The morning was gone and the crowd was drifting away, losing interest in a small woman holding a wee babe. Izzy held her breath as she looked over the dwindling numbers. "Sold," the man said, and slammed his gavel on the stand.

Izzy stood where she was, waiting. The rest of her life lay in some stranger's hands. A man made his way up to the platform, shouldering people aside.

"Dr. Keats?" Izzy almost wept in relief.

"I have need of a housekeeper," he said. "And someone to assist in surgery. Do you think you can do that?"

Izzy nodded quickly. "I will," she said. "Thank you, and God bless you."

"Don't thank me yet," he said. "You might grow to hate me before the next twelve years are over."

"You saved our lives," she said. "Both of us. I could never hate you."

"There are reasons why I left England, Izzy," he said as he handed the coin he owed for her over to the king's representative. "Life with me may not be easy."

Izzy tried not to shudder as she wondered what he meant. Dr. Keats helped her down from the platform and Izzy scanned the crowd, hoping beyond hope that she would spot Ewan. "Did ye see who bought Da or my brother?" she asked.

"I did not," Keats said. He smiled encouragingly at Izzy. "I did not mean to scare you, lass. And fortunately you went fairly cheap."

Izzy shook her head. "I promise I will work very hard."

"I am not questioning your worth as a worker," he said. "What I meant is that since you were so cheap, I have funds left over to buy you some clothes. And the babe also."

"You have done enough," Izzy said. "More than I can ever repay."

"Nonsense," Keats said. "First we'll get some clothes and then a nice meal."

"And then?" Izzy asked.

"Then we're off to the Carolinas, my dear."

"I wish she could be with us," Ewan said as he and his father watched Izzy and Dr. Keats from the shadows.

"It took all of Campbell's funds to buy you," Donald replied. "There was nothing left for her."

"Where we are going is not safe for a woman," William Campbell said. "And especially not for a wee babe."

Donald looked at the man who had purchased them. He was close in age to Ewan but had the looks of one who knew how to fight. Which was why he'd purchased Donald.

"Were you at Culloden?" he'd asked as soon as he'd taken possession of him.

"Aye," Donald answered.

"No love for the English, then?"

"None whatsoever," Donald confessed.

"There's a war coming. One to the west with the Shawnee

and another one soon against the king," Campbell said. "Are you of a mind to fight?"

"I havenae stopped in all these years," Donald said. "I can fight some more if need be."

"Are there any others like you in that lot?"

"There is my son."

"Fine," Campbell had said. "Let us see what his asking price is."

And so Ewan came to be with them. But not Izzy. There was no place for Izzy on the western frontier. From what Campbell said, it was a dangerous and violent place. Donald felt very much alive for the first time in years. Instead of hiding, he would be fighting again. And God willing, this time the English would be defeated.

"Donae worry on her, son," Donald said, placing a hand on Ewan's shoulder. "She is better off without us."

"Aye," Ewan said. "But it would be nice to ken where she is going, so we can find her again."

"We're all in God's hands now," Donald said. "All of us."

Chapter Twenty-two

South Carolina, March 1781

John stared around the tent and rubbed the sleep from his eyes. Another nightmare. One of thousands he'd had in the seven years since he'd arrived in the colonies. And Izzy was in every one of them. Why? Was it because he'd left her in the tollbooth? Was that not what she deserved for her betrayal? She'd seduced him, she'd used him, and she'd nearly cost him his career and sorely damaged his reputation. So why did she still haunt him?

How long until dawn? John pulled on his boots and scrubbed his hand over the stubble of his beard. The air was damp and cold and everything around him smelled, including his tent mates. He was sure he wasn't much better. How long had it been since he'd had a warm bath and a comfortable bed and a nice meal?

Years? Since he left England? Or just since revolution broke out here in the colonies? The English had not been able to claim the quick victory everyone expected, so his father's troops had been sent south with Cornwallis to capture Savannah and then Charleston in an effort to separate the south from the north and rally those colonists who still favored the king.

John's opinion was that those in charge had overestimated the loyalist population. But he was nothing but a lowly captain and his opinion on such issues did not matter. Nor did his father's where politics were concerned, since he was a bastard and only a major general, in spite of his excellent service to the king. Cornwallis was in charge now and the army had been ordered to secure the south. Outposts were placed along the border between South Carolina and North Carolina in preparation of taking that colony. With Clinton coming down from the north and Cornwallis's troops moving up from the south, Virginia would be caught in the middle and the war would end with an English victory. No doubt the loyalists would show up for the celebration.

The weather was cold, damp, gloomy. Typical for mid-March. John wrapped his cloak around his body and ducked out into the predawn mist. A lamp was burning inside his father's tent, as he'd known it would be. It seemed as if James Murray never slept.

John heard the restless coughs and snores from the tents around him as he picked his way through the mud and muck. How did anyone sleep anymore? There had been so much fighting, so much death, he could not remember what normal life was like. All he wanted to remember was a lovely summer afternoon on a hillock overlooking the sea and a pair of deep brown eyes that seemed to see into his soul.

Everything that came afterward, he chose not to remember. Because remembering brought pain. The betrayal, the beating, the humiliation of being sent home to his mother like a boy who'd misbehaved at school, his mother's death. One blow coming after the other until the weight of it all bore him down to nothingness. He existed, nothing more. Another day came and then another and then the war and he wondered at times how and why he survived it when others, more worthy, were killed and maimed each day.

Did he deserve to be here? That was not up to him. Did he want to be here? There seemed to be no choice about that either. He was a soldier, his father was his commanding officer, and he served both his general and his king. Everything else was just part of the day-to-day drudgery and misery that was life.

When had he become so bitter? He could trace his cynicism back to that moment he would never forget. The moment he learned that no one could be trusted, especially not those you loved.

The only person he could trust was his father. The father who sent him into battle to risk death day after day and year after year. A father who was even now planning the next battle.

General James Murray looked up from his portable writing desk as John ducked beneath the tent flap. "You are up early this morning," he said, greeting his son.

"I fear that for you it is still the same night," John replied, motioning to the scattered piles of papers and maps that covered every available surface of his father's tent.

"I slept for a few hours," James assured him. "You, however, look as if you didn't sleep at all. Do the nightmares still plague you?"

"No," John lied.

His father peered at him from over his half-moon glasses. "Are you hungry?" he asked.

"I could eat," he replied.

His father summoned a corporal who stood right outside the tent, and a place was cleared for both of them to eat. Breakfast arrived a few moments later. John looked dubiously at the meat on his plate. The countryside surrounding Hillsborough had long since been stripped of supplies to feed the king's army.

"I have a letter from Carrie," his father said when they'd finished their meal. John sat back in his chair and crossed his arms. His sister's marriage still rankled. His fondest hope had been that she'd find a wellborn husband in the colonies, but he'd never dreamed she'd fall in love with a red-haired Scotsman. John hated the upstart Carrie had marred, but his father had given her his blessing and was thrilled to hear of the two children she now had. He desperately wished to see them, but his duties and Carrie's safety forbade it. Her husband, Connor Duncan, had thrown in with the rebels. It was seldom that letters made their way through the lines, and his father treasured each one as if it were Carrie herself telling him tales of the life she'd chosen to live on the frontier.

I wonder what they look like, John found himself wondering. Did Carrie's children resemble her, or Duncan, or were they a mixture of both? He would find out, one day, if he survived.

"She says wee Jamie has become quite the marksman," his father reported, "and they are having trouble keeping Jillian away from the foals they are raising." John shook his head and grinned. It sounded as if the tiny girl named after their mother was just like Carrie.

James Murray paused and removed his glasses. He pinched the bridge of his nose. "My eyes are not as strong as they once were," he said, and handed the letter to John. "Not enough sleep and too much time spent poring over these maps and dispatches. Read the rest of it aloud for me, please."

The paper was well creased and John knew his father probably could recite it by heart. He didn't want to read the letter. He didn't want to hear about Carrie's happiness because it would mean that he was wrong about Duncan. About a Scot not being worthy of trust because they were all betrayers and they all lied.

And if he was wrong about Duncan, could he also be wrong about Izzy? His eyes scanned over the news about Jamie and Jillian to Carrie's report about the homestead, which he read aloud.

"We are prospering, in spite of the times. Indeed, I feel we are doing better than most. We have a fine garden and plenty of meat, thanks to Efrem, who decided to take the role of the Moravians and be at peace with everyone. Connor has urged me many times to go to Salem for safety's sake, but I will not leave this place that I have come to love."

"Salem is close to Hillsborough," his father observed. "Close enough that we could visit."

"We will be gone from here by the time she could arrive," John said. "If we could even get word to her."

James templed his hands. "True," he said. "True enough." He took a sip of coffee. "It is good that Efrem stays at their homestead while Connor is out."

"While Connor is fighting for the rebels, you mean?"

"He scouts for them," James said. "Carrie has never mentioned what he does, but I have talked to some who know of him. He is good at his job."

"So he is partially responsible for some of our recent defeats?" John jumped at any chance he could find to run the man down. Simply because he was Scottish.

"I believe he was at Kings Mountain this past fall," James answered. "One of the loyalists mentioned a man who matches Connor's description."

"You sound as if you are proud of him, Father," John said. "How can you forget what the rebels did to the loyalists after the battle? How many men died because of their cruelty?" Nine loyalist leaders had been hanged after the battle and of the six hundred who were marched to Hillsborough, only a hundred and thirty survived the journey.

"I find it hard to believe that Connor was a part of such doings." His father spoke with conviction. "I will never condemn a man for following his beliefs," James said. "Even if I disagree with them."

His father's steady gaze let John know that he was talking

more about him than Duncan. He turned his eyes back to the letter.

"Tell John," he began. Damn, he did not want to read any further. But his father's eyes were upon him, so he must go on. "Tell John that I love him and miss him terribly. Tell him I hope someday he can be at peace with himself." John read carefully, slowly, willing his voice not to break at his sister's impassioned plea. "I do not know what caused so great a change in him, but I pray every day that he will be able to forgive and forget. It terrifies me to think that he might die in this war without having the same sense of contentment I have found here on the Blue Ridge with Connor. Tell him above all that I wish for his happiness."

John resisted the urge to wad the paper up and throw it in the corner. No wonder his father had made him read it aloud. Instead he carefully folded the letter upon its well-worn creases and placed it on the portable desk. He sat back carefully in his chair and waited for his father to speak.

"You have never spoken of your time in Aberdeen," James began. "All I know of it is what Kensington told me in a letter."

"What did he say?" John asked.

"Merely that you had trusted someone you shouldn't have and that he felt it best for your career that you be posted to the colonies as soon as possible." He steepled his fingers and looked at John. "I have often wondered if it was a woman who betrayed your trust."

John leaned forward so that his elbows were propped upon his knees. He felt so very weary. He rubbed his chin across his clenched hands. Not one time in the past eight years had he spoke of his shame.

"I know you were lashed, son. I have seen the scars on your

back. But like Carrie, I wonder more about the scars you carry within you."

John looked up.

"Those wounds can fester inside until there is nothing left of what you once were."

"Have they?" John asked. "Do you not recognize me as your son?"

"I see a brave soldier who would lay down his life for his comrades," his father said. "But I no longer see the man I thought you would someday be."

"Am I a disappointment to you?" What would he do if his father said he was? John felt his heart leap into his throat.

His father leaned forward and clenched his shoulder. "Never," he said. "Never. I just want you to be happy, John, and I know that you have not been for a very long time."

John managed not to let loose a sigh of relief as he looked down at his knees. He could not deny what his father said. · He could trace back to the very second the last time he was truly happy. But what difference did that make now?

"Did you love her?"

He slowly nodded. "Yes." It was the first time he'd ever admitted it to anyone. Except for that day when he'd looked into Izzy's eyes.

No . . . that was the wine. . . .

He knew better.

"Rory was killed because of her," he said finally. "Her brothers were trying to break her father out of prison. She seduced me while her brother impersonated me by taking my coat and Sultan."

She drank the wine too. Could she not have been as much a victim of her brother's plans as he had been?

John quickly dismissed the thought as he looked at his father. "They were Highlanders. Her father fought at Culloden."

"As did I," his father pointed out. "And Connor's father as well. He died there on the battlefield. Right before his son was born . . . at Culloden."

John had never heard that bit of information before and looked up at his father with interest.

"It seems that Connor has a right to hate the English as much as you seem to hate the Scots," his father said. "Yet he loves your sister."

"Carrie had nothing to do with the war. She wasn't even born yet."

"As Connor had nothing to do with your own private war. Do not misjudge the man because of his heritage."

"I feel it is too late for that father."

James stood and gently touched John's shoulder. "It is never too late to do the right thing."

John let out a long breath. Could it be so easy?

"I must meet with Cornwallis," his father said, and John knew that it was time to go back to being a soldier instead of a son. He had much to consider. He stood to go.

He was surprised when his father stopped him by placing both hands on his shoulders. "You are a good man, John, and a good soldier. I know your mother would be proud of you, as I am," he said. Then his father embraced him. John felt like a small child again, safe, secure, and knowing that as long as his father was there, he had nothing to fear. But the moment passed as quickly as the embrace. His father gathered up his maps and papers and left without another word.

Oh, to be as innocent as a child again. . . . John went back to join his men and await the orders of the coming day.

Chapter Twenty-three

Izzy hung the sheet across the clothesline. She hoped today the laundry would dry. It had been so cold and damp for so long. The weather was as oppressive as the war. Every day gray and hopeless as food supplies dwindled beneath the constant foraging of either the colonials or the British. It was hard to say from one week to the next which army would occupy the town. She just wanted it over. This country had been at war practically since the day she'd arrived.

"Be grateful for what ye have," she said aloud as she yanked a pair of Elly's bloomers from the basket and snapped them open to hang on the line. "Ye've got a roof over your daughter's head, clothes on her back, and food to eat, such as it is."

Izzy closed her eyes for a moment and felt the sharp bite of the wind as it rushed through, tossing the clothes on the line and pushing the clouds above to the east. She opened them with a sigh as the wind promised more cold and more rain. She looked over at the bare patch of dirt at the back of the yard. The garden needed to be planted, but the ground was either too hard with frost or too wet with rain. Her two hens scratched at the dirt in their never-ending quest for food. She'd managed to save them from stew pots through all the occupations by hiding them in the cellar. It was Elly's job to watch for soldiers so Izzy would have time to catch them. They still had eggs and that was more than most folks. They had fared better than she'd ever thought possible that day she stood on the block with Elly in her arms. She was blessed.

Dr. Keats was kind. When he wasn't drinking. He had forewarned her and she'd learned to keep her door locked at night, just as she had with Angus.

A smile flitted across Izzy's face as she thought of Cook, Tommy, and Katty Ann. Even Davy. "I hope you are well," she said, and crossed herself in a quick prayer for her old friends before she went back to work. She did not dare think of them any longer. Because thinking of them would lead her to think of other things. Things she would rather not remember.

Like the look in John's eyes the day he thought she betrayed him.

"I did betray him," she admitted. She'd betrayed him by not telling him her real name, by not telling him her father was in the tollbooth, by not voicing her suspicions that day on a hill by the sea beneath the ruins of Dunnottar Castle.

The air had been warm that day. Their skin kissed by the sun. If she closed her eyes again and let the breeze caress her face, she could almost remember what it was like to be loved by John for one beautiful afternoon.

His face she would never forget. She saw it every time she looked at her daughter.

"Mama!" Elly called out from the back stoop of the house. She held an orange kitten in her hands. "Papa Keath is athleep on the floor." Izzy couldn't help smiling, even though the news was not good. Elly's front teeth had come out and she was having trouble with her *S*s.

Elly's announcement meant that Dr. Keats was drunk again. His drinking bouts seemed to be coming closer and closer together now and Izzy wondered how much longer she would be able to convince Elly that Papa Keats, as she affectionately called him, had a sleeping problem instead of a drinking problem.

"I'll take care of him, lamb," she said as she went up the

stoop and through the door. "Why don't you let your kitty play outside now?"

Elly smiled obligingly and went out into the yard. Izzy watched for a moment, as Elly put the kitten down in a patch of grass. The little cat headed for the garden and Izzy smiled in gratitude. At least she wouldn't have to worry about cleaning up after it.

If only Keats would be so obliging.

She found him on the floor of his office. The bottle lay beside him, empty, of course.

"Where do you find it?" Izzy wondered as she set the bottle upright. "I thought Cornwallis had taken everything." She moved behind him and grabbed him by his shoulders. She couldn't just let him lie on the floor. Not when anyone could walk into the house at any time looking for the doctor. It would not do for his patients to find him passed out cold on the floor.

"We must get ye to the couch at least," she grunted as she tried to move him.

"Wha?" His eyelids fluttered. "Ah, Izzy." He made a jerky movement and his hand hit her cheek. Izzy knew he did not mean to hurt her, so she pushed it away and pulled him back toward the couch. "You are a schweet woman, Izzzz," he gushed. "Too good for the likes of me."

"Aye, I am," Izzy agreed. "Get up on the couch now and sleep it off."

He managed to crawl onto the couch with Izzy's help and grabbed her hand as she turned to go. "Have I not been good to you all these years, Izzy?" he asked as he pulled on her hand. Izzy turned back. His red-rimmed blue eyes were strangely lucid, in spite of the drink.

"Ye have," she admitted. She stood as far away as her arm allowed. "More than I deserve."

"Yet you cannot bring yourself to share my bed," he said. His grip was tight as he pulled on her hand, drawing her closer.

Izzy looked down at the floor. The wood was well scrubbed. She kept it that way, working from dawn until dusk, cleaning and cooking and helping him with his surgeries and taking care of Elly, along with giving her some lessons so she could read and write. She worked until she was exhausted each day and then took Elly to sleep with her in their room with the door locked, hoping she would fall asleep and not hear Keats walking the hall and pausing by her room.

"I cannae," she said finally. Not when her heart still grieved. Not when the broken pieces of it belonged to someone else. She looked up at Keats. "Would ye make me?"

He dropped her hand and turned toward the back of the couch. "No," he said, and let out a deep sigh. A snore soon followed and Izzy knew he had passed out again. She closed the door behind her as she left, relief sagging her shoulders.

She leaned her forehead against the wall next to the door. How many more years could she fight this battle? Why should she? Wouldn't it be easier just to give in and let him have his way? Would it be any worse than being alone for the rest of her life?

Yet the thought of having Keats touch her made her skin crawl. He was at least twenty years older than she. His skin was flabby and his nose constantly red from drink.

He wasn't John.

"Worse things could happen," she sighed. They had. Yet she would not tarnish the few sweet memories she had by submitting to Keats. It seemed almost sacrilegious. She would hold those memories close and hope and pray that Elly would have a happier life. A pleasant life. A life of contentment. Was that too much to ask?

There was still work to be done. The laundry still waited. Elly still needed her lessons for the day. The bread should be turned.

"Start with the bread," she declared, and made her way to the back of the house. The dough was springy when she stuck her finger in, so she spread some flour on the worn surface of the table and turned it out to make into loaves. She peered out the window and saw Elly beside the shed where the garden tools were kept. The kitten hopped through the grass in pursuit of an insect and Izzy went back to her work.

She formed the loaves, covered them with a towel, and washed the flour and dough from her hands. She looked out the window again and her heart stopped.

Three armed men, militia from the looks of them, stood beside the shed. One of them knelt beside Elly with the kitten in his hands. They were all tall and lean, with long hair and unshaven beards. They cradled their rifles in their arms as if the weapons were a part of them.

Izzy ran out the door. "Get away from her!" she yelled as she ran toward them.

"Is that any way to greet your family, girl?" a familiar voice scolded. Izzy stopped in her tracks.

"Da?" His hair was pure silver now and fell down around his shoulders. Ewan stood beside him, straight and tall, with silver at his temples and scattered through the rusty color of his beard. The third man rose from his crouch beside Elly and he seemed to tower over Da and Ewan. His hair was as bright as copper and his beard was just the growth of a week or so instead of the fullness of his companions'.

Ewan opened his arms wide and Izzy rushed into them, crashing against his chest as he enfolded her. He smelled of wood smoke and damp woods and gunpowder. To her nose it was the sweetest scent in the world.

"How did ye find me?" Izzy cried. "Where hae ye been?"

"In the mountains mostly," Ewan said. "Fighting."

Izzy turned from Ewan and looked at her father. He placed a hand on her shoulder. "Ye look well, Iz. The doctor treats ye kindly?"

"Aye, Da," she said, and wiped her eyes with her apron. "He does. When he's sober."

"He's nay touched . . ." Ewan began, but Izzy stopped him with a quick look at Elly.

"Nay, Ewan. I am much as ye hae last seen me. Just older."

"As we all are," Da said.

Izzy knelt beside Elly. "This is your grandfather," she said. "And your uncle Ewan."

"Really?" Elly asked. "They are real?" Izzy had often told Elly of her family as she'd promised Ewan she would.

"Despite everything the Shawnee and the English hae done to make us not real," Da said to Elly. "She has the look of her father about her," he told Izzy.

"Aye," Izzy said. "She does."

"My father is a tholdier," Elly informed them. "Someday when the war ith over, he will come thee me."

Ewan and Da both looked surprised.

"She has flights of fancy," Izzy explained. "She's always looking out for the soldiers. It was easier . . ." Her voice trailed off as she wondered how she would ever explain to Elly about her father.

"She reminds me of my daughter Jillian," the tall man said, quickly changing the subject, for which Izzy was immensely grateful. "She's of the same size but must be older." He pointed to Elly's missing teeth. "Jilly is four."

"Elly is seven," Izzy said, "and small for her age."

"This is Connor Duncan," Ewan said. "A good friend."

Izzy dropped a curtsey. "Pleased to meet you, sir." She looked at Da and Ewan. "Come in the house," she said. "We don't have much, but I can feed you a bit."

"We'd better not," Ewan said.

"Keats is asleep," Izzy explained. "And will be for hours. And he cares not which side wins, as long as the tavern stays open."

The three men looked at each other and then in silent agreement followed Izzy to the house. She laid out a meal for them as best she could with what she had and they all sat around the table in the kitchen. She could not help noticing how quietly and efficiently they moved, as if every motion was thought out hours beforehand. And even though they filled the small kitchen, she sensed that in the wild they would be invisible and deadly.

Elly watched the men with quiet fascination and managed to work her way between Da and Ewan until Ewan picked her up without a word and put her on his knee. She settled back against his chest and Izzy's heart swelled at the sight. She quickly wiped her eyes as she refilled their cups with the chicory-flavored brew that served as coffee and sat down at the table.

"How did ye find me?" she asked.

"We heard tell of a Dr. Keats here," Da said. "So we came to see if ye were here."

"And here ye are," Ewan added. "We've asked around for ye every chance we got, but this was the first we heard anything. We saw that Keats bought your indenture, but we had no way of knowing where ye went after ye left the auction." He took a drink of his coffee. "He treats you kindly?" he asked again.

"He does," Izzy said. "I cook and clean and help him when I can. He's always treated us well and dotes on Elly. I hae no complaints."

"He drinks, does he?" Da asked.

Izzy quickly nodded and looked at Elly, who was playing with the fringe on the sleeve of Ewan's buckskin shirt. She changed the subject. "What happened to you two? You were together all these years?"

"Aye," Da said. "We were bought by William Campbell. He knew this war was coming and was making ready for it."

"There was no money left for you," Ewan added. "We wanted to keep you with us—"

"Where we went was no place for you," Da cut in. "We fought the Shawnee along the Ohio. It was nay safe for anyone. Connor's wife was taken by them."

"I got her back," Connor assured her. "We were lucky."

Izzy shivered. She had heard tales of Indian's atrocities. But for her the frontier seemed so far away. Like the legends of monsters in the lochs at home. Stories that frightened children, nothing more. Her father and brother were lucky to have survived.

"Where is your wife now?" Izzy asked Connor.

"We have a homestead on the Blue Ridge," Connor said. "We raise horses. I have a friend who decided the war was not his business. He takes care of my family and farm."

"He willnae let us meet his wife," Ewan said with a grin. "He is afraid I will take her away."

"Someday when this war is over," Connor said with his blue eyes twinkling merrily, "I will take ye there, Ewan. Then ye will see that she only has eyes for me."

Connor Duncan loved his wife. It was obvious. What a lucky woman she was to have such devotion. "How does she feel about ye being off fighting in the war?" Izzy asked.

"It is difficult," Conner said. "Especially since her father and brother fight for the English. They are both officers. I hae promised that I will not shoot them."

"The problem is they hae not promised the same," Da said.

"Hae ye fought many battles?" Izzy asked.

"A few," Da said as if it were nothing. "We fight with the Virginia Militia. As free men."

"Ye are not bonded?"

"Nay, Campbell freed us when we saw we would nae run," Da said. "I was glad for another chance at the British. For all their wrongdoings." He placed a hand on Elly's head and smoothed her hair. Izzy knew he was thinking of John and how he'd deserted her.

She did not blame John though. What man would want a woman who'd deceived him? Who'd lied to him?

"There will be a battle soon," Ewan said. "Close by. We will try to come again when it is over."

"Now that we know where to find you," Da added with a smile.

"After the war, I will make a place for us, Iz," Ewan said. "We want you with us. And Elly too."

"I hae five years left," Izzy said helplessly.

"There are ways around that," Da said. "The frontier is a big place. It is easy for people to hide."

"Da," Izzy said. "I cannae just leave. I owe Dr. Keats. Elly wouldnae be here without him."

"Are we leaving Papa Keath?" Elly asked.

"No, child," Izzy said quickly as she jumped to her feet and gathered the dishes. "And 'tis best if ye not mention to him what has gone on here today."

"Can ye keep secrets, sweet Elly?" Ewan asked.

"Yes," Elly said. "Mama thinks that I don't know about Papa Keath getting drunk all the time when she says he's just thleeping."

"Elly!" Izzy exclaimed in horror as the men burst into

laughter. They quieted quickly, however, when they heard a knock at the front door. Izzy quickly moved to answer it.

When she returned they were gone. Elly stood at the back door with the kitten once more in her arms.

"Will we thee them again, Mama?" she asked.

"I donae know," Izzy said. "But I hope so."

"I wish I could tell Papa Keath about my grandfather and uncle."

Izzy knelt before Elly. "Ye must not, sweet," she said. "We must keep their visit a secret so they will be safe. Do ye ken?"

"I do." Elly nodded. She put her kitten down and went off after it as it scampered away. Izzy stood and looked out the door, but there was no sign that the men had ever been here, except for the dirty dishes stacked next to the basin.

She was lucky it had only been Mrs. King at the door, looking for Dr. Keats. She had lied, of course, and told her he was out. Still, the woman had peered around her as if she'd heard the men's voices. There were those in town who sided with the English. It was best to tread lightly and not show an inclination to one side or another.

The truth was that her loyalty was divided. Her brother and father fought for the colonists. And John, wherever he was, fought for the king. She had no idea where John was, but she was certain he was here, somewhere, fighting the war. Just as she was certain he was still alive, somewhere. Her heart would know it if he were dead.

"God, keep them safe," she said to the sky before she turned to do the dishes.

Chapter Twenty-four

Today, finally, they would fight. John stood next to his horse in the predawn hours. The grass beneath his feet crackled from the heavy frost and his breath hung in the air like smoke. His stomach growled with hunger, but there would be no breakfast. The American army was within reach and after a long and sleepless night, Cornwallis was determined to do battle. He had chased Major General Nathanael Greene all over the south. It was time to confront him.

Reports were that Greene was being reinforced by the Virginia Militia, the North Carolina Militia, and the Continental army. Reports also said that the Americans had over twice as many men as the nineteen hundred English soldiers who were at this moment awaiting the order to march.

John was to ride with Lieutenant Colonel Tarleton's cavalry today since he was one of the few remaining officers with a mount. Cornwallis wanted them to find and hold the enemy until the main body of the English army could arrive. All around him horses stamped impatiently and the dragoons checked their weapons and the girths on their mounts.

He saw his father on his horse, up front, with the other officers, all waiting while Cornwallis conferred with a scout. Then suddenly the order was given and the troop of nearly five hundred riders and infantry moved out as one, traveling east on the Salisbury Wagon Road.

What would the day bring? Was it too much to hope that this battle would end all the fighting?

And then what? What would his life be like after the war? Would he survive to know? Did he care?

Now was not the time for such questions. Now was the time to concentrate on the task at hand. John checked his sword to make sure once again that the frost would not make it stick as the cavalry moved ahead. The weary infantry did their best to keep pace behind them. Tarleton, as usual, was anxious to do battle and pressed forward. Ahead, John saw the Quaker meeting house at New Garden, and suddenly the English were greeted by erratic gunfire.

Tarleton gave the command to fire and they returned the volley. John saw the American riders leaving the field and was not surprised when Tarleton issued the order to follow.

"It's a rout!" someone yelled as they pressed on.

But the rout did not last long. The Americans beat the British back under heavy fire. Tarleton once again gave the order to reform and attack. John hurriedly reloaded his pistol while holding his reins in his teeth. His horse danced around, anxious to run. The Americans took off down a long lane bordered with a high fence on both sides. John fought to get his horse under control as he looked ahead at Tarleton's route.

"Wait!" John yelled. "It's a trap!" He pulled at his horse's reins before the animal bolted after the rest.

Tarleton either did not hear, or did not care. He gave pursuit and the dragoons piled into the narrow lane. The Americans turned and charged. It was pure chaos. Horses and men went down. The fallen tripped up the rest and the troop became an easy target for the Americans. Tarleton realized his mistake and beat a hasty retreat with as many men as could follow. Most were taken prisoner. John rode with Tarleton down a narrow path that led southeast from the main road. The man was bleeding from his right hand and John realized that two of his fingers were missing.

They heard heavy gunfire to the west.

"It's the main army," someone said, and they turned their horses toward the sound. They came upon the Quaker meeting house again and saw the advance guard of the army firing upon the Americans they had just engaged. The American cavalry retreated while given cover by what seemed to be infantry and militia. The mountain men moved quickly and quietly, taking cover behind fences and trees while the regulars stood in the open and fired. John joined the ranks with what was left of the dragoons. The fighting between the lines became intense until the Americans realized that the rest of the English army was upon them. The militia faded into the trees and gave cover fire while the regulars retreated

John took a moment to wipe the sweat and powder from his face before he found his father at the front of his troop, which had just come into view.

"What happened?" his father asked.

"They were ready for us," John said. He walked his horse in a circle around his father's to allow the animal time to cool down. "The hotheaded fool led the troop into an ambush. Most were either killed or captured."

"Cornwallis wanted a battle; it looks as if he will get it."

"He will," John said. "Let's just hope he makes better decisions than Tarleton."

"Watch it!" Ewan had to catch his breath before he yelled at Connor, who seemed frozen in place. They had run for what seemed like forever to catch up with "Light Horse" Harry Lee and his riders. They were part of William Campbell's riflemen and experienced at war. It was unheard of for one of them to stand in the open, a clear target for anyone who could shoot a decent shot. At Ewan's warning Connor ducked back behind a thick oak to reload his rifle while Ewan fired and then moved behind his tree to reload.

"I think I saw Carrie's brother," Connor said calmly as he fired. "Mounted, behind the lines." He ducked back to reload and Ewan fired again. "Which means her father is here also."

"Perhaps you could invite them to tea," Donald said. He jerked his head back and they followed him as Lee's men turned to give them cover. "Catch up on the news and such."

Connor shook his head and grinned at Ewan as the three men ran through the dense trees. "Maybe even find a way to end the war?"

"If only they would go back to England and let us live in peace," Ewan grunted, jumping behind a fallen oak to reload. It seemed as if this war had lasted a lifetime. His entire life in the colonies had been nothing but warfare. Seven long years of fighting and surviving. But now that they'd found Izzy . . .

"Ye best point him out to us next time so we don't kill him by accident," Donald said to Connor. "It would be a shame to meet your wife as the man who killed her father and brother."

"Aye," Connor said. "I am certain she would not take kindly to that. When and if I see him again I will point him out."

"Fall back!" Campbell called out. Ewan peered over the fallen tree and then made a run for the rear when he saw that the riders were providing cover. He heard his father and Connor on his heels. Da panted hard. It was getting harder and harder for him to keep up, especially with the short rations they'd been on lately. How much longer would he be strong enough to fight? Today was not the day to worry about it. They could all be dead by noon.

I should have asked someone to tell Izzy if we fall. She would want to know. He was sure of it.

They kept on for the next mile or so until they saw the artillery. Campbell led them to form up on the south side of the road and Lee's riders fell in behind them.

"Do ye think they will hold the line?" Ewan looked down the row of men who were positioned behind a rail fence facing west. There were over a thousand of them, stretching from his position in the woods to the woods on the other side of a cleared and muddy field. The line of soldiers curved around on either side so the British would be caught in the middle with no place to go but back the way they came. If the line held.

"Some of them will," Da said.

Lee, who must have sensed the uneasiness of the men along the line rode behind them with calls of "Stand firm." And "I have whipped them three times this morning and we can do it again."

"The ones who hae not seen the English army marching upon them in all its glory will run for it," Da said. "And who can blame them, for 'tis a mighty sight indeed."

"It's a foolish sight if you ask me," Connor said. "Shooting at each other point-blank is no way to win a war. Especially on this terrain."

Ewan knew it would be hard for the English to march shoulder to shoulder through the uneven terrain covered with trees, stumps, and deadfalls. Harder still for the cavalry to navigate and the cannon to move.

"Aye," Da said. "The real fighting starts when the shooting is over and the bayonets and pikes and swords come out. It's easy to shoot a man. But kill him up close . . ."

Ewan turned his eyes to the west, his weapons ready and his mind on the men he would kill this day. He did not think on the ones he had killed in battle before this day. There were too many of them to remember.

Then there was the sound of drums.

★ ★ ★

They had to cross open and rising ground to get to the enemy's position. The soldiers marched, shoulder to shoulder, to the beat of the drum with their banners snapping in the brisk wind. The sunlight danced off the bright steel of the bayonets. It was an inspiring sight.

Yet John felt the men pause as he watched from his position to the south of the line. Why shouldn't they be frightened? Behind the fence that zigzagged across the rise, the rebels waited for them to come into range. General Webster must have felt the hesitation too, because he rode behind the men, giving them encouragement. An easy enough task for a man who did not have to stand and face a volley of gunfire.

The line moved on until the rebels opened fire. When the smoke cleared, John saw that nearly half of the men were down. Yet the soldiers closed ranks and moved on with bayonets fixed and their muskets pointed downward until they closed the distance to about fifty yards. Then they fired a volley into the rebels and with a huge shout charged toward them. The Americans in the middle fled, throwing down their arms and equipment before taking off.

"We've got them," somebody close to John said. But then a volley of fire opened up on the sides and the infantry was caught in the middle. The reserves were brought up to fill in the blanks in the line and soon the Americans were retreating on all sides.

The problem, John soon found out as his father gave the order to advance, was that the Americans retreated into a heavy maze of forest to the south of the line. It was impossible for the army to advance as it usually did. Especially for those who were on horseback. He had to wend his way around trees and through brush until he realized the men on foot were going faster than he was.

It was pure chaos. Small pockets of fighting broke out all around him as they caught up to the retreating Americans. A shot splintered a tree right next to his head and he ducked instinctively as his horse reared when a dead branch crashed to the ground right in front of them.

John fought his horse for control and realized he had lost track of his father. It was impossible to tell who was who in the dense forest and heavy smoke. Most of the group they chased was militia and wore homespun and buckskin that blended into the browns and grays of the surrounding woods.

He ducked again when a shot rang close by. He realized that he was a bigger target on horseback and quickly dismounted. John slapped the hindquarters of his horse and the animal took off toward the rear.

With pistol in one hand and sword in the other, he rushed forward to where the fighting seemed most intense.

John did not fear for himself as he knocked a man away with his sword. He was worried about his father. The higher-ranking officers were supposed to stay behind and let the soldiers do the fighting. Yet he knew his father had charged in with the rest of them.

It was impossible to tell. There were so many pockets of men fighting all around him. John realized his men were surrounded. The Americans were attacking from all sides. He heard the heavy sound of the artillery to the north as he ducked beneath a bayonet and sliced the back of the enemy soldier's leg with his sword. The man went down with a thud and John moved on. A horse screamed in fury somewhere before him.

It was difficult to make much headway. The terrain was uneven, covered with dead leaves and broken branches among heavy brush that jerked at him and tore his coat. Anywhere there was a place to stand, men fought hand to hand with bayonets and tomahawks and clubs. These were not regular soldiers, nor were they the typical farmers and storekeepers that made up the militia. These men were rangers, who had fought against the Indians. These men knew how to fight. And his father was somewhere in the midst of them.

Did they know that his father had fought the Indians alongside them? Would it matter that once they had all been brothers in arms against a different foe? Could his brother by marriage be in this fight?

Where is he? John slashed with his sword and pounded with his pistol, which had long ago been fired. He had no chance to reload. He blocked and he stabbed. He put his shoulder down and with a loud roar charged through three men when he saw his father up ahead, fighting from horseback against several opponents. These were men who knew that when the officers went down, the soldiers lost hope and scattered. He was fighting against men who knew how to fight a war against a mighty enemy.

The men pushed at his father's horse. They knew if they got him off the horse, they would have the advantage.

"*No!*" John yelled as the horse reared back. The men kept pushing and his father toppled off. The horse crashed down on top of him and rolled. John reached them just as the horse struggled to his feet. The animal staggered and John charged past it as one of the men raised his tomahawk to slash down at his father. John met him with his own blade.

He heard someone yelling his name as he fought. He heard the roar of cannon. He heard the screams of the dying. He heard several gunshots. Then something struck him hard, in the back, and he realized his father's horse had gone down and was taking him with it. He felt a snap, high in his leg, and saw a musket barrel coming at his face. He threw up his sword to deflect the blow, then all went black as he slid into the soft cushion of leaves and pine needles that covered the forest floor.

"Connor!" Ewan grabbed his arm. "We must go! We are behind the lines!"

"I cannae leave them." Connor shook off Ewan's arm. The look on his face was desperate. They had been fighting their own fierce battle against a squad of Hessians. Connor had suddenly broken away and run toward a group of men who were fighting a bloody battle with an officer on horseback. He yelled when the officer went down, then again when another man joined the melee.

"Would ye have me tell your wife that you are dead, along with her brother and father?" Ewan said. He quickly looked over his shoulder. He saw more green-coated Hessians coming their way. He had no idea where Da was either. Must he choose now between his father and his friend?

A shot whizzed by and both men ducked into a crouch. "We must go," Ewan said. "Now."

Connor looked around. Ewan knew he was memorizing the spot. "Aye," Connor said. "I will come back. I must be able to tell Carrie that I did right by them."

They ran silently through the woods, crouched low to the ground with their rifles ready to fire. The Hessians gave chase but they were clumsy and noisy. Ewan and Connor led them up a small incline where members of their company were waiting to fire upon their pursuers.

Ewan dove over the top of the incline and rolled onto his stomach with his rifle ready to fire. Da crawled up beside him. "I thought I'd lost ye back there," he said.

"Connor saw his wife's father go down. And her brother."

Connor stretched out opposite Da, and Ewan saw that his face was set and grim.

"He'll be wanting to go back," Da said.

"Aye," Connor answered. "I will. 'Tis my concern. Not yours."

"We'll come anyway," Da said.

"Aye," Ewan agreed. "We will." He took aim and fired and felt no satisfaction when he saw a green-coated soldier go down. Somewhere someone had lost a son, brother, father, lover.

When would it be over? When the last man standing said "enough"? Ewan rolled onto his back and reloaded as Da and Connor fired their weapons.

Chapter Twenty-five

"John." The voice came to him from a long tunnel. He recognized it as his father's, but it sounded so weak. So very far away. "Courage, John."

He should move. He wanted to but he couldn't. Nor could he see. Was it day? Was it night? Where was he? Why did he hurt? He wanted to blink, but his eyes would not move. He felt as if they were sealed shut. He tried to move his hand up to his face, but that simple motion was so painful that he could not stand it and merciful oblivion took him once more.

"John." The voice once again pierced the darkness that surrounded him. "I fear I will not last."

"Fa . . . Father?" Could his father hear his words? They bounced inside his head like the pounding of hooves but seemed weak to his ears.

He was wet. His face was soaked with rain. John managed to raise his hand and wipe the water from his face. He blinked and realized his eyes were sealed shut. He rubbed the rain into his eyelashes and managed to pry one open. He looked at his hand in the dim grayness that surrounded them. His fingers were covered with something dark. Blood? His head felt fragile, as if it might fall into a million pieces.

"John?"

"I'm here," he managed to croak out. He tried to look around, but everything was darkness and shadow and the rain pounded against his face. He knew there should be trees above him, but he could not see that far. He splayed his fingers in front of his eyes and saw the blur of his hand and nothing more. He moved his hand around his skull and winced. A memory flashed before him. A musket barrel coming at his face.

His stomach heaved. Bile rose in his throat. Luckily he'd had nothing to eat this morning. Was it the same day? Everything seemed so strange. Out of sequence. Confusing.

"Father?"

"I cannot move, John."

"The horse . . ." John swallowed. He could touch the animal. It lay across his lower body, pinning him to the ground. He felt strangely numb. He knew he was soaked, he could feel the water that puddled beneath him. He needed to move. He had to move. He had to help his father. He had to get to him.

John placed his hands against the animal and pushed, hoping beyond hope that he could slide his legs from beneath it. Instead, pain shot up his spine and into his head and the blackness overtook him once more.

When the voice came again, he could not answer. He felt his body floating. He floated higher and higher, until he hung among the treetops. John saw his body lying beneath the horse and saw his father sprawled just beyond and out of his reach. His father's body seemed contorted and unreal.

Broken.

"I'm dying." John realized it. Why else would his spirit leave his body unless he was dying? He knew his father was gone. There was nothing he could do to save him.

He looked down at his own bloodied body. He knew his skull was fractured, but there had to be more damage beneath the horse. Something that was killing him.

"So be it," he said. He looked heavenward, toward the rain

that pounded into his face. He was ready. There was nothing here to claim him. No one to miss him except a sister who was well cared for. No regrets . . . except one.

"Izzy."

Where was she now? Eight long years had passed. Was she still imprisoned? Surely not. Her crime was not so awful. Would he not have done the same to save his father? Would he have betrayed her?

He had no way of knowing. His life had never been that desperate. How could he judge her when he did not know what drove her?

"Forgive me, Izzy."

Where was he bound? Heaven, he hoped. Heaven with his father and his mother.

"I am ready."

He waited. He felt the pain in his head and the pain shooting up his spine and the numbness beneath. He was ready for his life to end. He was ready to end the pain on the inside, the pain in his heart, the pain in his mind, the pain from the memories of all the mistakes he had made since he'd met Izzy, since he'd left Izzy, since he'd come to the colonies and was too stubborn and too full of hatred to listen to anyone.

He heard a crashing noise, something coming, coming for him through the clouds and the fog.

A white horse, coming for him, at a full run. Sultan. How could it be? He reached his hand up, happy to see him. He was dead and Sultan was dead and the angels or the demons had sent his horse to take him to wherever it was he was destined to go.

"I am ready," he said to Sultan. "Take me to Izzy."

"I cannae believe it," Ewan said. "Did he say Izzy?" He looked at the face of the man who lay beneath the horse.

Connor's brother-in-law. "What did ye say his name is?" The man's hair was golden and his face, though heavily shadowed with the beginning of a beard still bore the sharp angles he remembered. He remembered the face because it reminded him of Donnie.

"I never said," Connor replied as he checked the wound on the man's head. "It is John Murray. Captain John Murray."

"He is Izzy's man, then," Da said. "And Elly's father."

"What?" Connor asked. He looked at the body of the horse stretched across Murray's lower body as if considering how to move it.

"It's a long story," Ewan said. "And this is not the time or the place." He sat back on his heels as the realization of the man's identify sank in.

They were disobeying orders by being here. After the retreat, General Greene had realized that the British army's losses were heavy. Unfortunately, the Americans were in no position to attack; their ammunition supply was seriously depleted. Campbell's men were to scout the British, harass them if possible, and report their movements back to Greene.

Connor had been impatient to find his wife's father and brother. So impatient that he'd struck out again as soon as he'd eaten. Ewan and Donald had gone with him. They'd shared too much in the past years to let him go it alone. If either his father by marriage or his brother by marriage survived, he would need help. The rain had started almost as soon as they left. With the weather working against them, and the necessity of circling around the British encampment, it had taken them a full twenty-four hours to find the place where the men had fallen. They stood now in the early morning rain among several bodies that the British patrols had yet to find. But none mattered to Connor except these two.

The father was gone, his body crushed when the horse fell

back on him. And the brother, Izzy's John, Ewan reminded himself, was not much better.

"We've got to get him to a surgeon," Connor said. "But first we must move this beast off him."

"Find a heavy branch," Da said. "Use it for leverage." Connor took off immediately to search while Da knelt down next to Murray.

"She'll want to know," Ewan said. But how would she feel about it? She'd never said anything about the man, one way or the other. Except on the ship, when she did not want him to know about Elly. But what about now?

"Aye," Da said. "She will. But it might be that she'd be glad of his dying."

"I donae think so," Ewan said. "I think she loved him."

"Still?"

Ewan took off his hat and wiped the rain from his face. "Did Ma ever stop loving you?" he asked.

Da looked at him. Ewan saw the pain there, the pain that his father always carried, the knowledge that he had chosen his king over his family.

"Nay. She did not," Da said. "And it killed her in the end."

"A broken heart is a broken heart." Ewan looked down at the pale and bloodied face. "He should know that it wasnae her doing. We should hae told him on the ship. There might not ever be another chance for them. He should know that he has a daughter. Elly should know her father. And Izzy . . ."

"Izzy should hae a chance to be happy," Da said. "I am not so sure that he is the one to make her so."

"At least she should have a choice in the matter," Ewan said. "We can gie her that much. We owe her that."

Connor returned, dragging a heavy branch behind him. Ewan helped him with it and they jammed it under the bloated carcass of the horse. They pulled up with muscles strained to the limit while Da pulled Murray's body from beneath the horse.

Murray groaned as Da hauled him out and a curse burst forth from Connor when they saw the thigh bone slicing through the cloth of his pants.

"I cannae believe he is still alive," Ewan said. The wound looked hideous and painful. They should have left him to die. They should have walked away. *I'd rather be dead . . . than this. . . .* Murray would lose his leg. Ewan had seen such amputations all too often during this war. Frequently the patient died anyway. Better to die a whole man than have bits of you chopped off on the surgeon's table.

"He is stubborn," Connor said. "Like his sister," he added with a slight smile.

"He will lose his leg," Da said.

"That is up to the surgeon," Connor replied as he knelt next to Murray. He tapped the man's jaw. "John," he said. "Wake up."

"We could take him to Izzy's doctor," Ewan said. "Dr. Keats."

Connor tapped his jaw again.

"I'm ready," Murray mumbled. Then he sighed as if all the air had left him. "Izzy."

"Gie him this," Da said, and handed Connor a pewter flask.

Connor opened it and jerked his head back as the smell reached him. "What is it?"

"Whiskey," Da said. Connor looked skeptical but lowered the flask to Murray's mouth and dribbled some in.

"Waking him might not be the best thing to do," Ewan offered. "Considering we hae to move him."

"I need to talk to him about his father," Connor said. He lifted Murray's head and poured more of the whiskey into his mouth. Murray moved his mouth and moaned a bit.

"John," Connor said. "Wake up. Carrie needs you to wake up," he added.

Murray's eyes blinked and then he opened them with a start. "Con . . . Connor?" he gasped.

"Aye. I saw you fall and came back for you."

"Father?"

"He is dead, John," Connor said, and bowed his head. "I am sorry."

Murray turned his head to where his father's body lay. Connor had closed the blank staring eyes when they'd arrived. Now the man looked at peace. But he'd died horribly.

Murray tried to move. "I must bury him." He groaned with the effort and grasped his head with his hand.

"I will," Connor said. "I will honor him. Ye have to trust me. Can ye do that?"

Ewan thought Murray would be sick. His body tensed as he saw pain flash across the other man's face. How much of that pain was Ewan's fault? Would Murray be here, fighting in this war, if he had not used him?

It was too late for regrets. Their separate roads had led each of them here to this meeting point. Connor was the catalyst. If not for him, Ewan could very well have met Murray in the battle and one of them could have killed the other. The important thing now was what happened next.

"We must get you to a doctor," Ewan said as he crouched on one knee next to Murray.

The man squeezed his hand against his forehead, as if to contain the pain that rocked his skull. "Do I know you?" he gasped.

"Aye," Da said. "Ye do."

"Who are you?"

"Ewan Ferguson. We only saw each other one time."

"Izzy? Izzy's brother?"

"Aye," Ewan said. Murray looked shocked.

"And her father," Da added.

"Izzy?"

"She's close," Ewan said.

Murray jerked as if to rise. He pushed against Connor, who still held him propped against his arm.

"Would you like to see her?" Ewan asked. Did he want to hear the answer?

Murray grimaced in pain and pitched forward. Connor caught him and eased him to the ground.

"Is he dead?" Ewan asked. Connor bent over Murray's chest.

"No. He is breathing."

Ewan let out a sigh of relief.

"He will never survive the trip to Hillsborough," Da said. "We'll be lucky if he survives the day."

"We must do what we can," Ewan said.

"You should take him to the British doctors," Connor said. "I can set his leg. Maybe that will keep them from lopping it off." His hands were efficient as he grabbed Murray's ankle and with one hand on the man's hip, pulled the leg out straight. They heard a pop as the bone settled back into place, leaving an ugly wound that covered half of the thigh. Connor quickly fashioned a splint from a branch and tied it on Murray's leg with strips of cloth from his pack. "They will not harm you if you carry a flag of truce and they see you are bringing one of their officers. Tell them about the others too," he added, his eyes going to the bodies scattered through the woods.

"What will you do?" Ewan asked as he looked doubtfully down at Murray.

"I must bury my wife's father," he said. "I owe him every-thing. It is the least I can do."

Da nodded in agreement. "Will ye be going for Izzy?" he asked.

"Aye," Ewan said. "As soon as we get him settled." They picked up Murray, Ewan taking his shoulders and Da holding his lower half. As they struggled forward with him, Ewan realized that Murray had not answered his question.

Did he want to see Izzy again? And more important, did Izzy wish to see Murray?

Chapter Twenty-six

Izzy slid from the bed and crept silently to the window so she would not wake Elly. Rain pounded against the roof, much like the pounding of hooves.

Was that why she dreamed of the horse? The snowy white horse? John had ridden a horse such as the one in her dreams. Sultan was his name. The same horse that Donnie rode to his death.

It would be morning soon, although it was difficult to tell with the gloom outside. Izzy perched on the sill and placed her cheek against the glass. Would she ever know a night when she did not dream of John? If only Elly did not remind her of him so. Yet she would not change a hair on Elly's precious head. If dreaming of her father every night was the price to pay for having Elly, then she would do so, gladly. Izzy looked at her daughter, who was nothing more than a little lump beneath the blankets with the orange kitten curled up at her back.

The dream troubled Izzy and she did not know why. She had never dreamed of the horse before, even when she'd watched John with the animal through the cracks in the wall on the ship that had carried them here. She'd watched him brush the horse's glossy coat and recalled the feel of his hands upon her body. She'd watched him comb Sultan's silky mane and recalled the touch of his fingers sliding through her hair. After all these years, she still could feel it if she closed her eyes, and especially if the sun was warm upon her face.

But not this morning. This morning the air was cold with

rain. Snow would be better. Snow would be pretty and cover the mud and gloom and despair that the war had brought. But it was not cold enough for snow.

She should have put on her robe. The cold penetrated the window and crept through the floor. Izzy pulled her feet up and stretched her gown over her legs until only her woolen-covered toes peeked out. Then she laid her head upon her knees and looked out the window.

There'd been news of a battle fought west of here. Were Da and Ewan in it? Had they survived? It had been so strange to have them show up after all these years as if no time had passed at all. But it had. Da, always handsome, always strong and glorious, now showed his years. Ewan had changed even more. With the gray sprinkled in his beard and around his temples, he seemed much more steady and mature than the last time she'd seen him. How much of the change was from the war and how much from knowing that because of his foolishness, Donnie was dead and they had all been transported?

There was no gray in her hair yet. But there were lines around her eyes and her hands were worn from years of hard work. And there were more years of hard work to come. Five more with Dr. Keats. Then she hoped to make a home somewhere with Da and Ewan if they were still alive. *Please, God, let them survive this war, and let Elly have a better life.* Was that too much to ask for?

A good life for her daughter. Better than the one she had. *Please, God, let her be blessed with love. Love that lasts a lifetime instead of one perfectly beautiful afternoon.*

Izzy heard the creak of the floorboards and turned to her door. It was locked, of course. She always made sure it was locked. Just as Keats always checked it to see if it was open.

She sensed his presence on the opposite side of the door and heard the handle move as he grasped it.

What would he do if one day he found the door unlocked? He would come in, she knew, but then what? Would he expect her to open her arms to him in gratitude, even with Elly lying beside her?

She was grateful. But . . . Izzy let out a sigh of relief when Keats moved on, as he always did, to his room. He must have passed out in his office again. What demons drove the man to drink as he did? It wasn't that he was a bad doctor. She had seen him do amazing things when he was sober. Things that she'd thought impossible. Things that saved peoples lives. He was caring also. A good man, except for the drinking.

Elly stirred beneath her blankets. Izzy watched as she stretched and yawned while the kitten did the same beside her. Elly sat up and blinked like an owl in the dim morning light. Then without a word she threw back the blankets and ran to Izzy, raising her arms so Izzy would pick her up.

"Why are you thitting all alone?" she asked. She climbed into Izzy's lap. The kitten jumped up on the sill and immediately swatted at the raindrops that trickled down the glass.

"I had a dream," Izzy replied as she tucked her daughter's golden head beneath her chin and wrapped her arms about her.

"Wath it a bad dream?"

Was it? Only because of the memories it brought. Only because of the confusion she felt. "No, sweet. I dreamed about a snowy white horse."

"Wath it pretty?"

Izzy smiled. "Yes. Except I think he would rather be called handsome or beautiful than pretty." She combed her fingers through Elly's hair as her daughter yawned against her breast.

"Ye can sleep some more if ye want. 'Tis a good day for sleeping." Izzy stood and put Elly on the bed.

"What about you, Mama?" Elly asked as she willingly climbed back beneath the blankets.

"Mama has to get to work."

That was all she had to look forward to. Work and worry. There was no need to dread it. It was her life. She would not complain, thanks to the joy she held in her arms.

"I best let the kitten out." Izzy picked up the kitten, which meowed in protest. "I am sure she will not like the rain."

"Don't leave her out in it." Elly yawned after her.

"I promise. I will look after her." Izzy dropped a kiss on Elly's forehead and quickly dressed before she went down to begin her day.

Izzy's day ended much the same as it began. The rain had not stopped and Dr. Keats was busy all day with patients who had minor complaints, mostly because of the damp and the cold. Life was better when there were patients. They kept Keats distracted and away from the bottle and he even managed to squeeze some time in for Elly's lessons in addition and subtraction. Despite the weather, Izzy felt content as she checked on Elly and saw her sitting at the table with her head bent over her slate. She chewed on her lip as she contemplated one of the problems Keats had written out for her. The kitten was beneath her chair, swatting at her feet as she swung them back and forth.

"I'm going down to the cellar to see what I can find for dinner," Izzy said.

"Yeth, Mama," Elly replied, caught up in her work.

It was getting harder and harder to find enough supplies to feed the small household. What she'd prepared for Da, Ewan, and their friend could have fed the three of them for half the week. There was no meat to be had anywhere. The two armies had cleaned everyone out and the food she'd put up last fall was quickly coming to an end.

Thank goodness for the chickens she'd managed to hide. At least there were eggs aplenty. Izzy shooed them through the small cellar window. The creatures were spoiled now and would rather be inside since she'd kept them hidden there during the occupations. She could not say that she blamed them. It was not a fit day out for man or beast or bird.

Izzy stood before the shelf and stared at the dwindling row of sacks and crocks that would have to get them through until the garden started producing and game became plentiful again. If she was lucky, maybe one of Keats's patients would pay with some type of food. What she wouldn't give for a nice ham.

She heard the creak of the stairs, but did not turn. It was most likely Elly, bored with her studies and the rainy day and needing a distraction.

"I wondered where you'd run off to," Keats said.

"I am trying to find something for dinner," she said quickly as she turned to face him. He stood between her and the stairs, a position that made her nervous.

"How about fish?" he said. "Thomas Brewster just came by with a nice trout."

"Wonderful," Izzy said as she sidled toward the steps. "I should get started."

Keats grabbed her arms. "Wait."

Izzy tried to pull away.

"Wait," he said again. He released her arms and Izzy folded them across her chest, her body taking a defensive position without her being conscious of it. Keats placed a finger under her chin and raised it. "Why do you always run from me, Izzy? I have never hurt you, have I?"

"No," Izzy replied truthfully. She was not sure if she liked the sober Keats any better than the drunken one. When he was drunk she could pretend he was not conscious of his actions. But this honest and sober Keats was more troubling. Because he expected honest answers. Answers he would not like.

"I have never hurt you and I've taken good care of you and Elly," he continued. She hated it when he used Elly as a weapon against her. "Yet you continually push me away. Why is that, Izzy?"

How many times had she answered this question in the past? How many more times would she have to answer?

I am so tired. . . .

Wouldn't it be easier just to give in? To give Keats what he wanted instead of fighting the battle day after day and year after year until she was too old, too ugly, too used up for him to care anymore?

Izzy looked at his bloodshot eyes, at his swollen nose, at his flabby paunch. It could be worse. He would not hurt her. He had saved her life, twice, and Elly's too.

Yet being with him would mean betraying John. She could not do that again. She'd done it once and would spend the rest of her life regretting it.

"I cannae give ye what ye want," she said. She could not stand to see the pain that would surely show once more in his eyes, so she looked down at the packed earth of the cellar. "Please donae ask me again."

Before, he'd always walked away, then spent the rest of the day drinking. That she could deal with. She knew there were reasons why he drank although he had never shared them with her, reasons that had nothing to do with her. Maybe he just used her rejection as an excuse to turn to the bottle.

Unfortunately, this time was different. He grabbed her arms again and pushed her against the shelf, pinning her body there with his. He covered her mouth with his lips. His breath was hot and sour and he pressed against her, moving his mouth to her neck when she turned away in an attempt to escape.

"Please," Izzy said. "Please stop." Tears came to her eyes as she fought him.

"I love you, Betsy," he said. "I've always loved you."

Izzy pushed as hard as she could. "My name isnae Betsy," she tried to say, but he covered her mouth again with his. She was going to be sick if he did not stop. There was nothing she could do. He was bigger than her, stronger. He owned her. She choked back a sob.

"Get your hands off her," a voice growled, and suddenly Izzy was free of Keats, who lay sprawled on the cellar floor.

"Ewan?" Izzy gasped. He stood before her with his face flushed a bright red and his eyes narrowed as he glared at Keats. He was also soaking wet from the rain. Elly stood behind Ewan on the steps with her fist rammed in her mouth as if she were afraid to speak. Izzy held out her arms and Elly jumped to her.

"What ith wrong with Papa Keath?" she sobbed. "Why did he hurt you?"

"Hush, sweet, he didnae hurt me." Izzy willed her body to stop shaking as she soothed her daughter.

"Who is this?" Keats demanded. "Your lover?"

"I am her brother, you gormless fool. I was on the ship." Ewan's jaw was clenched and his hands doubled into fists. A wicked-looking knife hung at his side, and there was a pistol stuck in his belt. Izzy knew he would not hesitate to use either if he thought it necessary. She stepped in between the two men as Keats clambered to his feet.

"Do ye nae remember me, man, or has the drink muddled your brain?" Ewan continued.

Elly buried her head under Izzy's chin and her body shook. Izzy knew she was terrified. She had to defuse the situation.

"Ewan," she said. "He didnae hurt me."

Ewan continued to glare over her shoulder at Keats, so Izzy put her hand on her brother's cheek to draw his attention away from the man.

"Why are you here?" she asked.

"I came to get you."

"Is it Da?" She swallowed back her fear, ready to face whatever news Ewan had for her. "Is he dead?"

"No." Ewan looked cautiously at Elly, who kept her head buried under Izzy's chin. " 'Tis your man."

Izzy felt the floor give way beneath her and Ewan grabbed her arms as she swayed with Elly in her arms. *John. He was dead?* All these years of wondering, all these years of wishing, all these years of wanting. And now he had died, still thinking she'd betrayed him.

"He was calling your name, Iz."

Calling her name? Why? Because he was dying? Because he was sorry? Because he still wanted her? Still loved her? *He was calling my name?*

"He's alive?" she managed to ask.

"Aye," Ewan said. "But bad off. We thought ye would want to know."

She nodded her head in agreement. "Aye . . . I want to know." She looked at Ewan. The brother who had always put their father above everything else stood before her, strong, dependable, and capable. "What should I do?"

"I will take ye to him. If ye want."

She nodded again. *Yes. I want. I want John. Still.*

"You aren't taking her anywhere," Keats said from behind her.

Ewan narrowed his eyes and his hand caressed the hilt of his knife. "Be thankful that I do not kill ye for laying hands upon my sister," he declared in a voice that made chills run down Izzy's spine.

"She is mine." Keats placed a possessive hand on Izzy's shoulder.

Elly shook in her arms. "Donae worry," Izzy murmured in her ear. How could she calm her daughter when she herself was terrified?

"As I said"—Ewan's voice was deadly—"I can kill ye now and no one would be the wiser."

"No, Ewan," Izzy said. Enough people had died for foolish reasons. "Despite what ye saw, he has treated me well."

"I am taking her," Ewan said. "And Elly. Ye will not touch her again."

"She owes me five more years," Keats protested.

Ewan pulled out his pistol.

Elly shrieked.

"Stop," Izzy said. "Please." She did the only thing she could think of to stop Ewan. She pushed Elly into his arms. He had no choice but to slide his pistol back into his belt as he sought to soothe his niece, who had dissolved into tears.

"There are many wounded?" Izzy asked Ewan.

"Aye. The Quakers are looking after them since both armies have left."

"Ye could go help them," Izzy said to Keats. "They will need doctors."

Keats looked at Izzy with pain-filled eyes. She could not help his pain, but she could give him an escape if he wanted it. "Yes," he said. "I will get my instruments." He pushed past Izzy and Ewan on his way out of the cellar.

Chapter Twenty-seven

He wasn't going to make it. Donald looked at the bruised, beaten, and sweaty face beneath the filthy bandage. John Murray would soon be a dead man, either from his broken skull or his crushed leg. He just wanted Murray to live long enough for Izzy to make her peace with the man.

Ewan had better return with her soon or the only peace she'd find would be standing over his grave. They'd carried Murray into the makeshift hospital camp under a flag of truce, and then Ewan had left, taking a few of the remaining English soldiers with him to show them where they'd found Murray so they could collect the dead and the wounded. The camp was nothing more than rows of cots with some canvases hung to shelter the patients from the rain. Surgery was inside a small cabin close to the meeting house, and wagons held the dead awaiting burial.

The Quakers at New Garden gave him a wide berth. Mostly because of the rifle that lay across his lap. They did not approve of violence of any kind. The doctors looked at Murray and offered to take his leg off, but Donald would not let them. When Murray faced his daughter, it would be as a whole man and nothing less. Donald had made his position clear and the doctors had left him alone after patching their patient up as best they could.

They all knew Murray would not live much longer. He was lucky to be alive at all. Since Ewan had left, the man had sunk into a delirium from his wounds and there was no rousing him. Occasionally he would speak as he tossed his head back and forth on the cot. Words like *father, mother, Carrie, duty, savages,* and *Izzy.* Donald could not help smiling when he heard his daughter's name. The man still thought on her.

Donald raised his hand when he saw Connor walking among the rows of wounded with two tin plates in his hands. He was covered with mud and soaking wet.

"How is he?" Connor asked as he handed a plate to Donald.

"Near death," Donald said. The plate contained a hearty stew and a chunk of bread, which he used to sop up the meal.

Connor flashed a quick grin. "Donae spare my feelings," he said. "Please."

"I ken he is your wife's brother," Donald said dryly. "But ye can tell by looking at him that he willnae last long." There was no need to mince words. Duncan's kinship with the man would not stop him from dying.

Connor dragged over a short stool, sat down, and dug into his plate. "I hae a friend," Connor said between bites, "Efrem, a Cherokee who is wise in the ways of healing. He might be able to help, but he is with Carrie, watching out for her."

"Ye buried her father?"

"I did," Connor said. "Beneath a dogwood. It will be blooming soon. Carrie would like it, I think."

"A better burial than he would have gotten from this lot," Donald said.

"He was a good man," Connor said. "I owed him much, including my life."

Donald nodded and gave Connor a few moments to collect himself.

"Tell me how ye know John," Connor said after a bit.

"I donae really," Donald said. "Except that Ewan used his horse to try to break me out of prison."

"What about your daughter?" Connor asked. "Ye said he was Elly's father?"

"Aye. Which makes her your niece."

"Then it is no wonder she resembles my wee Jilly."

Murray stirred feverishly on the cot. Connor pulled a kerchief from inside his shirt and stuck it out in the rain to gather water. He wiped Murray's face and let some of the water drizzle between his lips, but Donald sensed there was no love lost between the two men.

"Tell me the story," Connor said when Murray had settled.

"It seems the man here fancied me daughter," Donald began. He told Connor the tale, as he'd heard it from Ewan.

"Did your daughter know of the plan?" Connor asked when Donald was done.

"Nay, not according to Ewan. But Murray thought she did and that was enough to destroy Izzy."

"I would say it destroyed him too," Connor said. "He seemed to have an unnatural hatred for all things Scots when I met him. I can now see why. Carrie was puzzled also. She said the man I knew was not the brother she'd grown up with."

"My daughter seems to care for him. And he is my granddaughter's father. I know nothing of him beyond that. I cannae judge him as ye can."

"I am not sure I can judge him fairly," Connor said. "I spent more time thinking about how I wanted to kill him than anything else. From the first moment I met him we were at odds."

Donald settled his stool back against a post and crossed his legs in front of him. "Tell me," he said. "If by some miracle he survives this and I have dealings with him in the future, it would help me to know something about him."

Connor smiled. "He hated me from the start. That much was obvious. I think I understand his attitude now, but then I took it personally. Or course I had no love for anyone wearing the red coat at that time. For good reason."

"Most Highlanders can say that," Donald agreed. " 'Tis the way of things."

"Aye," Connor said. "What complicated everything was the fact that his sister caught my eye." He chuckled. "She nearly killed me come to think of it."

"From the looks of ye, I think ye survived," Donald said dryly.

"We nearly didnae," Connor said, suddenly serious. "We lost John's entire troop to an Indian attack up on the Blue Ridge."

"Shawnee?"

"Aye. I was to lead the British to Fort Savannah. It was back in '74. In May. They were just off the ship."

"As were we," Donald said.

"Carrie was determined to go with us. She wanted to see her father. And himself there was determined to march through the wilderness as if he were parading down the streets of London."

"Might as well have invited the Shawnee into your camp," Donald observed.

"I missed the signs," Connor admitted. "And he was not inclined to listen to my opinion on much. . . ."

"Because ye are Scottish."

"Aye," Connor agreed. He leaned forward and placed his forearms on his knees. "The fog was heavy that morning. My friend, Efrem, had come into camp the night before. We rose early and went down to the stream to bathe . . . and talk. Efrem was trying to convince me to cut John's throat and take off with Carrie." Connor tilted his head toward Murray. "As soon as I heard the first shot, I knew they'd come. My first and only thought was for Carrie. It turned out she was further down the stream, having a bath as well."

Donald knew what Connor was seeing in his mind's eye. He had seen it enough in his own lifetime. Different battles, different fields of valor, but always the same deadly results. "Ye did the only thing ye could do. Ye took the girl and ran."

"We did," Connor admitted. He smiled again. "Then she made us go back for him."

Murray chose that moment to stir. He said something unintelligible. Was he reliving the battle as Connor spoke of it? Connor wiped the man's brow again.

Murray settled again and Connor continued with his story. "We were too far into the wilderness to go back, so we traveled on to Fort Savannah. He blamed me for all of it." He stretched a long leg out and nudged a moccasin-clad toe at a rock that poked up through the damp grass. "He nearly drowned when we crossed the New River. Efrem and I jumped in to save him and still he wanted to kill me. Carrie nearly died too, from a copperhead bite. And all the while, we had the Shawnee on our heels. . . ." His voice trailed off and he scratched at the coppery beard that grew beneath his chin. "When we got to the fort, he threw me in a cell and ordered me lashed. He was full of hatred. And pride. I think he went mad a bit after his men were killed. He blamed me for it, ye ken."

"Pride can make men do strange things," Donald said.

"Aye," Connor agreed. "I think it nearly killed him when Carrie fell in love with me."

"He felt the lash himself," Donald continued. "Along with Ewan. The English made Izzy watch. We didnae see her again until we were put upon the ship. He was on it too. With his horse and his sister. And Elly was born on the voyage over. Izzy wouldnae let us tell him about her. He never even knew she was on board."

"Izzy . . ." Murray said as he tossed his head once again.

Connor wiped Murray's forehead again. "Luckily for me his father came and stopped my lashing. As I said, I owed the man much." He looked over at Murray, whose lips moved in silent communication with the demons who haunted his dreams. "I won his father's respect; I won his sister's love. I even wound up taking that beautiful white horse of his. I'm keeping Sultan safe on my homestead, where he's being put to good use as a stud."

"That might give him some comfort in spite of his hatred," Donald admitted. "We watched him on the ship with the beast. He treated him like a prince." Donald rose and stretched his arms over his head. The weather and Connor's story, combined with the intensity of the battle, had finally caught up with him. "I donae think Izzy ever got over him," he added. "She is much like her mother in that way."

"Once a woman gives her heart," Connor said, "it is hard to convince her to take it back."

Donald smiled as a vision of Ellyn filled his mind. "Aye," he agreed. "And since Izzy has given her heart to this man, I willnae have him die without knowing that she did not betray him. He will look her in the eye and ask her forgiveness."

I have not done much for her . . . my daughter . . . but this I will be sure of.

"I hope he lives that long," Connor said.

Izzy tucked the blanket in securely around the sleeping Elly. The road was practically impassible because of the rain, and the horse was uncooperative since Ewan had forced it from its dry stall and hitched it to the small buggy. He led it now, through the night, with Keats sitting on the seat before her, and Elly squeezed in beside her. Fortunately, the cover sheltered them from the worst of the weather. Elly lay with her head in Izzy's lap and Izzy kept a steady arm around her to prevent her from tumbling out. The kitten was curled up behind Elly's neck. They could not leave it behind. There was no one to care for it and Izzy knew the trip would be hard enough for Elly. The kitten would be a good distraction for her daughter.

She wondered how Ewan could keep going. From what she could tell, he had not slept in two to three days.

Izzy knew he was afraid they would not make it before John died.

Was she doing the right thing? Should she be making this trip? What if she went all the way to New Garden and John refused to see her? What made her think that he would forgive her now, after all these years?

He was calling your name. . . .

What about Elly? She had told her daughter only that they were going to help the wounded soldiers. The trip was enough of a distraction to keep Elly from wondering about the altercation between Keats and Ewan.

Thank God Ewan had showed up when he did. Could she have stopped Keats?

What was she going to do for the next five years? How could she keep fighting Keats? Ewan pretended she could just leave with him and Da. But she couldn't, not when she owed Keats her life as well as Elly's.

Worrying never solved anything, and it certainly didn't change anything. Izzy settled back against the corner and closed her eyes. She should sleep so she would be ready for whatever tomorrow might bring, but she knew it would be impossible. Opening her eyes, she focused on the lantern swaying on the hook by Keats.

How could Ewan see where they were going? The rain fell steadily and the mud sucked at the wheels. She was foolish to set out in this weather in the middle of the night. Foolish to think she would make it in time.

He was calling your name. . . .

John. Calling her name. After all these years.

Whatever would she tell Elly?

Chapter Twenty-eight

The rain, fortunately, was over. Unfortunately, the sun might not improve things much. Izzy pulled her cloak up over her nose to block the smell of dampness, illness, and death. There were too many people gathered in too small an area, and the smell assailed her nostrils as soon as they arrived in the small cluster of homes that was New Garden.

I never should hae brought Elly here.

Ewan held his niece in his arms. Deep shadows creased his face in the light of early morning. He seemed so exhausted. Izzy wondered how he could even stand, much less carry Elly, who looked around at everything with wide eyes.

Ewan's dark eyes darted around the scene as if he were getting his bearings; then he started off through the quickly erected shelters that covered rows of makeshift beds and pallets. Izzy and Keats followed behind his ground-eating stride. Izzy carried a basket with the necessities along with sheets to make bandages and some food. The kitten was stuffed in the basket too and occasionally meowed its distress. Keats carried his instrument bag and blankets.

It seemed strange to watch Ewan walk boldly through an English camp. At least Izzy thought it was an English camp since the Union Jack fluttered on a post in front of one of the cabins. But she saw soldiers from both sides, along with militia and the Quakers, all working side by side to care for the wounded.

At least this much is as it should be.

"You won't see any prisoners," Ewan said. "They are released now after the battles since neither army has a way to provide for them."

"What do the prisoners do then?" Izzy asked.

"Most from our side go home and tend to their families and crops. Some find their units and fight again."

"No wonder the war has dragged out so long," Izzy said.

Elly was taking everything in, her eyes wide. Izzy knew she'd have hundreds of questions for her later.

I never should have brought her. But what else could she do? There was no place to leave her. And what would she tell Elly when and if they found John? *Please God, let him be alive.*

Izzy stopped suddenly.

"Mama?" Elly said. Izzy could not look at her. She did not want Elly to see her tears.

"What is it?" Ewan turned to see what the trouble was. Keats stopped also. He reached out a hand, but then took it back as if afraid of what Ewan would do if he touched her.

Izzy looked at Ewan, who placed a sheltering hand over Elly's cheek. "I just realized," she said, "that I hae been waiting for this moment for so long . . ." Her mouth felt dry, so she tried to swallow and found that she could not.

"Iz?" Ewan sounded worried.

"I donae know what to do."

Ewan took her arm. Izzy felt his strength flow into her. Had he always been this strong and steady or had she just dismissed his good qualities in her anger at Da and Ewan's worship of him. "Ye will know when ye get there," he said simply, and took off again, pulling Izzy with him. And then before she could think, she saw Da and Connor Duncan beside him. They were beneath a canvas with five cots or so, each one holding an injured man. A Quaker woman sat by a post watching the patients. Izzy did not need to be told that these men had been left to die. She could tell by their injuries that there was no hope for them.

Da and Connor stood when they saw Ewan. Both men had their faces set in hard lines and both looked exhausted. As one they stepped apart and between them, on a cot, lay a man with golden hair and a bloodied face wrapped in a bandage.

"John." ·

"Come, wee gel." Da took Elly from Ewan. "Let us go see what we can find to eat."

Elly reached for the kitten, which purred loudly as Izzy settled it in Elly's hands. "Who ith that man?" Izzy heard Elly ask as Da walked away with her. Izzy did not hear his answer as she sank to her knees on the soaked earth next to the cot. Ewan grabbed a blanket and rolled himself up in it under the cot, where the earth seemed drier.

Izzy touched John's cheek. It was cold and clammy beneath the stubble of blond beard. Even though the line of his jaw was the same and his nose still straight and proud beneath finely arched brows, he was not at all as she remembered him. In her memories he was golden and warm, not this pale image of death that lay before her. He stirred, a bit, just enough to let her know that he still lived, but barely.

"What are his injuries?" Keats asked Connor.

Izzy pulled a handkerchief from her pocket and wiped away the moisture that covered John's face. The bandage about his head needed changing. The entire right side of his face was swollen and darkened with bruises.

"A busted head and a busted leg," Connor replied. He pulled back the blanket that covered John's body and undid the bandages that covered a horrible wound on his thigh. "I set it and hae kept it clean as best I could under the circumstances."

Izzy dug into her basket. She needed clean bandages.

Keats peered at the wound. "There are undoubtedly bone splinters in there," he said. "It might be best to take the leg off before infection sets in."

"*No!*" Izzy said, louder than she expected. "No," she said again when the two men looked at her. She turned back to John. He could not lose his leg. His pride was too great. It would kill him.

"Ye know he is my brother by marriage," Connor announced.

"Aye," Izzy said. "Ewan mentioned it."

"I willnae let anyone touch him with a bone saw," Connor said, and his blue eyes left Izzy's face to fix on Keats. "We hae kept it clean. There are plants and such that will help him heal. I hae a Cherokee friend who is wise in such things."

"Then let your Cherokee care for him," Keats retorted. "He is more likely to die from the wound to the head than to his leg anyway."

"Ye will not care for him?" Izzy asked, aghast. "Ye havenae even looked at him."

"I will not waste my time on someone who surely will die. Nor will I let you waste your time watching him die." He moved to grab her arm and she jerked it away.

"Why did ye come, then?" Izzy felt her anger rise.

Ewan sat up with a heavy sigh.

"Because your brother wanted to kill me," Keats said. "And I thought your man would be dead by now. He will be soon enough."

"You sound as if you want him to die," Izzy accused.

"I do. Then maybe you'll stop longing for him and realize what you have right in front of you."

"A drunk who frightens me night after night?"

"If you would show me some affection, I would not have

to drink." Keats's voice rose. "I saved your life and your daughter's and you still turn me away."

"Is that why you bought me? Because you wanted me?"

"No," Keats protested. "I bought you because . . ." His voice trailed off. The look in his eyes was desperate, but Izzy could not tell if it was because he wanted a drink or really did have feelings for her.

"I donae love ye," Izzy said. "I am grateful for what ye have done, but I cannae lie with a man without love."

"Nor would a true man want you without it," Connor said firmly as Ewan stood.

"Look at what love got you," Keats sneered. "Where was your love when you were dying in the cargo hold?" He swelled up, righteous with anger. "I remember him." He pointed at John, who lay lifeless on the cot. "He was on the ship with his sister—"

"My wife," Connor reminded him.

"He cared more for his horse than he did for you." Keats's tone was accusing.

"He didnae know I was onboard, nor did he know I carried his child. What happened between John and me is between us and no one else." Izzy stood her ground. "Nor is it my fault that ye drink yourself into a stupor night after night. That started as soon as ye bought me. Ye even warned me about it."

"Was that the reason ye left England?" Ewan asked. Despite his exhaustion, he stood like an oak beside her.

The doctor looked as if his head would burst. "Bah!" Keats grabbed his bag and stormed away.

"That will make it easier for ye to leave him," Ewan said matter-of-factly as they watched Keats fade into the crowd. Once more, he grabbed his blanket and rolled up beneath the cot.

Izzy looked at Connor; Keats was already forgotten. "What can we do for John?"

"If Efrem was here, he would know. But he isn't, so we shall have to make do."

"Can ye remember anything?" Izzy asked.

"Dogwood tea for fevers," Connor said. "There is also feverwort, but it is hard to find this time of year." He scratched his head as if that would help him think.

"Boneset in a poultice," Ewan grunted. "If ye can find it. Pack the leg in clay."

"That's right," Connor said. "Efrem set your arm when ye broke it."

"I didnae break it." Ewan yawned. " 'Twas a Shawnee with a tomahawk that broke it for me."

"What good is the clay? Willnae clay dirty the wound?" Izzy looked at the gaping hole in John's leg.

"I donae know, I just know that Efrem does it," Connor said. "Can ye stitch the gash?"

"I can," Izzy said. "I've done it many times."

"We can put on the poultice, cover it with a bandage, then pack it in clay," Connor said.

"Ye have to change the poultice every day," Ewan added.

"Of course it all depends upon me finding the plants," Connor said. He picked up his rifle and pack. "Dogwood willnae be a problem," he added as he left.

"Izzy," Ewan said, "do ye need my help?"

"Nay," she replied as she looked down at John. "I can do it. Get some sleep." She looked at John's leg. The wound was red and raw and Keats had mentioned bone splinters. Should they come out? To her mind it seemed best if they did. She looked once more at John's face. He had not moved except for the one time when she'd touched his cheek. It would be better if he did not move now.

Connor had stressed the importance of cleanliness. It was not something Keats worried about in his practice, but to Izzy it made sense. She needed hot water.

"I am going to get some hot water," she said.

"I will go," Ewan offered, and once more threw the blanket aside and staggered to his feet.

"I can go," Izzy protested.

Ewan grabbed her shoulders. "I cannae have you wandering about this camp by yourself," he said with a sleepy grin. "Remember what happened last time ye went off with a soldier?"

"Your lack of sleep has addled your brain," Izzy said.

"It isnae the first time," Ewan said as he walked away.

"Ewan!" Izzy called out. "Make sure it's boiling!" He raised his hand in agreement and moved on.

A pan sat on the ground with water in it. "At least I can clean you up a bit," Izzy said as she wrung out the linen handkerchief that lay in it. In the corner was a bit of embroidery and she read the initials. *JCD.*

"I imagine your sister made this," Izzy said as she wiped John's face. She removed the bandage from his forehead to reveal a deep gash. She probed at it with her fingers and John's face contorted in pain as he moved his head away from her hand. "Ye can feel that," she said. "Ye know someone is here, someone is touching you." She wiped the handkerchief across his forehead, down his cheeks, under his chin. "Do ye know that it is me?" she asked. "Do ye even remember me?"

John tossed his head back and forth. He shifted restlessly on the cot.

"I cannae forget, ye see," Izzy continued. "I see your face every day."

He jerked and Izzy remembered how he'd jerked when the whip struck his back, after his energy and will to fight were gone. Eventually, he'd collapsed against the post, barely conscious.

She had jerked too.

"Ye have a daughter, John Murray," she said. "I named her Ellyn, after my mother. I never knew your mother's name. Ye never mentioned it." Izzy looked down at her lap. Her cheeks flushed as she admitted, "Ye see, I remember every word ye ever said to me."

She wrung the cloth out in the pan once more and looked around for Ewan, but there was no sign of him. "I hope he has not fallen asleep by a nice warm fire, waiting for your water to boil."

When she turned back, eyes as blue as the summer sky looked up at her from a swollen face.

"John?" she said.

The eyes flared in what could only be astonishment. "Izzy?" He whispered her name, and then his long dark lashes fluttered and his eyes closed once more.

"Ye said ye would never think on me again," Izzy said with some satisfaction. "I believe I hae just proven ye wrong."

Chapter Twenty-nine

Donald had set up a little camp apart from the hospital tents, beneath a stand of pines. He had no idea where Keats had gotten off to, but he appropriated the horse and buggy before one of the English officers decided to confiscate it or, worse, eat the horse.

Connor had managed to scare up a rabbit while he was out hunting for plants, and Donald put together a stew with the meat and what he found in Izzy's basket.

He cut pine boughs to cushion the buggy floor for Elly, who napped there with the wee kitty. Ewan lay still as death on more pine boughs, wrapped in a blanket beside the fire. He had helped Donald to throw up a three-sided shelter of canvas beneath the trees and then they'd moved Murray into it. After that Izzy and Connor had applied balms, sewn wounds, and wrapped bandages, and now Izzy dribbled some sort of tea into Murray's mouth and rubbed his Adam's apple in the hope that he would swallow it. Donald did not care what they did as long as they got the result they all desired.

"He'd better live long enough to know the truth of the matter," Donald told the stew that had just begun to bubble in the pot.

"As long as you're asking the pot for help," Connor said, "ask if he can live long enough to see his sister also." He dropped an armful of pine boughs onto the ground. "I know it would make her very happy."

Donald grunted in response.

"I'd like to live that long myself," Connor added as he

yawned. The man was practically staggering. They had all gone nonstop since the morning of the battle. They needed rest or they would soon be dead.

"Get some sleep," Donald said. "And keep an ear out for Elly. I've got business to attend to." He took his pistol from his belt and his knife from his sheath. He would not use weapons in this battle, just words. Izzy would not want more violence. He hoped his words would be enough.

He felt even more tired than the younger men. He had never expected to live this long, much less to survive as many battles as he'd fought. His years had finally caught up with him. He was tired of the fight. He'd fought in two wars and lived off the land in the wilds of Scotland and the wilds of this new land. He longed for peace. He needed time to sit and reflect.

He had failed Ellyn and failed Donnie. On the other hand, Ewan was a good man, one who would find his own happiness. He was a man Donald was proud to call son. With a little luck, Ewan would find a wife and carry on the Ferguson name in this new country.

But Isabel still needed his help. He needed to find Keats. He needed to make things right for his daughter and for his granddaughter.

While out hunting plants and rabbits, Connor had learned that the English army had finally left Guildford Courthouse, where most of the fighting had taken place. Some one hundred and twenty wounded men from both sides were now in the care of the Quakers and scattered among the homes of New Garden. Cornwallis had sent word to Greene about the American wounded, and Greene had responded by sending men and supplies. Surgeons from both armies now moved among the wounded. Donald hoped to find Keats somewhere among them.

The British had claimed the victory, but Donald knew it was at a high cost. He also knew from watching the burial details that the British had suffered far more losses than the Americans, especially among their officers. The British army was in no shape to fight again, which was a good thing as far as Donald was concerned. He'd been fighting the British his entire life. He only had one battle left in him and it was for Izzy.

The Quaker church seemed to be the center of activity in the area, so Donald stopped there and asked after Keats.

After much discussion, someone remembered that the English doctor from Hillsborough was in the surgery, which was a one-room cabin off to the east. Donald recognized it by the washtub outside that held an assortment of limbs. Apparently Keats was putting his bone saw to good use. A scream of pain greeted Donald as he opened the door, and the smell of burning flesh assaulted his nostrils.

"There but for the grace of God go I," Donald said. The patient was mercifully unconscious, or dead, it was hard to tell which with all the blood and gore about. His leg, cut right below the knee, lay on the floor. Two men carried the man out on a stretcher, followed by a woman who looked as if she had survived hell. He and the doctor were alone.

Keats dropped the cauterizing iron back into the fire and wiped the blood from his hands on a towel before he looked at Donald.

"Has he died yet?" he asked.

"Nay," Donald said. "Nor will he, not if we hae anything to say about it."

"Stubborness won't save his life."

"Apparently ye don't know my daughter as well as ye think ye do."

"I have spent the past seven years caring for your daughter." Keats sounded as if it had been a burden.

"Lusting after her is more like it," Donald snapped.

"I saved her!" Keats snapped back.

"For yourself," Donald replied.

"I have never touched her," Keats protested.

Donald knew that he lied. Ewan had told him of how he'd found Keats and Izzy. "Never?" He arched an eyebrow. "Ewan said ye attacked her."

Keats opened his mouth to speak, then changed his mind and snapped it shut.

"Did Izzy ever tell you why she was transported?" Donald asked.

"No." Keats leaned against the operating table and crossed his arms. "What was her crime?"

"She committed no crime," Donald said.

Keats shrugged. "That is what everyone says."

"She is innocent," Donald continued. "Her only crime was trusting too much. She trusted her brothers and she trusted Murray. All of them wronged her."

"What does that have to do with me?" Keats asked. "I've done her no wrong. I saved her life and Elly's too."

"If ye really care for her, ye will release her . . . and help her."

"You mean help Murray, the man who abandoned her and his child."

"He did not know about Elly," Donald said. "But now he has a chance to learn the truth. We heard him speak Izzy's name when we found him. He still cares for her and ye know she still cares for him. He might not live, but Izzy cannae go on with her life until he forgives her. Izzy deserves some happiness in her life."

"You want me to release her from her bond?" Keats asked.

"Aye. And help her with Murray."

"When and if Murray dies," Keats said, "what will happen to Izzy?"

"We will take her with us to the Blue Ridge."

"It is dangerous there. The Shawnee . . ."

"When this war is over, more settlers will homestead there and the Indians will go further west. I have fought the Shawnee. They will stay west of the Ohio. There is no more danger from them now."

"What if Murray lives and still despises her?" Keats asked. "What if he hurts her?"

Donald was surprised. He had misjudged the doctor. He'd thought him lecherous and a drunk. Did he honestly care for Izzy?

"What if ye let Izzy decide, then?" he suggested. "On her own. With no obligation to you?"

"I have lost one woman," Keats said, his face tragic with his honesty, "and it nearly killed me."

"Is that why ye drink?" Donald asked.

"I made some mistakes." Keats covered his face with his hand. "Horrible mistakes. And it cost my Betsy her life. I do not want to have Izzy go through the same thing."

Donald nodded his head in agreement. If anyone knew how Keats felt, it was he. Hadn't his own mistakes led to Ellyn's eventual death? Yet Ellyn had chosen him. She knew the consequences when he went to war. She supported him. Still, she should not have died alone. But he was not a man who shared his inner thoughts much and certainly not with strangers.

"Izzy will never be truly yours," Donald said, "unless it is her choice."

Keats looked at Donald for a moment as if willing him to take back what he'd said. Then he let out a long sigh. "You are right," he said. "I will release her. The rest is up to her."

"What about Murray?"

Keats looked at the leg that lay where it had dropped from the surgery. "There is nothing I can do for him. He is in God's hands now. And Izzy's."

Chapter Thirty

He drifted. Somewhere between wakefulness and asleep, life and death. Drifting was peace, or so he hoped. He desperately wanted peace. Peace and forgetfulness. Death.

He saw faces. He saw his father, his mother, and Rory. All dead. He saw the faces of the men in his command who'd died in that ambush on the Blue Ridge. All dead. He saw the faces of the men he'd served with the past seven years. All dead. He moved among them silently, gratefully, easily, without the anguish, strife, and remorse that were always with him.

He hoped that the longer he drifted, the more easily the peace would come. He searched for peace, or so he told himself as he floated through the fog and clouds. Eventually he realized that the peace he searched for had a face and a name.

"Izzy."

He was sure he even saw her, once, among the faces of the dead. But the things she told him, when he saw her . . .

"You have a daughter."

Drifting was no longer easy. Drifting was confusing. Drifting was a struggle. He did not want to drift. He wanted answers. He needed answers. He needed to know if he was alive or dead. *Please, God, let it be dead.*

The fog and the clouds turned into quicksand. It grabbed him and pulled him and sucked at him. He had to fight it. He had to find the answers. If only he could escape. If only he could find his way back to where the answers were. But he did not know where the answers were. He'd been searching for them for such a long, long time.

"Are you my father?"

The voice was strange, one he'd never heard before. Whose was it? He had to know. He had to see.

"*Open your eyes.*" His eyelids weighed a ton and his head felt fragile, almost as if it would shatter into a million pieces. And there was more pain, and thirst and a hollow ache inside that meant he had not eaten in days.

"*I am alive.*"

He had to be; why else would he feel such pain? He opened his lids and found a pair of bright blue eyes in a tiny heart-shaped face staring down at him.

"Carrie?" he asked, his voice hoarse.

It could not be Carrie. Carrie was a grown woman now. Married, with children of her own. Or so he thought. It was hard to think, hard to concentrate, hard to know what was real and what was part of the drifting and dreams.

Who was this child?

"Mama!" the child called out, and backed away. She carried a kitten in her arms, or at least he thought it was a kitten. As she moved back, his vision became blurry. He could not see much past her, except light and the impression of movement. Above his head were shadows, without definition. Moving his head made him sick to his stomach.

A battle . . . His mind tried to sort things out. It was hard. *I am John Murray. Captain John Murray. I am in the colonies, fighting a war . . . with my father . . .*

"Father?"

"*Are you my father?*"

The memory flooded back. His father going down, with the horse, the battle in the woods.

Someone screamed his name. Someone told him his father was dead. Duncan? If Duncan was here, could Carrie be close?

"Where am I?"

"Ye are safe, John Murray," a voice said.

He blinked. He needed to see who it was because he could not believe his ears. A sweet face appeared before him with a cloud of red-blonde hair and deep brown eyes that saw into his soul. She had come to torture him. To condemn him as he had condemned her.

He closed his eyes. He could not stand to see the sorrow in those brown depths.

"John?" Izzy said. She touched his shoulder and he sighed deeply as he fell back into his dreams.

"Did he wake?" Ewan asked. The smell of the stew cooking had awakened him and he was eating hungrily by the fire. Connor was still asleep. It amazed Izzy that the men seemed to be able to sleep whenever they lay down. She felt as if she had not slept in days.

"He wath," Elly said from the end of the cot. "He looked at me. He called me Carrie."

"He's gone back to sleep now," Izzy said.

"Mama," Elly asked, "who ith Carrie?"

"His sister," Izzy said.

"Did you know her too?"

"Nay," Izzy said. "We never met."

It was getting harder and harder to avoid Elly's questions about the man they all anxiously cared for. She'd told her daughter his name, and that he was Connor's brother by marriage.

It did not help that Elly was a bright child. Nor did it help that Izzy had always told Elly her father was a soldier. She'd never dreamed John would come back into her life. Nor did she want Elly to learn John was her father and then have him die before her eyes.

She refused to consider the possibility that John might reject Elly the way he had rejected her. After all his talk about being the son of a bastard.

"Ewan," she said. "Can ye watch him? I need some time."

"Is everything all right?" He looked up, instantly ready to come to her aid.

"Aye . . . I just need to think," she said with a reassuring smile. She took Elly's hand and guided her to Ewan. "Ye must stay away from Captain Murray for now," she told her daughter. "Stay with your uncle for a bit."

"Yeth, Mama," Elly said as Ewan put her on his knee and fixed her a plate of stew.

"Izzy," Ewan called out after her. "Whatever answer you find, I will stand beside you."

Izzy turned back and nodded. She was too overwhelmed to speak. Too many years she had spent resenting Ewan and fighting Ewan because of his devotion to their father, not realizing that he was not only devoted to their father, but to the whole family. He had always loved her. She was the one who'd pushed him away and kept him out.

She saw the meeting house up ahead and hurried toward it. She had not been in a house of worship since she went to church with John and Edina, but it would be a good place to reflect. Out of habit she pulled her kerchief over her head and quickly genuflected when she entered. About halfway down toward the front she settled onto a bench and bent her head in prayer.

Her sins were many. That was obvious. How to learn from her sins, however, was not so clear. She was about to repeat the same mistake that had landed her in trouble in the first place.

Lying.

She'd never told John her real name, or that her father was an outlaw, because she was afraid the truth would change his opinion of her.

When he'd awakened earlier, she'd considered not telling him that Elly was his daughter for the same reason. She wanted John to forgive her for her lies and she wanted him to love her as he'd said he did that day on the hillside overlooking the sea. Would more secrets and lies be the means to that end?

There would be no more lies. John had never lied to her. He had been honest about everything. It was her lies that had made him think she had betrayed him. It was her lies that had kept him from believing her in the end.

"For I have sinned and fallen short of the glory of God," Izzy murmured. She knew it was scripture, knew she had heard it many times, but she had no idea where to find it in the Bible. She just knew the verse applied to her.

"No more lies, no more secrets . . . and please, God, if you could heal John and give him a chance to love Elly, that will be enough for me. Because I have caused both of them grief and loss."

Izzy crossed herself again as she finished her prayer. She wished she could light a candle for her mother and Donnie and John's father. There were not enough candles in the world for all the souls who'd left it. The best she could do was pray and be truthful with John and hope for the best.

But first he had to survive. He had to live. Izzy left the meeting house, resolved to do whatever it took.

The last time she had felt this hopeful was the day John took her to the fair. Almost eight years ago. It was true that confession was good for the soul. She even had a smile on her face when Da called out her name, but it quickly faded when she saw Keats was with him.

"We need to talk," he said when they caught up to her.

"I must get back to John."

"Listen to what the man has to say, daughter." Da took her arm to stop her. "Your man will keep for a while longer." He smiled and placed a kiss on her forehead. Izzy was stunned. She could not recall his ever doing that. Not even when he had poured his heart out to her that day they were sold.

"Your father has made me see the error of my ways," Keats said.

"He has?" Izzy asked. "In what way?"

"In all these years, I have never thought about what you wanted, Izzy. Only what I wanted. I expected you to come to me out of gratitude. I forgot that there has to be more than that between a man and a woman."

"Would you believe me if I told ye I hae just realized the same thing?"

"I am giving you your freedom, Izzy," Keats said. "You are no longer bonded to me."

Izzy felt as slack-jawed as she had when Da kissed her. She had always believed in the power of prayer, but this was almost too much. Any other time she would think that Keats was drunk, but now his eyes were clear and his stance strong.

"I am giving you the freedom to choose," he continued. "I know you will choose Murray, but if something happens and he does not survive or if for some reason he turns you away, then I hope you will consider me as an alternative. I would take good care of you."

"I know that," Izzy said. "And you hae been so good to Elly."

Keats took her hand and for the first time ever, Izzy did not pull away. "I was married," he said. "It came rather late in my life. Late for my Betsy too. But not so late that she could not have children." Tears welled up in his eyes and he wiped them away with his free hand. "She died giving birth and I could not help her. I did everything I could and it was not enough. I drank myself into a stupor and remained inebriated for years. Then I lost another patient because I was drunk. I left

England before charges could be brought against me. When I met you, and you and Elly both survived the birth, I thought it was a sign that I could have a second chance. I never considered what you wanted, Izzy. I hope you can find it in your heart to forgive me."

How could she refuse when it was the very thing she wanted for herself? "I do," she said. "I am so sorry I cannae give ye what ye want."

"That is not your problem, Izzy, it is mine," Keats said. "It is enough that you forgive me." He raised her hand to his mouth and kissed it in a gentlemanly fashion. "I also hoped to spare you the pain of watching your man die."

"I willnae think that way," Izzy said. "I must have faith that he will live and know Elly is his daughter."

"It might be that Elly is just what he needs to find the will to live," Keats said. "Knowing that you are here for him and Elly . . ." He smiled sheepishly. "It might be just what the doctor ordered."

"Aye," Izzy agreed. "It could be."

"Would you mind if I looked in on him? I would like to see how this Indian medicine works."

"I would appreciate that very much," Izzy said.

Chapter Thirty-one

Was he dreaming or was it real? He was fairly certain he was not dreaming. His body ached too much for it to be a dream. He was in an actual bed covered with soft sheets and above him he recognized the steep pitch of a roof. How long had it been since he'd slept in an actual bed under a roof? And whose roof was above him now?

John tried hard to remember as he stared up at the whitewashed ceiling. It was all so strange and confusing. Snatches of memory swirled around in his mind like eddies in a river. Ghosts danced in the corners, but his head hurt too much too concentrate. Even the light pouring through the window hurt his eyes. It was hard to focus, harder to see. Everything in the distance was distorted and he blinked several times, trying to clear his vision.

He felt clean and only pleasant smells greeted his deep inhalation. A quick but painful movement of his hand to his jaw let him know that he was freshly shaven. Someone had taken great pains to see that he was cared for, but he had no idea who it could be. Carrie perhaps? There was some vague memory of Duncan in his mind. Had he seen the man or was it part of the fever? How long had he been ill?

Every inch of his body ached. Especially his right leg. He needed some sort of relief and made a move to shift it from the stack of pillows that it rested upon. He was rewarded with a pain so intense that he saw lights dancing behind his tightly clenched eyes.

John let out a gasp as he fought against the tide of pain. He did not want to lose consciousness again. He felt that if he slid back into the fog, he would never find his way out of it. Finally the pain subsided and he relaxed against the bed, panting and covered with sweat. Instead of moving again he decided to try to take inventory of his body. He could see, not well, but he had his sight and was grateful for that. When he thought about it for a moment, he realized he could hear birds singing through the open window, and off in the distance he heard the clip-clop of a horse and wagon. Was he in a town of some kind?

A gentle breeze floated over the bed where he lay, bringing the scent of freshly turned earth. The air was cool against his bare chest and arms. Beneath the sheet he realized he was nude and still whole. His could move both hands, and he saw the points of both his feet sticking up beneath the sheets.

He breathed a sigh of relief. His biggest fear since becoming a soldier was losing one of his limbs.

Voices drifted to him. The low rumble of men and the lighter, higher voice of a woman. John closed his eyes in concentration, trying to make out the words and the voices, but they were too low and too distant.

He heard a creak, followed by a strange, soft thump-thump. He felt a movement next to him and opened his eyes to find a fluffy orange kitten sitting next to him, grooming itself with its tiny pink tongue.

"Who are you?" he asked in a raspy voice.

Mew? the kitten replied. It jumped on his chest, stuck its nose in his face and proceeded to sniff him curiously.

"I quite agree," John said in a whisper. His throat was too sore and too swollen to speak louder. His lips were dry and parched and he felt them crack as he moved them to speak. He lifted his hand and stroked the kitten, who apparently decided he was no threat; a rumbling purr came from its tiny chest.

Exhausted by that small effort, yet spurred on by thirst, he managed to turn his head and found a pewter pitcher and mug sitting on a tall table beside his bed. Water beaded the outside, so he knew that it was cold.

He'd never wanted anything in his life as much as he wanted a drink of whatever was inside the pitcher, but it seemed a million miles away. If petting the kitten was exhausting, then reaching for the table would kill him.

He heard another creak and turned his head to see a small form standing in the doorway. It moved closer and he blinked his eyes to help focus. He realized it was a small girl with bright blue eyes and long golden hair that tumbled over her shoulders. Dressed in a simple homespun shift, she smiled timidly and cautiously reached for the kitten.

John modestly pulled the sheet over his bare chest and then opened his mouth to speak, but nothing came out. He cleared his throat and was able to say in a rather weak voice, "Could I trouble you for a drink please?"

"Yeth, sir," she said, and John saw that her front teeth were missing. She quickly moved to the table and poured water into the mug. John managed to roll on his side as she handed him the mug. He had to stop a moment to fight the nausea that swept over his body at that small movement. Finally, he was able to take a drink. He had to fight the urge to down it all in steady gulp, taking slow sips instead.

The girl smiled again when he handed her the empty mug and he saw that her front teeth were coming in. Two white tips just showed through the pink of her gums.

"More?" she asked.

John nodded gratefully. "What is your name, young miss?"

he asked in a somewhat stronger voice as she handed him the refilled mug.

"Ellyn Ferguthon, thir," she said, and dropped a small curtsey.

"Ferguson?"

"Yeth, thir."

John studied the girl. Judging by her small size, she could not be more than four or five. And her last name was Ferguson. Was it a coincidence?

"What is your mother's name, Miss Ellyn?" John managed to croak out.

"Ithobel."

Images flooded his mind. Izzy's face hovering over him, wiping his brow, soothing his hurt and his fears. She had cared for him. It had not been a dream or a hallucination brought on by fever. She was alive and here in the colonies. How did she come here? When? Why? And she had a daughter. Did that mean that she also had a husband?

"Isobel Ferguson?" he asked as he tried to wrap his mind around the possibilities.

She nodded and her golden curls bounced around her shoulders.

"What is your father's name?" he asked, dreading the answer.

She shrugged her shoulders. "My father is a tholdier," she said. "He ith fighting in the war, juth like you and my uncle and my grandpa." The kitten chose that moment to bounce off the bed and skitter into the hall. Like a flash, the child went after it and disappeared from sight.

John fell back against his pillow. All these years he'd wondered and worried. And Izzy was fine. With her father and brother . . . and with a bastard child. It must not have taken her long to find another man. Two, maybe three years? Or maybe it had just taken her that long to have a child. Or maybe there were more. It was nearly eight years since he'd seen her. There could be four or five more running about. Some older, some younger . . . some . . .

"You have a daughter. . . ." Where had he heard those words? But this child could not be his. She was too young. What a foolish flight of fancy. A result of his fever, nothing more.

John squeezed his eyes shut. An overwhelming sadness washed over him. Was it because he was weak and hurt that he felt once again the pain of the betrayal? All these years he'd wasted, longing for a lost love. Why was he so shocked to know Izzy had not done the same? Why should she? He'd been a pawn in her game, nothing more. Something she'd used, just like his horse and his coat, to get what she wanted. Why would she even give him a second thought?

Why was he here? Why was he still alive? Why, when he wanted nothing more than to be dead?

Why?

"The man is awake," Elly announced as she bounded down the stairs and into the kitchen. Everyone stopped, as if frozen in place. Da and Keats were at the table and Ewan held an armful of firewood over the box beside the stove. Only Connor moved, placing the rifle he was cleaning upon the mantel, safely out of Elly's reach.

Izzy swallowed back the fear that rose in her throat. "Did he say anything?" she asked. She had not told Elly John was her father. She wanted to protect her from hurt in case John turned away. Izzy's heart wrenched at the thought. How could any father turn away from such a beautiful child? But pride had a way of making men do strange and horrible things. Connor had told them of the massacre on the Blue

Ridge. He had told them other things about John Murray, things that Izzy knew were a result of his experience in Aberdeen.

"He athed me for water and wanted to know my name," Elly announced.

The kitten ran to the door and meowed. Without even thinking about what she was doing, Izzy opened the door to let it out. "You go on out as well, Elly," she said. "It's too fine a day to be inside." Elly ran out. "Don't wander off," Izzy reminded her.

"I won't, Mama," Elly called back as she ran into the bright sunshine of early April.

The men all looked at her as she turned back after shutting the door. Ewan dropped his load in the box and sat down at the table. She'd been waiting for this moment since they'd carried John home from New Garden. Keats was not sure if he'd ever awaken from the blow to his head, but once they realized that his leg was not infected and was on the mend, Ewan and Connor added a wide plank to the back of the buggy so they could carry John back to Hillsborough and better care.

The men stayed on, even though it was dangerous for them. Anyone suspected of having dealings with "traitors" was in danger of being burned out or even hanged. But Connor felt he could not leave until he knew one way or another if John would live. Da and Ewan stayed because they would not go until Izzy would go with them. They slept in the cellar, stayed inside during the day, and only went outside at night so that no would notice their presence. They were good at blending in; they'd been doing it for years.

Even though she knew Da and Ewan were waiting for her, Izzy stayed because she had much to say to John. For two weeks she had cared for his wounds, bathed him, shaved him, dribbled water and broth down his throat, praying all the while that he would stir and open his eyes. Now that the time had come . . .

"You go first," she said to Connor. "He will need to know about his father."

"I have waited this long," Connor said calmly. "A few more moments will not change anything."

Izzy smoothed back the hair that escaped from beneath her cap. She wiped her hands on her apron, took it off, and replaced it with a clean one that hung on the hook by the door. She straightened the linen scarf that covered her shoulders.

"You look fine, Iz," Ewan said.

"A vision," Da agreed, and Keats nodded beside him.

Izzy gave Da a look. "Have you both gone daft?" She felt the heat rise to her face and placed the palms of her hands on her cheeks. "I look old and tired and worn," she said. "And I am suddenly terrified."

Connor shook his head and smiled. "Why is it that women think we are only concerned with their beauty?" He crossed the room and took Izzy's hands in his. He was so tall compared to her slight build that she had to tilt her head back to look into his vivid blue eyes. "Do ye not know that we men quake at the mere sight of ye? That we are more moved by your strength and grace than a pretty face? That the mere thought of ye leaving us is enough to make us quake in our boots and fall to the ground in despair?"

Izzy smiled at his foolishness as he chucked a finger under her chin. "Ye are beautiful and strong and I suspect ye are stubborn too. Ye would have to be to put up with the likes of my brother by marriage. I also suspect ye see things in him that he keeps buried deep inside because of his pride."

Izzy choked back a sob. No one but John had ever spoken to her so sweetly.

"Donae let his pride stop ye from having your say," Connor continued. "Nor your own pride," he added. "Ye have wasted enough time on the past. Now is the moment to think on your future. Ye can make it a better one, with or without him."

Izzy nodded. Connor was right. Her future and Elly's should not depend upon the whims of John Murray or George Keats or any other man. It was up to her. She could and would have a life on her own. She had survived this long without John. She could continue. The important thing was to tell him the truth about everything that had happened, including the fact that Elly was his daughter.

"Thank ye, sir," she said to Connor. "I think your Carrie is a lucky woman."

"I tell her so often." Connor grinned. "And plan to remind her of it when I return home."

"The sooner the better as far as I'm concerned," Da said. "Ye are about to eat Keats out of house and home."

Connor laughed. "We'd all be starving without me and ye know it. I haven't seen ye out on a hunt lately."

Izzy gathered her skirts and went up the stairs with the sound of their bantering in her ears.

Chapter Thirty-two

She was coming. He heard her footsteps on the stairs and in the hallway. There was no place to run, no place to hide unless he wanted to pretend to be asleep.

His pride would not let him do that. He had never been a coward and he would not begin now. Nor would he meet her again after all these years lying flat on his back. He needed to move. He pushed against the mattress and tried to raise himself so he could sit against the headboard. He was as weak as the kitten, weaker, if the truth be told. John closed his eyes as pain and exhaustion rolled over him. How could such a simple thing be so hard?

He closed his eyes, gritted his teeth, and pushed up with all his might, causing a pain to shoot up his hip and through his spine.

"Let me help you."

He felt her presence next to him and opened his eyes to see a flash of blue from her dress as she plumped his pillows and stuffed them behind his back. He settled back against them and sighed in relief as the pain in his leg subsided. She kept her head bent and turned away, straightening the blankets and sheet for him. He was suddenly conscious of his nudity and felt as exposed as if there were nothing covering him. His fingers twisted in the edge of his sheet and he pulled it up to his armpits and pinned it to his chest with his arms.

John cleared his throat. "Thank you, Is . . . Miss . . . Ferguson."

She straightened and looked down at him with her deep

brown eyes, and he felt the same familiar pull that had struck him every time he'd ever looked at her.

Why?

Her nose still had a smattering of freckles and there were lines about her eyes and a slight crease on either side of her mouth. The hair that spilled out from beneath her cap was the same reddish gold and held the same springy curls. He wanted nothing more than to touch the curl that dangled behind her ear. It was a foolish whim.

"I had thought we were beyond such formality, John," she said in her Highland lilt. "Do ye still hate me so much that ye cannae say my name?" She tilted her head to look at him. "Or hae ye just forgotten it?"

John cleared his throat again. He felt like a schoolboy beneath her steady gaze, and he had the strangest feeling that she might be teasing him. "I do not know how I came to be here, but I am exceedingly grateful for your care . . . Isobel."

She shook her head. "Always proper," she said, just as she had that day back in Aberdeen. The day she tricked him into leaving his coat behind so her brother could impersonate him.

"I have found that it is best to be proper when one is uncomfortable with one's surroundings." Damn his voice for making him sound so weak.

"Ye are an ass, John Murray."

John blinked. He felt as if she had slapped him. He'd been tricked, whipped, and shamed because of her. He'd been practically banished from his homeland. And she had the gall to call him an ass?

"I humbly beg your pardon," he said. It was the proper thing to say.

Izzy sighed and sat down on the bed. Right next to him. She placed her hand on top of his bandaged leg and he clenched his thigh, even though it pained him, because he could feel her touch through the blanket, through the sheet, and through the splints and bandages that covered it.

Damn her for still being able to affect him that way. Even after all these years.

"I am sorry," she said. She caught her lip in her teeth and looked at him. "Ye have been through a difficult time." She paused for a moment, got up, and wrapped her arms around herself as if she was cold. She walked over to the window and looked out. "Do ye remember anything of what has happened to ye?"

"Recently or in the past eight years?"

"Connor said ye were prideful," she replied tartly.

"Connor? Is Carrie . . ." he began hopefully.

"She is at their home. Connor is here. He's been waiting to see if ye'd make it."

"My father did not." He remembered that much. He recalled the battle. He knew his father was dead. He'd seen him in his feverish dreams.

"I am sorry for your loss," she said, and bowed her head for a moment before crossing herself. "Connor buried him. He is waiting to talk, when ye are able."

"Thank you," he said. He studied her as she once more looked out the window. There must be a reason why she'd come up first.

"Is there anything ye need now?" A tender smile touched her face. "Elly said ye were thirsty."

"Your daughter?"

"Aye." She looked at him expectantly. What did she want of him?

"She's a beautiful child," John offered.

Izzy smiled again and shook her head.

She is so pretty when she smiles. . . .

"Connor says she looks like her auntie."

Why was she telling him this? Why was she rubbing his face in the fact that she had found someone else? She was doing well, if this room was an indication of the house she lived in. Her sentence, whatever it was, must have been light. But why shouldn't it be? It wasn't as if she'd actually *done* anything wrong.

"Her father's sister?" John asked wearily.

"Aye."

"I take it he is a colonial soldier. . . ."

Izzy crossed her arms and looked at him, and once again he felt like a naughty schoolboy.

"Ye are daft and an ass," she said angrily as she placed her hands on her hips. "Can ye not tell that she is yours?"

"Do not try to trick me again." Did she think him such a fool? He felt anger flare up. "She cannot be mine. She is too young."

"She just turned seven. She is small for her age," Izzy proclaimed. "She was born on the ship. The same ship that carried ye and your sister over here."

John felt his jaw drop as he looked incredulously at Izzy. "That was you?" He shook his head. "Why didn't you tell me?" *Why didn't you tell me that you were so close? That you were alive and carrying my child?*

She looked away, as if she was finally ashamed of her actions. "Ye hated me for what ye thought I had done." Her voice dropped and he had to strain to hear her. "Ye still do. . . . I could not stand to see the pain in your eyes once more, nor could I stand to see ye turn away from your daughter."

John scrubbed his hand across his face. It was too much. There were too many questions, too much hurt, too much mystery, and too many years between them. "Why are you telling me this?"

"Because there were lies between us and I do not want any more."

"I never lied to you, Izzy."

She looked at the floor and he saw the life drain out of her as she sighed. "I ken." She raised her eyes and he saw the pain hidden in the darkness of their depths. "I should hae told ye who my father was. I should hae told ye my real name. I ken that Ewan had a plan, but I didnae ken what it was. I knew only that he had a seal and wanted me to write a letter. When ye said it was the wine that made us—"

John put up a hand to stop her. "Please," he said. "Go. Just go. . . ." He did not want to hear any more. He did not want to relive that day. He did not want to know that he had a daughter and that he had missed the first seven years of her life. He just wanted it all to be over.

Izzy nodded and with her knuckles wiped away a tear that slid down her cheek. She stopped at the end of his bed. "If ye cannae accept her and love her, then please do not tell her that ye are her father," she said. "I willnae have her find her father and then lose him. I would not wish that pain on anyone."

She looked at him with those damn eyes of hers and he wanted to stop her. To say that it did not matter what had happened before. He could not make the words come. Instead, he nodded to show his agreement concerning her daughter. Their daughter.

"I will send Connor up," she said.

"No," John said. He did not have the strength or the courage to face Connor Duncan at the moment. "I'm tired. I need to sleep."

"Aye," she agreed. "Ye probably do."

John closed his eyes as she left. Once again he could not stand to see the pain on her face.

★ ★ ★

When he opened them again he found Connor Duncan sitting in a chair beside his bed. He had to blink a few times to get his eyes into focus, but there was no mistaking Duncan's large build and long red hair. He had not changed much since the last time John had seen him.

"Carrie?" John's voice was still hoarse and weak from disuse. Why did he always feel so inadequate whenever Connor Duncan was around?

"She is well last I saw her," Connor said. "She will be happy to know that ye are the same."

"Am I?" John asked.

"Ye have made it this far. Ye will live."

John looked stonily past Connor to the window. Dusk must be close; the light outside had dimmed.

"Ye donae need to be so happy about it," Connor said dryly. He leaned forward and struck a match, holding the candle beside the bed. "I am anxious to be home and tell her the news. Can I tell her that ye are well?" he asked.

"Tell her that I am alive," John said. "It is more than I expected."

"Ye donae sound greatful for it," Connor said.

"I was not given a choice in the matter."

Connor shrugged his shoulders. "I believe ye were outvoted if your choice was death."

"What of my father?" John asked. "I know that he died but . . ."

"I buried him beneath a dogwood tree," Connor said. He took a packet tied with string from inside his shirt. "He had these papers in his boot and coat." He handed them to John. "There is money inside too. I will leave it to ye to divide with Carrie."

John nodded.

"I will take ye to his grave when ye are able. If ye want."

"Thank you," John said. "I suppose the papers are her letters."

"She missed both ye and your father," Connor said. "It was her greatest wish that he see his grandchildren. If not for the war . . ." He leaned forward with his hands clasped before him and his elbows propped on his knees. "I hae found recently that we hae more in common than I originally thought."

"Father told me," John said. "About your father being at Culloden, just as he was."

"Did he tell ye of my mother?"

"No," John admitted.

"My mother was raped and hanged in front of me when I was ten years old. By English soldiers who then sold me into bondage."

Ten years old. When he was ten years old he was in school, playing games with his friends. "You were not without your reasons for hating me," John said.

"I had a severe dislike for any man wearing a red coat," Connor said. "I still do," he added with a grin. "But 'tis a good thing I did not expand my hatred to all the English, or I would hae missed out on the best thing in my life."

"Carrie."

"Aye. Carrie." Connor sat back as if he was more relaxed now. Perhaps he thought the most difficult part of the conversation was over. "I donae ken what it is like to have a brother or sister," he said, "as ye are the closest I will come to it. Efrem is like a brother to me. It was his ways that healed your leg," he added. "Therefore I donae ken what it is like to hae to choose between family and friend." He looked pointedly at John. "But there is one thing I do ken. Hate is a cold and lonely companion to spend your years with. I ken that Carrie would not want that future for you, her only brother. Her only kin."

"You want me to forgive Izzy and her family for what they did to me?" John asked. "Why should I?"

Connor shrugged. "Why not forgie them?" He stood. "I will tell Carrie ye are recovering and that ye hope to visit. Ye can pick up your horse when ye come," he added with a sly grin. "He has earned his keep." He left the room on silent feet.

John looked out the window. It was full night now. And he was so very tired.

The last thing he saw before he closed his eyes was his red coat, cleaned, brushed, and hanging from a peg on the wall.

Chapter Thirty-three

Was there ever a more stubborn man on this earth than John Murray? Da could certainly compete, and Ewan, even Keats. But John Murray and his pride . . .

For the past two weeks he had clung to his pride as if it were the only thing keeping him alive. Connor had talked to him and left for his home on the Blue Ridge. Da and Ewan felt it best if they did not antagonize him, so they kept to the shadows, only slipping out at night to hunt or fish to keep the larder supplied. The garden was weeks away from producing. Izzy looked out the window at the rows of tender green shoots that were finally poking their heads through the dark earth after the long hard winter. Da and Ewan were asleep now, in the cellar after a night of hunting. A wild turkey lay on the table, cleaned and ready for the oven, and Izzy washed her hands after rubbing the skin with dried herbs.

Keats had been surprised and impressed by John's recovery once the fever broke. He still had some difficulty seeing things that were far away, but his vision seemed to be improving every day. Swelling in the brain, Keats called it. Once it was gone, he should be fine.

His leg was coming along nicely also. Izzy heard him thumping around upstairs with the crutch Ewan had fashioned for him. John did not know it had come from Ewan. Izzy just placed it by the bed one morning when she carried up his breakfast.

Another few weeks and he should be ready to go.

"And then what?" Izzy said to the window as she wiped

her hands on a towel. Where would he go? Back to the war? According to the news that Da and Ewan gleaned, the war was not going well for the English. They controlled the ports of Wilmington and Charleston, but the country beyond that belonged to the Americans. There were reports that Cornwallis was moving his troops north to the tidewater area of Virginia. "Good riddance," Izzy said.

Would John follow them?

He'd not said a word to her about his plans, about Elly, about anything. He responded to her care with quiet politeness, nothing more. She carried his meals, she kept him clean, and Keats helped him with his baser needs. She had no idea what he was thinking, none at all. Just a few weeks earlier she had been so sure about everything. Now she was just resolved. No matter what John did, with or without him, she would make a home and a life for Elly and her family. Life was too precious and time to short to waste it on worry and regret.

Elly bounced into the kitchen with the kitten chasing after her hem.

"Where have you been, lamb?" Izzy asked.

"Talking to John," she replied. Elly rose on her toes and peeped into the pot that sat on the stove top. Her teeth had grown in, which changed her appearance. She looked older now, more her age, even though she was still so very small.

"Ye are calling him John?" Izzy raised an eyebrown in question.

"Yes, Mama," Elly replied. "He asked me to. He said since we were friends now, I should call him John."

Izzy spread jam on a piece of bread and set it before Elly as she slid into a chair.

"He said ye are friends?" Izzy asked. That seemed to be a step in the right direction. "What do you and your friend talk about when you go visit him in his room?"

"We talk about my lessons and my kitty and what you are doing." Elly bit into her bread. "Today we talked about Papa Keats."

"And what did you tell him about Papa Keats?"

"I told him that he likes to drink whiskey and that Uncle Ewan tried to hit him when Papa Keats hugged you in the cellar."

Izzy clapped her hand over her mouth at Elly's matter-of-fact tone. Elly continued as she ate. "He asked me if you liked it when Papa Keats hugged you and I said no because you lock your door every night so Papa Keats won't come in and wake us up."

"Father, forgie me," Izzy whispered, and crossed herself. She should have realized that Elly was old enough to figure out what was going on. At least Keats had left her alone since their return. And he had freed her from her bondage, even given her the papers to prove it. Having Da and Ewan around was a good influence on the man, who was at the moment out attending to his patients. Since her family was camped in the cellar, Keats felt it prudent to see his patients in their homes rather than in his office. He made his rounds every day with the horse and buggy. Izzy had a feeling he was stopping at the tavern a good bit too, but as long as he left her alone . . .

The water on the stove came to a boil and Izzy poured it into a shallow bucket. She added more well water to it until it steamed and a touch of her fingers satisfied her that it would not burn.

"Work on your lessons," she told Elly as she slipped a bar of soap and the razor in her apron pocket. "And keep the kitty away from the bird." She threw a towel and washcloth over her shoulder and took the steaming bucket with her up the stairs to John's room.

He stood before the window with his back to her. The late

morning sun poured through the glass, surrounding him with a golden haze. The light made his nightshirt transparent and showed the long line of his arms and legs. His hips were narrow and his belly lean from his long years in the army. But his arms were sure and strong as he rested them solidly against the eaves on either side of the dormer window. She knew he placed them there for support as he eased his weight down upon the broken leg. Izzy watched as the muscles that were tensed across his shoulders relaxed and he leaned forward a bit, as if testing the leg. He raised his heel from the floor and peered down at his foot. His hair fell forward around his face and the sun lit it with bright gold.

"Like an angel," Izzy whispered, echoing Cook's words from long ago. Before she'd met John, she never would have thought a man could be beautiful, but John truly was.

How did one repent after hurting an angel? Was there enough penance in the world? She did not deserve him, yet she still wanted him with a burning desperation.

He turned his head and smiled slightly, as if he were proud of what he had accomplished. He turned in place with a bit of a limp and faced her.

"I have heard from Elly that we are to have roasted turkey for dinner," he said. The look on his face seemed odd to Izzy. Almost wistful in a way that confused her. "And it seems that it is time for my bath," he added with a look at the bucket.

Heat flared up from her chest to her face. Izzy set the bucket down next to the small stool and turned away, toward the bedside table. There was nothing there to catch her attention, so she turned back to look at him. "It is hot," she said, hoping he would think it was the water that caused her to flush instead of the sudden rush of yearning clenching her insides. She had bathed him many times since his injury. She'd seen him naked and helpless in the past few weeks. This was the first time in a long while that she'd seen him so vital . . . so alive.

John limped over to the wooden stool and sat down. He looked at Izzy expectantly from beneath his hair. Was it the sunlight that made his eyes seem so very blue today? Or maybe it was just his mood? "No crutch," he said with a smile when she did not speak.

"Very good," she said. "I suspect you will be climbing the stairs next."

"That is my hope. I have to admit I am tired of looking at these four walls." He scrubbed his hands back through his hair. "I also have to admit that I long to soak in a tub."

"As do I," Izzy said. "I am afraid that Dr. Keats doesn't have the same longing. He considers tubs to be a waste of space. I have to make do by standing in the laundry tub and pouring water over myself." She blushed again. John, always proper, must be mortifed at her openness about her bathing habits. She busied herself by placing the razor and soap on the table.

John ran a hand over the bristle on his jaw. "I would think someone as tiny as you could scrunch up in the tub."

"You either underestimate my size or overestimate the size of the tub, sir," Izzy said. "Either way, it is an uncomfortable fit. Elly manages quite nicely, however."

"She is small like her mother," John admitted. "She also reminds me greatly of Carrie."

"Is that why you spend so much time talking with her?" Izzy asked. "Because you miss your sister?"

"I thought you wanted me to get to know my . . . daughter," he said with a catch in his voice. He cleared his throat. "Isn't that why you brought me here?"

"It was one reason," Izzy admitted. She remembered her

promise to God and herself. No more lies between her and John. Unfortunately, he did not want to hear the truth; he'd made that much obvious the day he woke.

John nodded, seemingly content with her answer. He also seemed content to let her minister to him, even though he was quite capable now of doing it himself.

She wouldn't complain. He would be gone soon and she was determined to enjoy every minute that he was here. Especially when he was being so pleasant. She dropped the washcloth in the bucket, wrung it out, and placed it over his jaw while he leaned back obligingly. Izzy lathered the soap across his skin after the washcloth cooled and gently dragged the razor over his beard.

He kept his eyes open and upon her face, unnerving her. His hair was in the way, so she pushed it back and he raised his eyebrows; he did not dare speak lest she nick him with the blade. The wound on his head had scabbed over and was fading away. There would be a scar, but his hair would hide most of it.

"I will fetch the pitcher so I can rinse." She looked intently as his face to check for stray whiskers as she wiped it with the towel. John kept his eyes upon her, then suddenly he reached a finger up and tugged on a curl that had fallen from her cap.

"When did you start wearing caps?" he asked. "I like how your hair used to look."

"A mess?" Izzy asked. A warm glow filled her at his touch. At his gentle teasing. He was teasing her, wasn't he? It was so hard to tell with John. "It seems like I never had time to even brush it when I worked for Master Rabin."

"I remember that day we went to church," he said. "It was beautiful. And it smelled wonderful."

His eyes were honest and open, as they had been in Aberdeen.

"Are ye talking about before or after I fell in the river?" There was no need for her to get excited. They were just talking. Still, talking was a nice change from his usual polite silence.

A smile flitted across his face. "I am eternally grateful it was you that fell in and not Edina. I fear I never would have gotten her back to the surface."

Izzy laughed. He *was* teasing. "Ye have a way with words."

"So do you," he said, serious once more. "I know you can read too. Who taught you?"

"My mother," Izzy said, happy to answer him. They had never really talked much about her family because of her secrets. "She was well born, educated, and then she met Da. She taught Ewan and me and then I taught Donnie."

"While your father was hiding in the mountains?"

"Aye," Izzy said. "We didnae hae much. She did the best she could." She rinsed the washcloth in the bucket again and held it in her hand with the soap wrapped inside.

John looked at her as if he were studying her very carefully. Then he undid the tie at his neck and slid his nightshirt down over his arms until it pooled at his waist, revealing the lean muscles across his chest and shoulders. They flexed as he looped the sleeves so it would stay in place. His build was long and lean. He did not have Ewan's thick muscles, created by years of hard work. Instead he had an elegant grace that disguised his strength. Every move he made seemed sure and strong. Izzy well recalled how it felt when he'd carried her from the water. It was if she weighed nothing.

He was different, somehow, today. Before he had ignored her as he accepted her care. He was always exceedingly polite. But today his eyes were upon her. His gaze unnerved her, so much so that she silently offered him the washcloth.

"You do it," he said. His eyes stayed upon her face. "Please?"

Izzy nodded and moved behind him. He leaned forward

with a sigh, placed his elbows upon his knees, and dropped his chin to his chest.

She had seen his back many times during his recovery. But not like this. Not bent and exposed to her as it was the day he was whipped. The only difference was that this day the sun shone clearly upon his flesh, highlighting every ridge of each scar that crossed back and forth, the evidence of each stroke he'd received. Strokes that should have fallen on her.

Tears filled her eyes and trickled down her cheeks as she wiped the soapy cloth across his back, over each scar. There were five more than Ewan had. All because of her. She rinsed out the cloth and cleaned the soap from his back.

Who had tended his wounds? How many days had he spent lying on his stomach cursing her for the pain she'd caused his body, his heart, and his spirit.

A sob was wrenched from her and she dropped the wash-cloth in the bucket. She gathered up her skirts to run, but John grabbed her arm and spun her around to face him as he slowly and painfully rose to his feet.

"Izzy," he said in a hushed whisper. He placed a finger under her chin and raised it so that she had to look into his sky blue eyes.

"I am sorry," she sobbed.

"Don't," he said. He smoothed a tear away with his thumb. He gave her a half smile, crooked and fleeting. He stroked his hand down her cheek and picked up the curl that dangled behind her ear. He pulled on it, gently, then slid his hand up her head and pushed her cap off. She felt it slide down her back and then there was a tiny puff of air as it hit the floor.

Izzy trembled. She felt her entire body shaking and she could not stop it. John studied her face as if trying to look inside her soul. He smiled again as he twisted his hand in her hair and pressed her face toward his.

His lips touched hers tentatively, as if he were afraid. Izzy let out a small gasp of surprise and when her lips parted he took it as a sign of encouragement. He turned his head slightly and moved his mouth over hers. His tongue touched her lips and Izzy's arms circled his neck. She leaned into the strength of his arms.

John enclosed her in his embrace and she twisted her hand into his hair. His hands roamed her back and she felt the heat of his bare chest as he pushed her against his body. Closer. Tighter. But not close enough. Not tight enough.

Izzy felt all her fear, all her frustration, all her loneliness melt away. This was as it should be. Except she wanted more. John did too. His hands moved down her back to her thighs. He gripped them, squeezed them, never breaking the kiss. Izzy pressed herself against him and realized that he was totally and thoroughly naked. She felt his desire pressing against her and her body responded in kind. She wanted to be closer. She wanted more. The only way to get it was to take her clothes off. She shifted away. Suddenly he staggered and the nightshirt, which had slid down his hips when he stood up, tripped him and he toppled.

"Your leg!" Izzy exclaimed as he pitched forward and she fell back. They crashed onto the bed with John on top of her. When his forehead crashed into hers, Izzy felt all her breath leave her body and John grunted in pain. She saw stars and knew he did too. He rolled onto his back, moaned. When Izzy opened her eyes, she saw his face contorted in pain.

She finally was able to suck in a breath. She scrambled to her knees. "Please forgie me, I forgot about your leg."

John pushed her away as he pulled the sheet over his nakedness. "It's fine," he gasped. "Really." He pulled the sheet tighter, but it only accentuated what he was trying to hide.

He wanted her. Badly. He pushed her away. "Just go," he said. "I need to rest."

Izzy moved off the bed. She put her hands to her face and pushed back her hair. Her cap lay on the floor and she picked it up. The movement made her dizzy and she swayed for a moment.

"Izzy?" he said.

She turned to face him.

"Are you hurt?" he asked.

She touched a finger to her forehead. "Nay," she said. "Just a wee bit sore."

As John pulled the sheet up under his chin and closed his eyes, she realized she had lied to him again. She hurt so much she wanted to die.

Chapter Thirty-four

Why was it every time he followed his heart instead of his head, he wound up in trouble? He was no better than Keats. The man had owned Izzy and forced himself on her. He knew that much from talking with Elly.

Had Izzy been with Keats? Did he really want to know? Did he want to know for a fact that because of his pride and stubbornness he'd sentenced Izzy and his own daughter to a life of servitude with a man who had abused her?

What would he have done if he'd known Izzy was carrying his babe? Could he have walked away from Izzy and his own infant daughter?

You were so filled with hate you would have taken Elly and left Izzy to her fate.

John sat on the edge of the bed. He was lucky he'd fallen when he did. Lucky for Izzy that he did not take her on the spot.

She was willing. . . . She would not have denied him. But was it because of guilt? Or did she truly want him? She'd said there would be no more secrets between them. If only he'd listened to her in Aberdeen, let her explain . . .

"Damn," John groaned. He looked at the pail of water, now cold, and his nightshirt. The smell of roasted turkey drifted up the stairs. The house had been remarkably quiet since Izzy had left. She'd left him alone. And why shouldn't she? She was right. He was an ass. A complete and stubborn ass of a man who'd put too much stock in his pride and what people thought of him.

So many mistakes. So much time lost and wasted. So many lives ruined.

He heard a sound from below. A door closing and voices in the yard. Dusk had come once more. John hobbled to the window and saw two men standing in the yard talking to Izzy, who held a basket of clean laundry under her arm. He recognized her father and her brother, who had remained out of sight during his recovery. By all rights they should want to kill him for what he'd done to Izzy. He watched as they disappeared behind the shed and into the dim light of evening, no doubt to go off and hunt for game. Izzy set the basket down and walked back toward the garden.

When she came back in, Izzy would carry his meal up to him as she did every night. Wouldn't if be nice if he went to her for a change?

He limped to the bucket and finished washing. He scrubbed his hair as best he could and rinsed it with the pitcher of fresh water that always sat on the table by his bed. It was tepid but he did not care. He'd experienced much worse in the field during the past eight years. He combed the strands with his fingers and tied them back.

His clothes were clean and mended and hung on pegs. He had some trouble when he got to his breeches. He quickly unwound the bandages from his thigh and tossed the splints away. The gash in his leg was healed but still red and raw and his thigh tender. He rewrapped the linen bandages around it for support and pulled on his breeches.

His boots were blackened and polished and inside was a packet that contained what little money he possessed, along with the things Connor had taken from his father. He pulled them on with difficulty and stuffed the packet inside one. The weeks of lying flat on his back had softened him.

He reached for his red coat and then changed his mind.

There would be no army between them. No war. No duty. No lies. It would just be John and Izzy from now on.

And Elly.

It was his first trip out of the room. The upstairs hallway showed four doors, all closed, though candlelight showed beneath one of the doors. He supposed one room was Izzy's and one belonged to Keats. The stairs came up through the center of the house. The house seemed deserted as he made his way down the stairs. He was careful with his wounded leg as he eased his way from step to step. A lamp glowed from one of the downstairs rooms. He looked inside and realized that it was the doctor's office. There was a desk and a sofa. The door to the room opposite was closed. John figured it must be the room where Keats treated his patients. He followed the smell of roasted turkey to the back of the house, where there was a kitchen and a dining room.

The turkey sat in the middle of the worktable. Part of the breast was gone, along with a drumstick. Izzy's father and brother had probably already eaten. There were two dirty plates sitting on the counter. A fresh loaf of bread sat on a board with a knife beside it and there were some boiled potatoes in a pot on the stove. His stomach rumbled; he had not eaten since breakfast.

He had more important things on his mind.

He made his way through the kitchen and out the back door. There were three steps down. The laundry basket sat on the bottom step. John saw a glow of white in the darkness. The wide linen scarf Izzy wore about her neck.

And the cap too, most likely. He should have thrown it away. He would. As soon as he could snatch it from her head.

"Isobel," He called out. At same time, he heard a noise. A sound like breaking glass and the pounding of a horse galloping on the street.

She turned. Whether at the noise or his calling her name, he did not know or care. She dropped the weeds she was pulling as he took a limping step toward her. He took another step and she moved hesitantly toward him.

John opened his arms and she ran to him. She stopped suddenly right before him and looked up at him with her deep brown eyes unfathomable in the darkness. He took her hands in his.

"I cannot pretend that I can make up for the harm I've caused you—" he began.

"Nay—" she interrupted, and John placed a finger against her lips.

"Hear me out, Izzy," he said. "My pride hinders me most of the time. I think I have it whipped into submission at the moment, so let me speak."

She smiled and nodded.

"I cannot make up for the past, for what you had to bear alone. But if you will have me, I would like to make the future better for both of us."

"What are ye saying, John Murray?"

"I've got some money. I can buy your bond from Keats. No matter what the price. If I have to, I'll work for him. Whatever it takes." John squeezed her hand. "And then, when you are free, you can decide . . . Izzy . . . Will you marry me?"

"Ye would do that for me?" she asked.

"Anything Keats asks."

"He's given me my freedom. He gave me a choice."

"And what do you choose?" John asked hopefully.

"I choose you," she said. The glow from the fire lit her face and showed the happiness brimming in her eyes.

The glow from the fire . . .

A horrified look came across her face and John turned to see the windows at the back of the house shining with light.

Flames flickered in the room where he slept and smoke poured from under the eaves.

His mind raced. He had not lit the candle, he was certain of it. But there had been a light in one of the rooms.

"Elly," Izzy gasped. She started to the house and John grabbed her.

"Where is she?"

"Asleep. The room next to yours." She wrenched herself away from him. "I hae to get her."

"No!" John said. He gripped her shoulders and they both flinched as the windows above them exploded from the heat and rained glass down upon them. "Stay here."

"Elly!" Izzy screamed. Her face was ghastly white and her eyes wide with terror. John shook her.

"Stay here," he said. "I will get her."

Izzy put her fist to her mouth as sobs racked her body. John knew that she realized she was not strong enough to fight the flames and the heat. She could not carry Elly down the stairs if she was hurt. God help them if the child was already dead. Izzy would just throw herself into the flames and die with her. He could not lose both of them. Not when he'd just found them.

"I will get her."

The heat was unbearable. Flames licked at the ceiling as he ran into the house and up the hall to the staircase. Keat's office was an inferno. It must have started there. John touched the banister and yanked his hand back. It was like a hot iron. The top of the staircase was still passable, but the roof above was aflame. What would he do if he got up there and could not reach Elly?

His leg throbbed but he could not let it stop him. He raced up the stairs, ignoring the pain. His lungs ached and his throat burned. The fire roared like a demon giving out a battle cry.

A battle he could not lose.

"Elly!" he called out when he reached the top of the staircase. He choked and covered his nose and mouth with his hand. His face felt raw and his hair steamed. His room was to the right and so was the fire. That entire side of the house was aflame and going fast. Smoke billowed through the hall and blinded him

"Elly?" He moved to the left, stuck his hand out, felt the wall, felt the door. It was hot, but not unbearably so. It was also locked.

He had to balance on his bad leg and kick with his good one.

God, give me strength. He stumbled through after the second kick at the lock.

"Elly?" he called out. The bed was against the wall and empty. Flames came in behind him, traveling along the ceiling and to the wall around the window. How could the fire move so fast? He turned in a circle. There was a table next to the bed, a washstand with drawers, and several articles of clothing hung on pegs. There was only one place she could be. His thigh screamed its agony as he crouched on the floor and looked under the bed.

Elly was there, curled up with the kitten in her bloody hands. Obviously the kitten knew enough to escape, but Elly held it in a death grip.

"Let us leave this place," John said encouragingly. Elly nodded and scooted out enough for John to grab her and the kitty in his arms. The kitten buried its claws in his chest as he pressed Elly close.

The fire had spread. "Try not to breathe," he said to Elly. His lungs felt as if they were about to explode. The entire ceiling was alight and the fire had burned through the wall along the staircase. It was the only way out. He felt the heat and the flames licking at his back as he moved to the stairs. A crash sounded behind him and Elly screamed. The roof was caving in. John placed his foot on the first step and felt his leg give way.

"*No!*" he wailed. He pitched forward and caught himself on the banister. He heard the sizzle as his palm and fingers burned, but he maintained his balance and kept going. The front door loomed before him. *Please, God, let it be unlocked.* He had not the strength to kick through another one.

He stumbled forward and miracously the door opened. Ewan Ferguson stepped through and caught him just as he fell forward. Ewan carried all of them out into the yard.

"Elly!" Izzy shrieked. She threw her arms around both of them and John clutched Izzy to him as Ewan propelled the entire group away from the house. They collapsed to the ground in a heap with the kitten yowling in anger and frustration between them. Ewan scooped it up as Izzy rained kisses on Elly and John.

"Ye saved her," she sobbed, and her hands explored Elly's face and arms and legs to make sure she was whole.

She reached for his hand and realized it was burned when he flinched. She turned it palm upward and placed a gentle kiss on it. John ignored the pain in his hand and in his leg and placed his palm against her cheek.

"No, Izzy," he said. "You saved me."

"We saw the flames," Donald explained later that night when they were far enough away from Hillsborough to feel safe. They were camped in some deep woods along the edge of a river. They'd made their escape with John, Izzy, and Elly, along with a very upset kitten, in Keat's buggy. The kitten was stuffed in the basket of laundry along with whatever supplies they could scrounge from the shed. They even had the turkey, which Donald plucked from the kitchen moments before it was engulfed in flames.

"No need to waste food," he had said when Izzy cried at his foolishness.

The horse had trotted up pulling the empty buggy moments after their escape from the house. The buggy was empty because Keats was hanging dead from a tree in the front yard with a note attached.

Let this be a lesson to all who help the rebels.

Retribution from the Tories for the cruelty after the battle at Kings Mountain. They'd killed Keats for taking in two colonials without knowing that an officer in the king's army was also in the house.

"We thought the fire might mean trouble," Ewan added.

"I am just happy that you came back," John admitted. "I doubt I could have done much more."

"Ye did enough," Donald grunted. He rose from his place by the small fire. "Let me put the wee one to bed in the buggy," he said, "so ye can get your rest. We've got a long way to go."

"Where are we going, Da?" Izzy asked as she reluctantly handed the sleeping Elly up to her father.

"To the Blue Ridge, of course," he said. "Yer man here needs to see his sister."

Your man . . .

"There's a town near there called Abington," Ewan said. "I ken that they are in need of a printer."

"And how do you know that?" Izzy asked.

"The last one died at Kings Mountain," he said. "I seriously doubt that a new one has shown up yet."

"A printer," John repeated. He tightened his good arm around Izzy while she spread salve over his burnt palm. "It sounds like a good life. Especially since I know of a good apprentice."

"And that would be you," Izzy said. "As I am the one who actually knows how to do the job."

"As long as there is a priest," Donald said. "So ye can marry her. I'll not have my granddaughter a bastard all her life."

"I fully intend to marry Izzy as soon as possible," John assured him. "Because I have always loved her," he added.

Izzy smiled beside him. "As I hae always loved ye," she said.

"We can stop in Salem," Ewan said. "The Moravians can marry a man and a woman just as well as the Catholics." He yawned widely and followed Donald to the buggy. "We will gie ye some privacy," he said with a wink.

"The sins of the father," John said. Elly would not be called a bastard child. Not as long as he was alive. It was not her fault her father was a fool and full of pride.

"Pride goeth before the fall," he said.

"Quoting scripture?" Izzy asked. She snuggled up next to him and pulled the blanket up over them.

John leaned his head back against the oak tree he was leaning against. "It's something Rory said to me when we first came to Aberdeen. It was the day we first met actually. *Pride goeth before destruction and a haughty spirit before a fall.* But I have decided that falling is not so bad. Not when there is someone to catch you."

Epilogue

The valley seemed to hang right below the treetops. There was a meadow covered with tall grass and speckled with blue flowers. Horses browsed peacefully among the grass and all raised their heads as the little party came down the ridge.

A creek wound beside the trees, and a cabin sat beneath a copse of hemlocks. Smoke poured merrily from the chimney and there were clothes hanging on a line and drifting in the breeze. There was a huge shed off to the side and beside it a fenced-in pasture that held a snowy white horse. The stallion perked its ears toward the group who walked down the trail.

They'd given up the buggy long ago. Elly and Izzy rode the horse and the three men walked alongside with packs on their backs and rifles in their arms. They each had the long loping stride of men who were used to walking.

Connor, easily recognizable by his height and his red hair, walked out of the shed and placed a hand over his eyes to shield them from the sun as he looked at the visitors. A wide grin split his face and he motioned to a boy and sent him running to the house. Mere moments later, a woman came out. She looked at the visitors, let out a shriek, gathered her skirts, and took off at a run. The little boy and a little girl followed her.

John ran to his sister. She flung herself in his arms and covered his face with kisses as she laughed and cried at the same time.

"You're alive. You're here!" Carrie exclaimed. She stopped

her merry dance and looked at him. "Oh, John—" She touched his face with her hand. "You are happy."

"I am," he said. He held her away with his hand on her shoulders so he could look at her. "You are so beautiful," he said. "I think I had forgotten how beautiful you are."

Carrie placed a hand over her stomach. "The babe makes me glow," she said. "There will be another Duncan come winter." She drew her children to her. "This is your uncle John," she said. "This is Jamie. And Jillian." The boy had red hair and bright blue eyes like his father. The girl was the image of Carrie. And the image of Elly.

"Hello, Uncle John," they both said.

John heard the approach of his family. He turned and gently lifted Elly down, then Izzy. He took their hands, one on each side and turned to Carrie.

"This is my wife and my daughter."

Vexing the Viscount
by Emily Bryan

Read ahead for a sneak peak.

Item: One clay lamp after the fashion of an erect phallus.
—from the Manifest of Roman Oddities,
found near London, England
3rd July, in the Year of Our Lord 1731

"Hmph! I wonder if that's life-sized," Miss Daisy Drake murmured as she leaned down to inspect the ancient lamp. Talking to herself was a bad habit, she knew, but since none of her friends shared her interest in antiquities, she often found herself without companions on this sort of outing.

"Of course, it would be on the most inaccessible shelf in the display case." Solely to vex her, she suspected. Daisy scrunched down to get a better look at it. The clay lamp was only about four inches long, but in other respects, so far as Daisy knew, was perfectly life-like. She opened her small valise and drew out paper, quill and inkpot in order to take a few notes. "Where does the flame come out?"

"Right where one would expect," a masculine voice sounded near her. Daisy's spine snapped suddenly upright.

The crown of her head clipped his chin with a thwack and she bit her tongue.

"Oh!" One of her hands flew to her throbbing mouth, the other to the top of her head where her cunning little hat was smashed beyond recognition. Her sheaf of papers fluttered to the polished oak floor like maple leaves. The small inkwell flew into the air and landed squarely on the white lawn of his shirt-front.

"Oh, I'm so dreadfully sorry." Daisy dabbed at the stain with her hanky and only succeeded in spreading it down his waistcoat. A black blob dribbled onto his fawn-colored breeches. At least, thank Heaven, plastering the man with ink covered her unmaidenly interest in that lewd little lamp. "How clumsy of me!"

Then she made the additional mistake of looking up at him. Her mouth gaped like a cod for a moment. She forced it closed by sheer strength of will.

He'd grown into himself since she'd seen him last. His fine straight nose was no longer out of proportion to the rest of his face. As he rubbed his square jaw, Daisy saw that the little scar on his chin was still visible, a neat triangle of pale, smooth skin. She'd recognize that anywhere.

After all, she'd given it to him.

His curly dark hair was hidden beneath a dandy's wig. Oh, she hoped to heaven he hadn't taken to shaving his head as some fops did. Uncle Gabriel was a dogged opponent of the fashion. Said it was nothing but French foppery. Since Uncle Gabriel's opinions were only slightly less authoritative than a papal bull, the aversion to wigs had rubbed off. Besides, hiding a head of hair like Lucian's was almost sacrilege.

An ebony wisp escaped near his left ear.

Good. Daisy breathed a sigh of relief. His dark mane was one of Lucian's finest points, after all. Not that there weren't plenty of others.

His full lips twitched in a half smile.

"An interesting piece, isn't it?" He was still the same old Lucian. Still direct, even at the expense of propriety. He wasn't going to play the gentleman and pretend he hadn't caught her ogling that Roman phallus.

"Indeed." Surely he understood her interest was purely intellectual. "Obviously a cultic object of some sort. It is certainly a curiosity."

"It is gratifying to meet a young lady who is…curious," he drawled.

Daisy lifted her chin in what she hoped was a confident manner. "Antiquities give us but a glimpse into the lives of the ancients. That lamp merely poses new questions."

"Ah, yes, and you raised some intriguing ones," he agreed, one of his dark brows arched. "I'd be happy to help you discover the answers."

Was he suggesting something improper? If he was, it would serve him right if she gave him another scar. Daisy might be innocent yet, but thanks to Isabella she was not wholly ignorant of men.

"You owe me no further assistance. Not after I ruined your shirt. And your waistcoat. And your—" She shouldn't have allowed her gaze to travel the ink's path down the front of his breeches. To cover her embarrassment, she sank to the floor to retrieve her scattered notes.

"Think nothing of it." His voice was now a deep rumble instead of the adolescent squeak she remembered. "I should be more careful where I put my jaw. I do hope you have not suffered an injury to your head."

His eyes were even darker and more beguiling than she remembered. The fact that she even had a head temporarily escaped her notice.

"Please, allow me." Lucian knelt beside her and helped her reassemble her pages. Then he offered his hand to help her up and she took it.

Had someone loosed a jar of Junebugs in her belly?

"Thank you, my lord," she murmured, for lord he was.

Lucian Ignacio de Castenello Beaumont. Son and heir of Ellory Beaumont, Earl of Helmsby. Daisy assumed Lucian was now styling himself Viscount Rutland, one of his father's lesser titles, since the earl was still very much alive.

But Daisy remembered him as Iggy.

His ears had turned an alarming shade of red when she called him that. He complained Iggy was not dignified, as though a skinny, dirty-kneed twelve-year-old was capable of anything remotely like dignity.

But he was no longer twelve. Lucian must be two and twenty by now. The last time Daisy had heard his name bandied about in Polite Society, the sober matron doing the talking lowered her voice, but the words "rake" and "wastrel" were unmistakably used.

Neither of which did anything to slow her racing heart, Daisy admitted with a sigh.

She accepted the stack of papers from him, casting about in her mind for the right thing to say. "There's no salvaging your ensemble. I'll have a new suit of clothing made for you."

She could afford to be generous. After all, she'd discovered the family fortune beneath the stones of Dragon Caern just when other members of the nobility were losing theirs in the South Sea stock swindle.

"I wouldn't hear of it," he assured her smoothly, though she'd heard his father had invested heavily in the failed company. Perhaps his mother's family was still solvent. She'd been a contessa in her own right in her homeland. All vestiges of Lucian's Italian accent were gone, erased by a few years at Oxford, no doubt. Daisy thought that a terrible shame.

"I've been meaning to retire this suit in any case," he informed her. "The style is tres passé, n'est ce pas?"

That would be a pity since the cut of that green frockcoat does wonderful things for his shoulders and as for those bree— Daisy caught herself before her thoughts completely ran away with her, but lost her fight with the urge to gape at the way his breeches molded to his thighs.

His smile broadened.

"I see my lord has become an avid rider," she said because no other coherent thought would form in her mind.

Only the regular exercise of squeezing a horse between his legs could account for his musculature. She was glad he'd finally learned. He certainly had no aptitude for it on his first and only visit to Dragon Caern.

"Indeed, I ride daily," he said, flashing a fine set of teeth. "But how could you 'see' that?"

Her mouth formed a silent 'oh' and she mentally cursed herself. She was acting like some pudding-headed debutant.

"Riding improves a man's…posture." Daisy bit her lip to keep from babbling further. A guilty blush heated her cheeks. She sidled away from the case where the phallic·lamp was on display.

Lucian looked around the nearly deserted exhibit hall. "It seems there is no way for us to be properly introduced, but perhaps you will allow me the honor of giving you my name."

He doesn't recognize me!

How was it possible that she could carry about his image in her head for all these years and he should have completely forgotten that Daisy Elizabeth Drake even existed? Bristling with indignation, she took another step backward to put more distance between them.

Before she could remind him that he should know her name quite well, the door behind her swung open and whacked her soundly on the bottom.

"There you are, Rutland." A monocled gentleman waved Lucian in with urgency. "We've been waiting for you."

Daisy recognized him as Sir Alestair Murray, head of the Society of Antiquaries. She'd petitioned for admission several times only to have Sir Alestair black-ball her membership on account of her gender. The man cast a quick dismissive gaze over her and turned back to Lord Rutland.

Murray's eye-piece dangled from its silver chain when he noticed the ink stain marring the viscount's finery. "Good God, man, what's happened to you?"

"It was—" she began.

"My fault entirely," Lucian finished for her. "I will be in directly, Murray."

Lucian turned back to Daisy. "Perhaps once I've delivered my presentation, we may continue our discussion. I'd enjoy learning what such a charming young lady finds so…curious in these dry halls." He made an elegant leg and shot her a wicked grin. "And for your information, the answer is no."

"No?" Her brows nearly met in a puzzled frown.

"It's not life-sized."

✂ ☐ **YES!**

Sign me up for the Historical Romance Book Club and send my FREE BOOKS! If I choose to stay in the club, I will pay only $8.50* each month, a savings of $6.48!

NAME: _____

ADDRESS: _____

TELEPHONE: _____

EMAIL: _____

☐ I want to pay by credit card.

☐ **VISA**　　☐ **MasterCard**　　☐ **DISCOVER**

ACCOUNT #: _____

EXPIRATION DATE: _____

SIGNATURE: _____

Mail this page along with $2.00 shipping and handling to:
Historical Romance Book Club
PO Box 6640
Wayne, PA 19087
Or fax (must include credit card information) to:
610-995-9274

You can also sign up online at **www.dorchesterpub.com**.

*Plus $2.00 for shipping. Offer open to residents of the U.S. and Canada only.
Canadian residents please call 1-800-481-9191 for pricing information.
If under 18, a parent or guardian must sign. Terms, prices and conditions subject to change. Subscription subject to acceptance. Dorchester Publishing reserves the right to reject any order or cancel any subscription.